Other books by the author
Raven's Realm Series
Raven's Child
Windows to the Soul
Chaos Within
Immortality
Darkness Falls

I0638916

Women of Ravenwood Series
Fallen
Unspoken Oaths

Gods & Dragons Series
Brothers
Victory
Beyond Valhalla

Immortal Series
Whispers of the Immortal
Tears of the Immortal
Soul of the Immortal
Fall of the Immortal
Echoes of the Immortal
Quest for the Immortal
Reign of the Immortal

REIGN OF THE IMMORTAL

Immortal Series
Book Seven

M.J. Spickett

No part of this book may be reproduced by electronic or printed means without express written permission by the author.
Northern Gem Publishing (2024)

ISBN: 978-1-998318-17-9 eBook
ISBN: 978-1-998318-18-6 Paperback
ISBN: 978-1-998318-19-3 Hardcover

www.mjspickett.ca

Library and Archives Canada Cataloging in Publication
Spickett, M.J., 1976-, author
Quest for the Immortal / M.J. Spickett
Issues in print and electronic formats

I. Title.

Art by Rosel Graphic Designs

Dedication

To Priya and Ashley, who kept me encouraged and focused while writing. To Jayden and Harley, who put up with my craziness and continues to do so as I keep writing.

AUTHOR NOTE

MJ Spickett is a Canadian Author. Most locations within her novels focus on Canada and England, and, as such, words and spacing may appear differently than they would in America. For example, we like to use "U" and "Z" in many of our words, for example "honor" (US) and "honour" (Canadian). We write grey with an "e" not with an "a." My editor is also Canadian and is helping me keep to Canadian standards. As well, although it is normal for Americans to use a single space at the end of a sentence, Canadians tend to double space. This also makes it easier to read and give an extra pause to help readers digest what they just read and better comprehend it. These are not spelling or formatting errors but simply the way we are taught to read and write.

Canadians tend to be a complicated group but that's also what makes us special.

To my Canadian readers...celebrate your uniqueness and continue writing.

Chapter One

The flash of silver caught Alex off guard. The assailant came out of nowhere, brandishing a dagger before he quickly buried it to the hilt in Lucas's stomach. Lucas didn't cry out. The only sound to pass through his lips was a soft grunt as knife twisted to do the utmost damage. Kyra jumped into action, bringing the reality of the situation to Alex. He caught Lucas as the larger man's legs gave out, and curled around his beloved, protecting him as their child fought against their attacker. She displayed a power and skill they had not known her capable of. Her human form changed to something made of energy and pure light. Many would mistake her transformation for that of an angel, but she was something far more dangerous than a make-believe angelic being. Alex's focus turned from Kyra to the man in his arms. He tried to stop the bleeding, but it was like an endless stream. It covered him and the ground beneath Lucas, like thick red wine that could never been scrubbed away.

Worry filled Lucas's face but not fear, as if he had yet to realize the seriousness of his injury. The worry was not for himself or even Alex, but rather their daughter. He watched her with keen eyes, mouth moving as if calling to her. All that came out was laboured breathing. Nonetheless, there was no fear. Not of the power Kyra displayed, nor when she tore out the other man's heart, letting his body deteriorate into dust. When the helicopter landed to take them to safety, Lucas smiled with relief and squeezed Alex's hand. There was strength in his grip, and for a moment, Alex believed everything was going to be alright.

Kyra had defeated Archer, saved them and the hybrids. Once they got Lucas to the hospital, his wounds would be tended to and he would heal. They should be celebrating, but such thoughts were premature. Once they were safely in the helicopter and it took off, a strange light, like a laser, cut through the sky. The building they were on only a few short minutes ago, imploded, collapsing in on itself one floor after another. Those still inside were crushed to death, with no chance of escape. Hundreds of hybrid Celestials, who were just freed of Archer's control, were gone within an instant. Lucas's heart stopped at almost the exact moment the building was hit. Alex was too preoccupied with what was transpiring outside to notice until Lucas's hand slipped out of his. There was no reviving him. Both Alex and Kyra did everything in their power to save him. Kyra's power was drained from the battle with Archer and unable to use it to heal him. Lucas was gone and with him, a large chunk of Alex as well.

The scorch marks near the lake were still visible even after the snow and freezing rain. Neither stuck to that section of ground, as if some strange force protected it from the elements. Grass did not grow over it. Leaves did not fall upon it, nor snow, or rain. It tormented Alex to no end. A reminder of the one he lost and was forced to cremate on that very spot. He stared at it from his spot on the porch, unable to look away even as the wind howled around him and the temperature dropped. Sometimes, he could almost swear Lucas was standing there staring back at him, trapped, unable to take the short stroll that would bring him home. It was a silly thought. Lucas was gone, his body cremated and soul moved on to the great beyond. There was no coming back from that.

There was a bad storm on the horizon. He should be inside taking refuge. After all, the view would not change no matter how long he watched it. That one spot of ground would remain the same. Lucas would not suddenly appear out of the woods to tell him everything was okay and the last few months were merely a dream. Lucas was gone, his ashes, what little Alex could gather, were stored safely in the small canister that hung from a gold chain around Alex's neck, next to an almost identical one that held Owen's, Lucas's older brother. In a twisted sort of way, the brothers had been reunited, but not the way Alex would have preferred. They had both died protecting him. It was part of the reason he tortured himself now; sitting out in the sub-freezing cold, staring at the site of Lucas's pyre when he should be inside, monitoring the radio channels for any chatter from the local military. Sooner or later, they would come for him and his charges, it was only a matter of time.

Let them come, he thought.

He lifted his mug to his lips, thankful he had the forethought to bring his coffee outside with him. It was getting cold but was still hot enough to break the chill that was beginning to take hold. Since Lucas's funeral, it had become a ritual to make a mug of coffee, sit on the porch and simply stare at the scorch marks as if his will alone had the power to bring his husband back from the dead. Rain or shine, snow, or blizzard, he always came out first thing in the morning and spent almost the entire day sitting on the porch, watching…waiting for something to happen. The handheld radio sat on the table next to chair, humming faintly as it dialed through frequencies to pick up possible military movement through the region. His home was well defended. In recent years it had been upgraded with state-of-the-art government defenses making it one of the most secure places in Canada. However, that same government had come under threat and only a few months ago had been taken over by a foreign entity. What was once seen as a sanctuary for hybrids – people born half human and half Celestial – was now viewed as a threat. That made Alex a target, as it did the dozens of people in his care.

That number was growing every day as more and more hybrids found their way through the Ishpatina Ridge. It was a long and dangerous trek. Located ninety kilometer north of Sudbury and the highest point in Ontario, people had to hike in almost fifteen kilometers from the nearest highway to reach the Sanctuary. The terrain was rough. People had to climb through the mountains to reach him. His home was in a valley area between two ridges. A large lake allowed for water planes to land close to his home. It was a no-fly zone to commercial and most private planes. The only exception was the supply plane that came once a month. It was the only way in or out, other than making the long trek to the highway. The chalet sat upon a decommissioned military base. Everything that marked it as such was gone now or cleverly hidden underground, designed to rise out of the ground should there be a threat to the current inhabitants. It was a little gift given to Alex and Lucas to protect their daughter before the world turned upside-down. The military no longer had access to it. That had been severed shortly after Earth Defense Command were forced to disband in Canada. Of all the insane things to happen, Alex never expected the attack on EDC headquarters to lead to the group being disbanded. It made sense given what now controlled the government, but they were one of their few resources Alex had.

Living so far from the city, with no direct access to the highway was not easy. He would need to ride an ATV or snowmobile almost two hours – depending on weather conditions – to reach the highway and then another hour or two to reach the nearest town. Not exactly ideal without a car or truck. Flying was questionable as most of the lakes were would either fully or partially frozen over in the winter. He didn't trust his little personal plane to handle the ice. EDC had a special ice breaker that would come out to make sure there was a safe path for the supply plane to land. That, like Lucas, was gone now. Alex felt unprepared for that. If it wasn't for the vast supply of vacuum sealed military rations stores in the cellar and in the Sanctuary, they would be starving right now. As it was, they had enough to do them over the winter and into late spring…provided they didn't get many more hybrids within that time.

The bitter cold finally became too much for him. With a sigh, Alex dumped his now cold coffee onto the snow. A small laugh escaped him. Lucas would approve of him turning to pristine white snow a dirty mud colour. Hell, the man didn't even like peeing outside – and it had nothing to do with the cold or public nudity. It was simply the way Lucas was. Sex…that was more than okay outside. He wouldn't have cared if anyone walked in on them…expect their daughter. Those were things children were not meant to see, regardless of Kyra being a grown woman now.

4

He gave the scorch mark a fleeting glance. He could almost see Lucas looking back with that devilish smirk of his. That spot had more history than merely being were Lucas was cremated. It was also the first place they made love after moving here, many years ago, late in the evening, long after Kyra went to bed for the night. Alex had almost forgotten about it. For a moment, the sadness he felt whenever he looked at the burnt earth lifted. It was only for a moment, but it was enough to get him to go back inside just as the storm fell upon the ridge. While the snow may not cover where the pyre had been, it did obscure Alex's view of it, breaking the spell it held on him.

Inside was a complete contrast to the outside. It was warm and bright with a merry glow emanating from the glassed-in woodstove in the middle of the living room. He barely remembered stoking the fire before going outside. For one brief moment, he thought Kyra may have come home and done it for him. In the winter months, it was the primary source of heat as the solar panels weren't always reliable during the winter, nor was the generated. Storms like this one had a tendency to knock it out, cutting the power supply entirely. Should that happen, Alex was prepared to work on it at first light. He could handle a night with only the woodstove. He hoped that the power didn't go out, though. It wasn't the chalet he worried about. The Sanctuary, hidden deep within the mountain, served as home to dozens upon dozens of hybrids. Their only source of power came from the generator and solar field. With luck, the storm wouldn't be as bad as it felt. His entire right side ached, from his amputated right leg all the up his hip to the right side of his face, pressing against his ruined ear. It was one of those times it was just better to go to bed and deal with everything in the morning.

Of course, going to bed brought about the entire reason he had gone outside rather than snuggle under the warm comforter on his king-size bed. He would be alone. Lucas wasn't there to share it with him and that was something he could not accept. Not yet. Instead, Alex forced himself to stay awake as he did every night. He sat on the sofa, facing out toward where the pyre had been with a fresh mug of coffee in his hands, his laptop open on his lap. The curser blinked steadily as it waited for him to type. He and Lucas were working on their next book regarding the history of the underground temples, what they now called Sanctuaries. Alex was the lead investigator. He knew just about everything there was to know about the temples and alien technology hidden within. Lucas was an expert as well, having lived through much of the same as Alex. Yet, Alex could not so much as type a sentence. He stared at the screen, silently willing his fingers to move and transcribe his knowledge to the screen, but nothing happened. His mind was blank, the passion he once felt gone. What was the point anymore?

An alarm jarred him out of his thoughts. The edges of his laptop lit up as security protocols took over and a new screen popped up.

"You've got to be kidding me," he grumbled as six orange dots appeared on the screen.

There was an invisible shield around the former military compound. A laser grid ran along the perimeter and hundreds of feet into the sky. It was designed to pick up certain energy signatures. Humans were blue, alien – or Celestial were red, Shadows were black, and hybrids orange. It was easy to tell them apart by the body heat. Human possessed by Shadow-beings registered as black along with the Shadows themselves as their core temperature dropped to levels that would kill most humans. Some fool hybrids must have thought they could outrun the storm. That meant he had to go get them before they froze to death. And yes, hybrids could die from the elements, it just took a little longer. They were only a few kilometers east of the chalet, but in this weather it might as well have been twenty or more kilometers.

His shoulders fell as he placed the laptop on the coffee table. At least rescuing hybrids was better than moping about the house, wishing Lucas was with him.

He grabbed his one-piece snowsuit and tugged it on, then his heavy boots. His hat and rabbit fur mitts hung next to the woodstove beside his boots to keep them warm. One of the snow mobiles was parked next to the porch, already fueled and ready to go. All he needed was the sleigh to transport the newcomers. He grabbed the keys to the garage and the walkie-talkie.

"Kyra?" he called into the walkie-talkie.

There was static for a moment.

"Hey, Dad," came the response. "Are you alright?"

"Yeah, fine," he lied. He tried to keep his voice steady. The last thing he needed was Kyra worrying about him more than she already did. "Look, the storm is picking up. We have six hybrids coming from the east. I'm going to pick them up."

"Wait, I'll come with you," she insisted, ever the attentive daughter.

"They're only a few kilometers from me. I'll be there and back before you make it home. I'll bring them directly to the Sanctuary. If you don't see us in an hour…" His voice faltered. His gaze shifted back to where the pyre was in longing.

"I'll come find you," she assured.

He nodded to himself. With one last look at toward the pyre, he slipped his goggles over his eyes and pulled the scarf up over his nose. There wasn't much time before the storm got too severe to rescue anyone.

The snow mobile was safely parked in a lean-to. It kept the majority of the snow off it. Alex checked the gas tank to make sure there was enough fuel, then straddled the vehicle. The engine roared to life, sounding far too loud in the quiet wilderness, despite the wind through the trees. Removing his hat and goggles, he replaced them with a helmet that sported a full-face visor. They were anti-fog and allowed him to see much better than the goggles. He turned on the onboard computer and tapped into the network to access the location of the newcomers. The garage was on the other side of the perimeter. He sped toward it, stopping within feet of the double doors. There was no point turning off the engine. He yanked open the doors. The sleigh was to the left, within feet of the door. As was a jerry-can of fuel. It took some work, but he managed to drag the sleigh outside and hitch it to the back of the snow mobile. After closing up the garage once more, he was off, following the tracker to the approaching hybrids.

It would have been easier and considerably faster if it were daytime and the weather was clear. Living in the mountains, even in the valley region, meant the terrain was not smooth. What trails there were, were covered in snow and near impossible to find. He had to make his own. With only the light from the snow machine's headlight, it was not an easy task. It took a notoriously long time and with every passing minute, Alex's anxiety grew. The hybrids were within the shield but there was always a chance something else had come in with them. He wasn't about to allow that to happen again. Not after the love of his life was murdered before him. He may be devoted to saving hybrids but his duty was to his family…what was left of it. If anyone tried to harm Kyra, he would end them, human, hybrid, Celestial, or Shadow.

The snow was deep. Far deeper than he anticipated. It hid many dangers that would not be found on one of the well traveled paths. He missed the days when the rangers would come through and blaze a trail. While there were still members of Earth Defence Command, they were under deep cover which meant their usual obligations to the Sanctuary were no longer in affect. Not when their every move was being monitored. A curse escaped him as he hit a hidden bump, causing the snow mobile to tilt dangerously to one side and almost overturning the sleigh. The headlight bounced over the trees and fallen logs. He was forced to stop or risk damaging the vehicle.

He looked left then right. There had to be another path. The snow mobile had reverse but it would be difficult to back-up with the sleigh. It was near impossible to see anything with the increasing snow. He would have to chance it, if only a few feet, just enough for him to turn without hitting the fallen logs. Very slowly, very carefully, he backed up, his focus on the sleigh to make sure it stayed straight and did not jack-knife. Last time he did that he broke a ski. Once he was sure he had enough space, he faced the direction he wanted to go.

A surprised cry escaped him as a young girl appeared out of the darkness. She was pale faced and clearly not dressed for this sort of weather. She was a shivering mess. Alex stared at her in shock, his face hidden behind the visor, but mouth wide open. More people appeared behind her.

Alex shook off his surprise and lifted the visor of his helmet.

"Is this everyone?" he called out over the howling wind.

His computer said there were six hybrids and he counted six, but that didn't mean there weren't others. He glanced at the monitor to see if there were anymore humans or – God forbid – Shadows and Celestials were nearby. Nothing else appeared on the monitor.

"This is all of us," a youth said through chattering teeth.

The children looked frightened, as if they were not expecting to have found, and had all but given up.

Alex squinted. It was a boy, no more than fourteen or fifteen years old. The entire group were children, the oldest appearing around seventeen, the youngest approximately four. None of them dressed for the weather. His heart broke as he took that in. Where were their parents?

"Alright, everyone in the sleigh. We need to get you out of the cold." He gestured at the eldest youth. "Help me turn the snow mobile enough to pull out of here and then climb in with the others."

The two oldest kids helped the younger ones into the sleigh then gave Alex a hand pushing the vehicle around the fallen logs until it was in a safe enough area to turn it and the sleigh around. Once they were secure in the sleigh with the others, Alex gunned the engine and made his way toward the Sanctuary.

From the corner of his eye, he saw movement in the woods and a flash of red. He slowed down for a moment and looked back, but nothing was there. He glanced at the monitor just to be certain, but nothing else showed up on it. It had to have been one of the trail cameras and blowing wind distorting the natural shadows of the woods. Whatever the case, he needed to get these kids to the Sanctuary where they would be safe and warm. Anything else in the woods could be dealt with in the morning.

Normally, he would have taken them to the chalet to warm up before heading to the old mine that served as the gateway to the Sanctuary, but he couldn't bring himself to do that. He wanted to be alone in his home, not surrounded by strangers let alone children or teenagers. He needed his privacy to process his thoughts and emotions, regardless what others may think. So, he took the well-worn trail to the abandoned mine. Unlike the other trails, this one was used all year round and was well maintained no matter the weather. One of the hybrids had even gone as far as to light the trail. Not by ordinary means. In fact, only other hybrids and those "touched" by the Celestials like Alex could see it due to the young woman's gifts. Normal humans and Shadows could not see the path and would quickly be turned around as a defensive gimmick. Alex wasn't sure how her power worked and dared not ask. Too many hybrids had gifts that made little to no sense. Nonetheless, with the path clear and lit, they made it to the Sanctuary in no time.

To the average person, the opening to the old mine looked like any other, a cave carved into the mountainside long ago. It went in a ways before large metal doors blocked the entrance. Alex drove the snow mobile into the tunnel a dozen feet or so thanks to snow being blown into it, then parked it. He asked the hybrids to get out of the sleigh while he accessed a panel next to the doors. The security for the Sanctuary was a two-part authentication system requiring both facial and DNA recognition. It went beyond that really. Both the facial and DNA scans also measured his core temperature to ensure he was neither Shadow possessed or Celestial possessed. Despite the fence surrounding the property, there was always the possibility of one getting through and they were not taking any chances. The process only took a few seconds. Before long, the sounds of gears turning and the metallic whine of the heavy doors scrapping against one another could be heard as the large doors opened. Beyond them was a simple lift.

Alex frowned at it, tempted to tell the newcomers to go the rest of the way without him. They would exit inside the Sanctuary. He didn't need to lead them any further. He inhaled deeply and buried his anxiety under the grumpy, gruff exterior. He created the mask to shelter himself from becoming emotionally attached to any of the new hybrids that now resided in the Sanctuary. He had one simple mission, get them to Kyra then go back to the chalet and pretend they weren't there. He simply wanted to go home and mourn Lucas in peace. He wasn't ready to deal with the rest of the world yet.

Nonetheless, he escorted the newcomers onto the lift, made sure everyone was accounted for, then the mine doors sealed close behind them. He took them down the shaft to the cavern that housed the Sanctuary. It was over a hundred feet underground. The further down they went, the warmer the air became until Alex found himself stripping off his winter coat, gloves, and scarf. He had a tendency to overheat whenever he visited in the winter. Normally that wasn't a bad thing, but today he just wanted to be in and out without getting pulled into some new drama with one of the new residents.

The shaft automatically lit up as they descended deeper underground, causing the minerals in the rock walls the sparkle like jewels. The younger hybrids gazed at them in wonder. Alex watched them, his gruff mask of indifference slipping as he gazed at the young girl. Kyra had the same expression when they first came here. That same wonder and excitement, as if realizing she was finally home. The hybrids seemed to be born with a sense of the Sanctuary as home, even if they had never been to one of the underground temples before. It could also be the fact that, like the Celestials they had almost a hive mind. They were merely answering Kyra's call for all hybrids to come to the safety of the Sanctuary. Whatever the case, the fear left them the moment they began their descent, knowing this was where they were meant to be. That contentment grew as they entered the vast cavern that housed the Sanctuary.

The cavern was a busy hub of activity. People moved about, helping one another, or chatting. It was brightly lit, the overhead lighting mirroring natural sunlight. It should have been dimmed for this time of the evening but recently, Kyra had ordered it to remain on at all times. She was unwilling to take any chances with Shadows making their way into the cavern.

Alex spotted her at the top of the alien temple with Liam and Winston, the latter of which was suspended from the ceiling with a number of gadgets strapped to him and a tablet in hand. Alex raised a curious brow. He knew they had been working on the energy grid in an effort to make the Sanctuary self sustainable should the government suddenly cut their power supply or the generator and solar power system go out. They didn't have the proper tools, nor the funds for such a large conversion. Obviously, this did not deter Winston.

The lift came to a stop and Alex gestured for the newcomers to depart. He was intent to leave immediately. That plan quickly went up in flames when Naomi called out to him. The young woman greeted him with a large grin before shining that infectious smile on the new hybrids. Any fear or tension that was left in them quickly melted away. Naomi had a gift for calming one's mind. Not so long ago she used it to manipulate people. Now she used her gifts to put people at ease. Given the number of people displaced by the Shadows hunting them, it was a much-needed reprieve.

"My name's Naomi," she told them with a small nod. "We have hot food and drink ready for you in the mess hall. Once you've eaten, we'll find huts to house you. Are you all one family?"

They shook their heads.

"That's alright," she assured. "We'll set you up with Watchers. They'll help you adjust and bring you up to speed on what's going on."

She gestured toward her helper, a young man in his late teens. Almost every hybrid in the Sanctuary were teenagers or children. There were very few adults to care for them all. The older ones cared for the younger ones. It was not the ideal set up. The Watchers were a mix of EDC agents who choose to stay and protect the hybrids and spirits, otherwise known as Guardians, who were not displaced when Kyra's power had gone berserk months ago.

Naomi caught Alex's arm as he turned to leave. He looked back at her but didn't shake off her hand as he normally would. She knew better than to try her mind tricks on him.

"She needs to talk to you," the young woman told him.

He glanced toward Kyra. Just the thought of climbing up all those temple steps brought a sharp pain to his stump. He and Lucas often took the winter off from their research to write up their findings from the rest of the year. The weather had a negative affect on his bad leg. There was no way he could make the climb today, and Kyra knew it.

"Not Kyra," Naomi assured him. She must have read his expression. "Marie."

That was even worse. Alex's face pinched at the very thought of speaking to the Celestial. She was nice enough, but for an alien creature she acted all too human. It unnerved him. Ancients only knew how long she had actually been on this planet. Then there was also the fact she was his "biggest fan," having collected his books and researched him thoroughly...and what he knew about the temples. There were fans and then there were the ones that could quickly turn into the horror fiction "Misery." Especially with Alex's tie to the temple. He was the "key" to opening it. The mark was literally on his right hand, allowing him access to the Vault and Void, and every other corner of the alien temple. All thanks to another woman obsessed with the beings hidden within it. Marie had not asked him to open anything for her but it was just a matter of time.

"You can tell her she knows..." he began, turning back to the lift.

13

"...where to find you," Marie finished. She stood between him and the lift, a small frown pulling her lips downward.

Naomi gave her a small nod and left them. Alex gave the girl a sideways look. Naomi was normally full of sass and ready with some witty comeback. However, when it came to Marie, she was docile and ready to do as she was told without question or even a word exchanged. It unnerved Alex. His mind was tied to their hive mind and it took all his strength to keep himself separated from them. He may not be a hybrid but he had once been possessed by a Celestial. That connection never goes away. Hence his dislike of Marie. She may have a human body but a Celestial possessed it. There was no telling if the true Marie even existed anymore.

"Make it quick. I'm not staying long," he told her. He folded his arms across his chest. It was hot in the Sanctuary. He was beginning to sweat.

"Why are you helping us if you hate us so much?" Marie asked.

Alex stared at her in disbelief. The question was straightforward but it felt as if she had slapped him in the face. His frown deepened.

"I don't hate the hybrids," he reminded her. "They have no control over what they are." He took a step forward, getting in her face. "Nor do Liam or Kyra. They were born the way they are, but you...your kind possessed and slaughtered humans like me and forced us to breed with you. A lot of these kids grew up not knowing what they are and now they're being hunted and killed. Just like before. Or have you forgotten about the Great Rebellions that nearly eradicated your kind and wiped out most of your original hybrids? The difference this time? Your little Shadow puppets have turned against you and are leading the fight." He let that sink into her head. "It's only a matter of time before they make it past our defenses and then...all this will be for nothing."

Surprisingly, Marie nodded, a look of understanding filling her eyes. It could have been an act, after all, Celestials were good at

14

mimicking human emotions, but there was something in Marie's eyes that was very human.

"I know," she said. There was a small tremor to her voice. "That's what I'm afraid of. Kyra is trying so hard to protect us. As our Queen, she feels it's her duty…" She raised a hand to stop Alex as he went to interrupt. "She's pushing herself too hard. She's going to burn out. She refuses to face the hard fact that this 'Sanctuary' cannot sustain all of us for much longer."

She was right and Alex hated that. "What do you propose?"

"There are other temples. Perhaps ones that are safer, where the Shadows can't reach us…" She gestured to the lights hanging from the ceiling that Winston was once again working on. "…with an active orb. The longer we rely on artificial man-made lighting the sooner we waste away."

It was the first time Marie had asked about an orb. Alex had only seen one temple with an active one and that was in the Arctic. The American government had attempted to recreate it, believing it was a power source for the temples. It was like a small sun. It had turn a frozen tundra into an oasis. Could it do the same here?

"I don't know of any active orbs," he answered honestly. "Even if I did, they're highly radioactive. It could kill them."

"Yes," Marie responded, as if that was the entire point. "The Shadows cannot survive its light, even within a host. However, the children will thrive. There would be plenty of food and…"

"No," he answered sternly. "I'm not condemning them to radiation poisoning just so you can have your power back." He walked past her to the lift. "You'll have to make do like the rest of us."

"It's for them, not me," she argued. She hurried after him and grasped his arm. "You know just as well as I do that we can't keep living like this. We're running low on rations and…"

He shook her hand off. "We'll make it work."

He stepped on the lift, shut the gate, and began his ascent. Marie watched him for a moment before shaking her head and walking away, clearly not happy with their conversation. Neither was Alex. How dare she demand he find them another temple, let alone an orb that could wipe out ninety percent of them. It was madness.

His gaze flicked to the top of the temple. Kyra was watching him, a questioning look on her lovely face. He raised a hand to her and she waved back. He was happy to see she was in her true form, no longer hiding under an illusion to appear more human. Her pale skin and flowing white hair gave her the appearance of an angel. His heart swelled with pride at how well she was caring for everyone. She had become a great leader in the short time since they opened the Sanctuary to hybrids.

He hated to admit it, but Marie may be right. They may need to find another location that could properly sustain them all. He simply had no clue where to find one or if a temple with an active orb even existed anymore. They wouldn't be the only ones searching for it either. If the Shadows found it, they would have it destroyed immediately.

It felt like a losing battle.

Chapter Two

Alex awoke to the smell of freshly perked coffee and bacon sizzling on the stove top. Music played from the radio in the adjoined kitchen with a familiar voice humming along to the song. It was a familiar thing to wake up to.

He slowly opened his eyes and glanced toward the kitchen. Kyra was puttering around, making breakfast as she did those rare occasions when she was home. Since Lucas's death, she had taken it upon herself to check in on Alex every morning, despite no longer living at home. He knew it would not last forever. Now that she was Queen of the hybrids, she had other duties. Even if she wasn't, sooner or later she would have to go back to living her own life without worrying about him. For now, Alex planned to enjoy every moment he could with his daughter.

He carefully sat up, letting the comforter she must have draped over him fall onto his lap. He must have fallen asleep while working on his manuscript. His laptop was closed and safely on the low table in front of the sofa. His mug of coffee from the night before was ice cold next to it.

"Good morning, Daddy," Kyra greeted him. She replaced the old mug with a fresh one then placed a large plate of scrambled eggs, bacon, and rye toast on the other side of the laptop.

Alex's mouth watered at the smell of the food. He couldn't remember the last time he had taken the time to cook himself a proper meal. "Good morning, angel. I thought you'd be busy settling the newcomers."

She nodded as she headed back into the kitchen to fetch her own food. "Naomi and Marie have that covered. I'm more concerned about keeping the power on. We're starting to have rolling power outages. Probably due to the storm…but all it takes is one for the Shadows to find their way in."

That was why Marie approached him about finding an active temple and orb, Alex mused. He didn't say anything, unsure if Kyra even knew about what Marie was proposing. If she did, Kyra didn't say anything as she sat in the armchair across from him, her plate balanced on her lap. They didn't normally eat in the living room. It felt odd doing so.

"What do you propose?" he asked.

Her shoulders tensed ever so slightly. She stared at her plate for a moment without answering. Marie *had* gotten to her as well.

"You once told me about the Arctic temple…the one with the orb that had an oasis. It was like this one but alive," she began.

Alex's lips pressed together. It had been a cautionary tale of how dangerous the temples could be, of how toxic the orb was. It was as powerful as a small sun, bringing life to the frozen lands while poisoning those who ventured into the cavern. Many had developed cancer and blood poisoning, dying months or even years later. Lucas had nearly died.

"If you recall, the Oasis was also extremely dangerous and highly radioactive," he reminded her.

"That's not why you're scared," she pointed out. "You never told me what happened there. The whole story, not the abbreviated version."

He shook his head. Marie had triggered enough of those memories last night, he did not want to dwell on them now.

"Dad…"

A sigh escaped him. "Remember when I told you I was once possessed by a Celestial?"

"Yes."

"I never told you how." He glanced toward a framed drawing of the Arctic temple that hung on the western wall. "It was a few years after your father and I became a couple…before we married. We were still trying to figure what we wanted in our relationship. We loved each other but we didn't see eye to eye on how to proceed. At one point I just needed time to myself. I ended up going for a walk and…got kidnapped by an occultist and his followers." He rubbed at the scar on the palm of his hand, the ancient alien markings still as crystal clear today as the day it was burned into him. "They used me to hurt Lucas, tortured me, raped me, took me to that temple, then…sacrificed me." He looked up, catching the surprise in Kyra's face. "I died in order to free a Celestial. That thing brought me back, possessed me, and turned me into a sex crazed murderer. Then it tried to harness the power of the orb. It was during an eclipse. The power…" He was rambling, the memory still fresh after all these years.

A shiver ran down his spine as he remembered the power that coursed through him. The feel of another being inside his body with him. If there was another temple like it, there was no telling what would happen should the hybrids find it. It could bring salvation or utter destruction.

Kyra stared at him, shock written across her face. "Why didn't you tell me? Dad…I…had I known…"

He blinked away the moisture that filled his eyes. "It was a long time ago, and it's not exactly something you share with your children." He took a deep breath. "Look, there may be another Oasis. It's possible, but can you say with all honesty that you trust Marie not to be after the power of the orb for herself? That she won't use it to bring other Celestials back? They've already shown they can attack Earth from space. They killed hundreds of hybrids when they imploded that lab. What's stopping them from killing everyone in the Sanctuary?"

"Me."

"You're one person, Kyra. You're powerful, but that power is still new. We don't know its full extent or how it would hold up against a Celestial. Right now, our best bet is to stay here."

"For how long? Until the power gives out completely or we run out of food? What if someone gets seriously hurt or sick?" She placed her plate on the table then leaned forward, her elbows on her knees. "We need to face facts. Things as they are now is not a viable solution. If we can't find another temple then we need to move everyone somewhere else. Denmark as offered asylum to many of the European hybrids. As has Norway and Iceland. It's not the ideal solution but we won't be hunted there and we can use the Void to cross to a temple there."

He shook his head. "Kyra, they've all been destroyed."

Her face twisted into a disappointed scowl. "What if one survived? This one did. It can't be the only one. Originally, you and Papa thought there could only be a dozen temples like ours, then there ended up being hundreds, all over the world. They may be gone now, but there has to be another one, maybe undiscovered? And maybe…just maybe…it can support us, even half of us. If we can find one…"

"No."

"But…"

"Canada is not the only place with hybrids," he said sternly. "There could be millions and all of you need Sanctuary…some place safe. It's not only our government and the Shadows hunting you down, but also the Celestials. Do you really think they would have killed those hybrids if they actually cared about their creations?" He stood, his food only half eaten, and took his plate to the kitchen. "There will be no accessing the Void. Everyone is to stay here. Elizabeth will be here with supplies few days. We'll make do."

With a sigh, she followed him and scraped her leftovers in the garbage. "For how long? Sooner or later, we're going to be overwhelmed with refugees. We don't have the equipment or room to expand."

She placed her plate in the sink, gave his arm a squeeze, then headed up to her bedroom. It wasn't used anymore, Kyra had moved to the Sanctuary after the first group of hybrids arrived, but the majority of her belongings were still there.

She was right though. They had to make a decision on what to do and where to go as more and more hybrids arrived. Initially, the Celestials hid the temples underground to escape the rebellion that had all but destroyed them some twelve thousand years ago. Or so Alex thought. Now he wondered if they were placed where they were in preparation for the hybrids. With so many destroyed over the last two decades, there were very few safe places for them now. That still didn't explain the Celestials attack on the lab in Ottawa, or why they willingly wiped-out hundreds of hybrids in one blast. How did they even know about them hunting Kyra? Was it even the Celestials that fired the laser? Right now, they were merely assuming it was them. What if there was something even more dangerous out there? How many beings had access to a space laser?

He instinctively glanced toward the remains of the burial pyre, wishing Lucas was there to tell him he was overreacting and that everything will be fine. Even if his spirit had become one of the Guardians, a protective spirit that guarded the temple, it would be better than this…this nothingness that came after his death. He used to be able to see the Guardians, but they were gone now as well. Everything that helped him cope all these years since his first encounter with the temples and Celestials was gone. Except for Kyra. For now, at least. He was not fool enough to believe she would stay with him forever. Once she found a new Sanctuary for the hybrids, she would leave with them. After all, she was their Queen, and Queens protected their people at all cost.

"What am I going to do, Lucas?" he whispered.

Regardless if he saw or felt Lucas or not, he still felt the need to talk to him. Sometimes it helped him think and clear his mind. It took away the heavy feeling that seemed to weigh down his heart.

He washed the last of the dishes, placed them in the dry rack, then headed back to the living room. He still had to finish his manuscript. Even if it was never published, it had to be done. If only for his own sanity. He sat back, the laptop opened and file set where he had left off the night before, but the words wouldn't come to him. His mind felt blank. Upstairs, he could hear Kyra rummaging around in her room, the wooden floors creaking ever so slightly under her feet.

He tapped his fingers lightly against the side of his laptop, his mind slipping away from the work at hand to the last time he was in the Vault hidden deep within one of the temples. It was an alien space ship and while the one they had in this temple no longer seemed operational, neither was the Void or portal. He avoided the Vault as much as possible. There were some memories he simply didn't want to dwell on. The rest of the temple looked and felt Aztec, allowing him to escape into his Anthropologist roots. The Vault and the Void were alien and made the memories of the Celestial that possessed him all those years ago come roaring back. He spent over a decade trying to rebuild his life and have a family. He did not need to be reminded of the horrible things he had done while possessed. What he needed now was to be left in peace. The last time he was in one of the Vaults, it had been to destroy the Void within. The Shadows had opened it to free more of their kind in. Kyra had been taken captive and forced into it. Alex had followed after her, becoming trapped in a realm between realms. Lucas had gotten them out. Just in time, too. They sent bombs to destroy the Void. There was no way for the Shadows to return, at least not through that portal. There were others. Interdimensional travel systems that could not be destroyed by mere human devices. If even one was still active, they were all in danger. If the one in their Sanctuary was to be activated it could bring the Shadows directly to them, or worse, the Celestials.

Kyra sighed as she weaved her long hair into braids. She couldn't believe how stubborn Alex was being. She understood his fears, but nothing like what had happened to him in his youth was going to happen again. No one was trying to summon the Celestials. She certainly wasn't. She'd rather have nothing to do with them, despite her heritage. Her job was to protect her people and that meant finding a safe place to live where humans couldn't find them and the Shadows could not survive in. Everything Alex and Lucas taught her said that a Sanctuary with an active orb was the safest place. It was light all the time with few to no natural shadows because white the orb may have been the source of light, it was cast everywhere, reflecting off just about every surface. She had read every research paper and journal both her fathers had every written on the subject. It was the only logical chance the hybrids had of surviving. Where they were now was only a temporary solution. The Sanctuary was dying. Without an active orb, it would only be a matter of time before they did, too.

The elastic she was using snapped as she tried to wrap it around the end of her braid. She cursed under her breath. That was her last one. Today was already off to a shaky start, she didn't need anything else to happen. Nonetheless, she needed to keep her hair tied back, and she didn't want to wear a pony tail or bun. Perhaps there were some in the guest room. Elizabeth usually used that room when she visited. It was a mix of a guest room and office that Lucas would use when he needed privacy. Now it sat empty until Elizabeth's return. Thankfully, that was only a few days away. Kyra was looking forward to spending some much needed time with her aunt. Hopefully, she could break Alex out of this funk he was in. Lucas's death had taken a lot out of him…a lot out of both of them, but they had other problems to deal with. Finding a safe home for the hybrids was only one of them. Preparing for the next possible attack, either from the Shadow-beings or the Celestials was the other.

She went into her aunt's room and to the tall chest of drawers that was shoved into the closet. Living in the mountains limited the outfits most of them wore. They all practically lived in jeans and t-shirts or sweaters in the winter. Elizabeth only kept the bare essentials for on her visits, including extra hair elastics and bobby-pins. Kyra finished her braids and let them hang over her shoulders. At least her hair was out of her face while she worked. They had a lot to do at the Sanctuary. They needed to get the lighting situation fixed. They needed to UV to help grow what little crops they could underground. It also helped nourish the hybrids. They thrived in the sunlight. Underground was not the way they should be living. She knew Alex understood that, it was just frustrating having no other choice.

She looked at herself in the mirror, thankful to actually have one to look into to. There were no mirrors in the Sanctuary. Not because they weren't allowed but simply because no one had any and to have them shipped in was a waste of time and resources. So, when she came home, she allowed herself to indulge in the small pleasures that came with it. Perhaps, if she hadn't taken a moment to look at herself, she may have missed the white envelope on the desk across from the mirror. Curious, she went to the desk and picked it up. At first, she thought it was something Elizabeth had forgotten on her last visit and would have left it alone. However, it was addressed to Alex and Kyra. That didn't make sense. All mail that came in was left in the kitchen to be read and then filed away if important. Most of their mail was electronic. Usually sent by email. A physical letter was rare. Her fingers traced over the returning address. She didn't recognize it. Why was a lawyer from Toronto sending them mail? She opened it as she left the room.

"Dad, when's the last time you checked the mail?" Kyra asked as she descended the stairs.

He shrugged. "A month or so."

They rarely got mail and when they did they normally only received it when Elizabeth visited. They had a Postal Box in Temiskaming Shores which she would go to, collect mail, and bring with

24

her. She only came once or twice a month, depending on her schedule. The last few times there was nothing but letters from the government, formally requesting his appearance. There may have been one or two court summons as well. All of which they ignored. The main branch of the Canadian government had been taken over by the Shadows and he had no interest in dealing with them.

"Well, you might want to check this out," Kyra insisted. She sat across from him, her gaze fixed on the letter in her hands. "It's from a lawyer…Papa's lawyer."

He glanced at the letter. Why would a lawyer be reaching out to them now? And why? They had already dealt with a lawyer regarding Lucas's Will. The reading of the Will was scheduled for this Summer in London. However, this one was Canadian, the return address from a law firm in Toronto.

"Let me see that," he said.

Kyra handed the thin piece of paper without question, looking just as perplexed as Alex felt. "Did Papa own property here?"

"Not that I know of."

His brows furrowed as he read the letter and then reread it, confusion growing with every passage. It was dated two months ago, not long after Lucas's death. Considering they had not made a grand announcement that Lucas had passed away, it seemed a little suspicious. Why would Lucas retain a second lawyer in Canada? Why not tell him? Besides, if he owned more property in Canada than what they had and sold in Massey, it made even less sense. If there was one thing he knew about Lucas, it was that he never did anything without reason. Given the fact they rarely left their home in the mountains and always stayed in hotels or resorts when they traveled, this felt more like a hoax than anything else. Perhaps the Shadows were trying to lure them away from the safety of the barrier that surrounded their home. There was no other logical explanation.

"What are you doing?" Kyra asked as he stood.

He strolled past her to the wood stove and went to throw the letter and envelope into it. She saved the letter before it could be consumed by the flames.

"Shouldn't we call them and see if this is legit?" she asked. Her eyes were wide in surprise at his actions.

"It's an obvious trap. There is no lawyer. Your Papa never owned any property in Toronto. He would have told me," Alex pointed out.

Kyra didn't answer as she went to the kitchen and grabbed the satellite phone off the counter.

"Kyra, no."

She dialled the number listed in the letter. Of course, the girl wasn't going to listen to him. She was as strong willed as Lucas. Alex pinched the bridge of his nose as he sat back down. This was futile at best. It was all a shame. There was no lawyer, no property, no buildings that Lucas owned. Even if he had purchased them with Owen way back in the day, he would have told Alex. After all, why would a lawyer be calling them if he hadn't added said property to his Will? It didn't make sense for Lucas to have two Wills, one in London and the other in here in Canada. Having more than one Will wasn't unheard of. In fact, it was practical when it came to property, but it seemed a little over the top. Lucas was a practical man and had his fair share of secrets, most of which Alex had been fortunate enough to learn over the years. This didn't sit right with him.

"Uh huh," Kyra murmured.

She returned to the living room and sat down again. A pen and paper were held in one hand. She placed them on the coffee table and began jotting down the details she was being told. Alex tilted his head to read it. Her penmanship left a lot to be desired. It was not as crisp as it was when he taught her cursive as a child, but it didn't take long to realize that she was writing down a series of addresses and a website. He raised a brow in silent question.

"Yes, we'll be there tomorrow at one," she told whomever she was speaking to before hanging up.

"No, we won't," Alex objected.

She gave him a hard stare. "Yes, we are. Papa owned multiple properties. I'm not talking about land. Buildings. Actual buildings. Three apartment buildings and two skyscrapers."

"Bullshit."

She blinked in surprise. It was rare for Alex to swear. With an audible sigh, she took his laptop, minimized the program he was using, then clicked onto the internet icon. Their internet access, like their phone, was through satellite and it wasn't the most reliable. The website she wanted came up and she silently read over the page. A moment later, she stood, carried the laptop with her, then sat next to Alex so he could see it as well. What the website displayed took him by surprise. There was an image of two skyscrapers close to the Lake Ontario shoreline with the Toronto skyline behind them. At first there was nothing noticeable that would tie Lucas to them. Then, at the bottom of the page read O&L Griffiths Foundation. Alex remembered the O&L Griffiths Foundation. Owen created it to support Lucas's research as an Archeologist. After Owen's death, everything went to Lucas, but there had been very little talk of it. Lucas took a job as a guest speaker at a variety of Canadian Universities, often traveling for days or even weeks on end. He never mentioned another source of income. After the fire that destroyed their home in Massey and sent them into hiding in the mountains, he had reframed from teaching to focus on their family. They rarely left home and when they did it was for small family vacations. They had been to Toronto several times but not once had Lucas mentioned owning any buildings or skyscrapers. You would think if someone owned such things they would point it out to their loved ones.

"Papa and Uncle Owen must have bought them when they were in their twenties," Kyra mused. She opened the menu and read through each page.

"Check the source code," Alex instructed. "It will tell us when this website was created. If it's new…then this is a scam."

"Dad…"

"Please."

She took a deep breath through her nose before doing as requested. She right clicked on the home page then selected *View Source Code* from the pop-up menu. A panel opened on the right with all the HTML for the webpage. Every detail for the page was displayed before them, from the date of creation to layout. It took a quick search to find the publication date, but when they did, Alex was even more confused.

"Twenty-five years," Alex whispered in disbelief.

"That's the skyscrapers," Kyra reminded him.

She opened another website. This one showed a series of apartments. They weren't as tall or fancy as the skyscrapers, but still elegant. Kyra repeated the process to find the date this website was originally created. Again, it seemed to be twenty-five years.

"That's not possible. He would have told me. Why wouldn't he tell me? Tell us?"

Kyra shook her head. "I don't know. Either way, we're meeting with the lawyer tomorrow and sorting this out."

It still felt like a trap to Alex. "No. We can't take the risk. We have hybrids migrating here on a daily basis. Who's going to watch for them and monitor the temple? If the shield comes down, no one knows how to fix it."

"Winston can handle the shield. And Marie is more than capable of running things until we get back."

He began to object but she cut him off before he could say a word.

"Dad, we need to find out if this is real or not. Maybe…maybe we can sell all five buildings. If anything, it'll get us the money we need to house the hybrids. If people are living in the apartments, we can set a clause where whomever buys them has to allow the people living there to stay at the same rent they're paying now." Her gaze searched his, obviously still seeing the doubt within them. "And if it's a trap…you get to say you told me so before I kill them."

Kyra's proclamation may have shocked some, but after everything they had been through it seemed like the natural response. Alex nodded in agreement. He normally stood against killing, but after Lucas's death, right and wrong had become blurred. Besides, anyone they faced off with now was likely possessed by one of the Shadows and already dead, their body animated by the creature within it.

"Fine," he agreed.

As much as he didn't want to go, he had to admit his curiosity was piqued. Why had Lucas kept these buildings secret all these years? And how did the lawyer learn of his death? There were only three people who would have made the announcement: himself, Kyra, or Elizabeth. If Elizabeth did it then that meant Lucas had trusted her with his secret instead of him, his husband. That brought up an old sense of betrayal that Alex had not felt in many years.

Chapter Three

The shaking in his hands wouldn't stop as he pressed the phone to his ear. It was cold out, but he needed to get out of the house to catch his breath. He should have been packing, instead he stood on the patio as Kyra started up their small private plane, waiting for Elizabeth to answer his call. They didn't usually fly during the winter. The lake was frozen but there were pockets of water here and there that could cause issues should one of the pontoons dip in and get caught on the ice. It would be better if the lake was either completely frozen or completely thawed. This in between stage was due to the numerous waterfalls and fast flowing rivers. The lake never fully froze over.

"Alex, is everything okay?" Elizabeth answered.

Her concern surprised Alex for a moment before he remembered they had agreed to limit their communication due to the ongoing aggression from the government. The anger he felt momentarily subsided.

"Yeah...no..." He took a deep breath. "Did you know Lucas owned property in Toronto? Apartments and skyscrapers?"

There was a long moment of silence. That alone told Alex everything he needed to know. Lucas had confided in her but not him.

"I assumed you knew," she finally answered.

He knew from the tone of her voice that it was a lie. "Did he tell you why he purchased them?"

There was an audible sigh on the other end of the phone. "They're income properties. Owen bought them years ago when the market was cheap and they were trying to break away from their family. He added Lucas's name to them to ensure he had an income after their father disowned him. From what I know, he had very little to do with them other than insuring a maintenance crew took care of the buildings and tenants. Alex…it wasn't something he was trying to keep secret from you. After Owen died, he simply cut himself off from his former life to be with you. Losing Owen shattered him."

That was the truth. Owen and Lucas were tied at the hip. There was rarely one without the other. When Owen died, Lucas had been lost and alone for the first time in his life. In many ways, it was that loss that brought about the bond between Alex and Lucas. Alex had fallen in love with both brothers shortly after they met. His relationship with Lucas began as purely sexual while he shared a more emotional bond with Owen. Would he and Lucas have become a couple had Owen survived? Or would Alex have ended up with the older brother? Guilt churned in Alex's stomach at the mere thought of being with Owen instead of Lucas. Sure, they had a threesome and he cared for both dearly, but how different would his life have been had he married Owen and not simply been haunted by his spirit?

"Alex?"

"Hmm…"

"Are you alright?" Elizabeth asked.

"I don't know," he answered honestly. He glanced toward the plane as Kyra waved to him. Singling she was ready to leave. "Can you meet us at the lawyer's office?"

He could almost see her nod.

"Of course. Anything you need."

31

He pursed his lips in thought. "I need you to do a background search on this lawyer. Tisdale & Associates. I want to know everything about them before I meet with them."

"You've got it. Fly safe."

He hung up, still bitter that she knew about the buildings Lucas owned and neither had bothered to tell him. Sadly, that was more common than he wanted to admit. He didn't have time to feel sorry for himself. Whatever Lucas's secrets, he would learn them in time.

Kyra waited for him on the dock, a worried expression on her face.

"Are we good to go?" she asked.

She didn't bring up the conversation. She likely overheard his conversation with Elizabeth. Her hearing was uncanny. Regardless if she meant to eavesdrop or not, she likely heard every word he and Elizabeth said. Her power had increased considerably since absorbing Archer – the hybrid who had killed Lucas. His power now flowed through her. They were not yet sure of the extent, and honestly, Alex was afraid to test it. His mission had always been to protect his daughter and keep her alien heritage a secret. After the attack in Ottawa, that was much harder now than ever before.

He glanced out over the icy lake. "You sure you can get this bird in the air? There's an awful lot of ice and snow."

"It's not snowing or windy," she counted, reminding him the storm from the night before was over. "It may be a little bumpy, but we'll make it."

Her lips turned downward in a small frown as she looked out over the partially frozen water. No doubt she was thinking of Lucas and his fear of flying, especially in such conditions. Had he been there with them, he would have told them to wait until spring to deal with the lawyer, or better yet, do everything over video conferencing. It wasn't a bad idea. They had satellite internet and a strong enough bandwidth, if not a little shotty at times. It was military grade after all. However, that was also the problem. There was no telling who could be spying on their internet activity. If this lawyer was legit, then they had to meet him in person.

"The weather in Toronto looks good. We should be able to land at the island with no problem," she continued. She stepped aside to let him in.

The plane was small: a Hartzell Propeller, which was considerably smaller than the plane they would normally fly; a Canadair CL-215T. It was less likely to attract attention and didn't need as long of a runway, or in this case, length on the lake, to take off. Alex slid into the co-pilot seat only to frown when he noticed his cane resting next to his seat. His bad leg was bothering him, but he thought he had done a better job of hiding his discomfort. He glared at Kyra as she took her seat but she ignored it. Instead, she slid her headset on and took the controls of the plane. Slowly, she backed it away from the pier. The vehicle turned until the nose faced out over open water. There was a moment of bobbing before the plane began moving forward, slowly accelerating. It bounced several times as she slowly pulled the throttle back, but soon they were in the air and flying over the mountains.

Alex put his headset on then stared out the side window at the world below. His gut churned with anxiety at the thought of leaving his home. Without Lucas, the chalet and the temple hidden beneath it, were his only sanctuaries.

Both headsets were connected to the onboard computer. A touchscreen monitor was set in the center. To Alex's surprise, it came alive with Liam's perplex face looking back at them. The young man was blind, unable to see those around him but able to sense their unique energies. He was for all intents and purposes, Kyra's right hand.

"Winston has the new computer system up and running," Liam reported. His pale, sightless eyes directed toward Kyra. "We're tracking you. So far the airspace is clear. Winston has taken it upon himself to keep it that way. Any air traffic that he can't reroute won't be able to read your identification. You'll look like any other private plane with a fake ID number generated anytime they try to scan you."

"That includes military aircraft?" Alex asked. They were nearing the edge of the no-fly zone where they would be vulnerable.

"There are two CF-18 Hornets patrolling north of us. Winston believes you're cloaked from them. If they do turn to intercept…" He whispered something off screen, likely to Winston. "We'll reroute them."

"What about potential new hybrids and possible unwanted visitors?" Alex asked. He couldn't bring himself to say the Canadian Armed Forces. They were supposed to be on the same side until the government was taken over by the Shadows.

Liam nodded. "We have people patrolling. Don't worry, everything's fine. Enjoy Toronto."

Alex gave a snort while Kyra grinned. She liked the city while he was happier in his solitude.

"We'll be back tomorrow," he reminded the young man.

"Or the day after," Kyra teased. "We may hit up the aquarium or do some sightseeing. I haven't been to the CN Tower in a long time." She flashed her father a grin. "Oh, come on, diner at the CN Tower…we haven't done that in ages. It'll be nice."

He bit the inside of his mouth and looked away from her. It would be nice if they weren't missing a certain someone.

She sighed loudly. "We'll see you tomorrow, Liam."

She didn't say anything after Liam logged off. Her gaze focused on the sky before them, as she flew the plane up over the grey clouds to where the sky was clear and sunny. Alex glanced toward her, noting the small frown that pulled on her lips. She really did want to do more than see the lawyer and figure out their new mystery. Visiting the aquarium and CN Tower had not been mere quips or jokes, she truly did want to go out and do something like they used to be Lucas. She spent most of her life in hiding, training for the day she would face off against not only the Shadows but her own kind. The last few years had been hard on her, not just Lucas's death - that was still relatively recent – but the years working undercover for Earth Defense Command, trying to find and save hybrids. She never really had a normal life. Perhaps it wasn't such a bad idea to have some father-daughter time.

"We'll do lunch at the CN Tower," he conceded. "Dinner is too expensive and not worth the money. Lucas paid well over $500 dollars last time."

A tiny grin tugged at her lips. "That's because it was your anniversary and he bought their most expensive wine." Her gaze met his. "Imagine if they had the real expensive stuff in stock."

That brought a whimsical smile to Alex. Lucas would have happily purchased a bottle of wine worth well over ten grand if it was available to him. He had done it numerous times for their collection that was now worth well over a million dollars. It would not be unlike him to buy one for their anniversary. Lucas had acquired a small fortune throughout his life and rarely spent any of it. It simply continued to build with interest.

He pushed the last thought down. This was the first time he and Kyra had left their mountain home in months. He couldn't keep burying himself in his sorrow. It wasn't something Lucas would want him to do. Especially in front of their daughter. This trip, regardless the reason for it, would give them time to heal without the constant reminders of what happened. If it was a trap…they would deal with it, but a few days away from all the chaos that surrounded their home was a small blessing.

The flight was uneventful. The CF-18 Hornets flew past them, conducting a visual fly-by but otherwise left them alone as they continued to patrol the region. There were a lot of pilots in the area with small aircraft so it wasn't unusual see one close to the no-fly zone.

They arrived in Toronto in the early afternoon. The waters of Lake Ontario were wide open and not frozen over, the temperature considerably warmer than that of Northern Ontario. Kyra guided the plane over the water to the airport as she spoke with air traffic control. It wasn't long before they were okayed for landing, their small plane equipped to land on both land and water. They touched down on the runway and taxied toward a spot indicated by traffic control. Kyra waited a few moments before shutting down the engines, her keen eyes scanning the area around them to ensure they weren't led into a trap and have to make a hasty departure. Alex watched as well, his nerves on end. Nothing happened. No police or soldiers came charging at them. No weapons were aimed toward them. It was just a quiet sunny day in Toronto.

Alex exchanged a look with his daughter, relief putting a smile on his face. She looked more sober, her head tilted to one side as if listening to someone or something. Her appearance changed a moment later, her white-blond hair darkening to brown and pale skin tone taking on a healthy tan. It wasn't her normal human disguise but rather that of an older woman in her mid to late forties. He didn't bother to ask why she took on such an appearance, he trusted her instinct. She had an uncanny ability to take on the right form needed for just about any situation. This was proven correct as they exited the plane only to be met with a security guard.

"Doctor Miller," the man called. He jogged toward them, waving one arm and clearly out of breath.

Alex glanced at Kyra, a small grin tugging at his lips. The disguise now made sense.

Kyra hefted her bag over one shoulder, an annoyed expression on her face. "Yes?"

The security guard stopped in front of her, huffing as he bent over, one hand on his knee. He was an older gentleman, possibly former police, and sadly out of shape. "We heard about the mishap earlier this year, with you plane being stolen. I need to check your ID."

"As you can clearly see, it's been recovered."

"Yes, ma'am. Protocols."

She rolled her eyes. "Shouldn't this be done inside?" she questioned. She pulled out a passport from her bag and handed it over to him. "Happy?"

He looked it over carefully before handing it back to her. "Yes ma'am. Thank you."

She gave a curt nod then walked past him. "Call a taxi, please. We need to get to downtown."

"Of course! There should be some just outside the airport. This way."

It wasn't nearly as cold in Toronto compared to the Ishpatina Ridge. While the mountains surrounding the home provided a lot of protection, it was also bitterly cold. Toronto was several degrees warmer and within the downtown core it would be warmer still due to the heat produced by the number of people, large buildings, and traffic. Even though Alex enjoyed visiting the city, it was too busy and noisy for his liking.

"Elizabeth should be here by now," he remarked. He glanced skyward, hoping to see her larger transport plane that she flew from base to base, carrying either supplies or soldiers, but there was no sign of it. Concerned, he followed Kyra and the security guard into the airport terminal.

Kyra shrugged. "She's probably running late."

Alex wasn't so sure. Elizabeth was their direct line to the EDC outside the Sanctuary. She moved through the ranks quickly and in only ten short years became a general. She was their eyes and ears withing the Air Force. However, despite her rank, she was notoriously late. It was something Alex should have been accustomed to by now.

"Can I use your phone?" he asked. A smartphone was no good in the mountains, but Kyra kept one on her ever since her last assignment. It was automatically paid every month, regardless if she used it.

She gave it to him without question.

He gave her a grateful smile and dialed Elizabeth's number. He held the phone to his ear and wait…and waited, and waited. There was no answer. While that wasn't unusual for Elizabeth, it was concerning.

With a sigh, he gave the phone back to his daughter. "I'll try again later."

Kyra took his hand and gave it a squeeze. "I'm sure she's just running behind."

He nodded. Hopefully, that was all it was.

The security guard took them to the taxi stand just outside the airport, going as far as opening the car's door for Kyra and shutting it as soon as she was safely inside. He wasn't as courteous to Alex. The anthropologist simply gave him a nod before sliding in next to his daughter.

"Is it me or was that weird," Alex asked as they pulled away.

"That security met us at the plane?" she asked. She leaned forward to speak with the taxi driver. "Wellington West and York, please." She sat back down. "Someone gave them a heads up."

"Which means they'll be watching us," he concluded. "It was a bad idea to come here."

She nodded. She kept her voice low for only him to hear. "Perhaps, but I intend to find out why this lawyer contacted us. If it's a trap…then I'd prefer to face them head on here rather than hiding in the mountains. Sooner or later, they'll come for us there."

"What if it's a divide and conquer technique?"

"Then I pray our security is enough to keep the others safe." She turned in her seat to face him. "Regardless how you feel, we need to find a safer place. It's only a matter of time before the…they're no longer safe."

Alex glanced at their driver. They should wait until once they were out of the vehicle to speak about the hybrids and their current situation. Kyra reached over and took his hand, giving it a gentle squeeze. It reminded him to take a deep breath. No matter what happened, they were in this together. He squeezed her hand back. Despite everything that had happened, they were still together. That was all that mattered.

The taxi weaved through traffic as it left the small island and made it's way into the city. It was slow moving, the afternoon rush hour having taken hold of the downtown core. After ten minutes, the driver pulled over, having reached the intersection of Wellington West and York. Kyra thanked him and paid him in cash, then she and Alex exited the taxi, their bags in hand. It was an odd place to get out. The lawyer's office was nowhere near their location, neither was a hotel. This was a business district. Nonetheless, Kyra took his arm and began leading him down the street. For her to do this there had to be something wrong.

"What's going on?" he asked. He glanced over his shoulder. All he saw were people rushing from place to place.

"We're being followed," she responded.

He looked back once more but could not see anyone following them. In fact, no one was even looking in their direction. "I don't see anyone."

She didn't look back. That didn't surprise him. She saw or felt things he could not. He trusted her completely. If she said they were being followed then they were being followed. They moved quickly down the street then turned a corner. She held his marked hand, the one scarred by one of the Celestials' artifacts. It began to tingle, the sensation of her power building and flowing from her to him. It wasn't immediately clear what she was doing. She didn't pause or stop as they moved. Alex caught his reflection in one of the windows and almost stumbled at the image that looked back at him. He looked like a young man, half his age, dressed casually in jeans and a warm jacket. Kyra's appearance had changed as well, now looking her age but with brown air pulled into a ponytail. Her clothing had changed from warm and practical to a short skirt and hooded bomber jacket, paired with knee high boots. They were clever disguises but only bought them a few minutes at most. If regular humans were following them then they were fine. If a Shadow or Shadow possessed person was following them, then they would be able to detect Kyra's and his energy signature, something that was unique to each individual. It would be near impossible to lose them. However, while this was part of Old Toronto, the original ten blocks that form the city in the later 1700s, there was a lot of foot traffic. They turned up Bay Street and cut through a courtyard to Jordan Street. At the next corner Kyra changed their appearances again before ducking into a café. She whispered something under her breath as they passed through the door, her fingers grazing over the metal doorframe. Whoever or whatever was following them did not follow them inside.

"Now what?" Alex asked.

She let go of his hand and stepped up to the counter.

"We eat," she answered.

He shook his head as she ordered food and drink for them both. Kyra certainly took after Lucas more than him. She was very take-charge. A born leader. Lucas would be proud if he saw her right now. No wonder they always shared such a close bond. They were quite literally daughter-like-father. That similarity brought a source of comfort to Alex. Such a small thing gave him confidence that Kyra could handle anything that was thrown at her.

They found a seat in the back of the café, away from the windows but with the door in full view. A small laugh escaped Alex. The location brought about a forgotten memory of Owen. Many years ago, he and Owen had gone to a café and sat in a similar spot to watch the door in case someone was following them.

"What?" Kyra asked, surprised by the outburst.

He shook his head. "I was just thinking about your Uncle Owen. He was protective, like you."

A small smile lit her face. She hid it behind her coffee cup and sipped at the hot brew. Alex didn't want to admit it, but he missed Owen. They had only known each other a few short days, but his spirit still lived on, even if Alex could no longer see it. He felt it.

"What time was that meeting tomorrow?" he said. He took a bite of his scone, his coffee still too hot to enjoy.

She lowered her cup and licked her lips. "1 pm. We'll need to find a hotel for the night."

Her gaze moved toward the door. Alex knew better than to turn and look. It would draw unwanted attention to them if they both stared out the door.

"Our stalkers?" he asked instead.

"They passed by," she informed him. "Remind me to thank Marie when we get home."

"Why?"

She blinked slowly as she turned back to him. "Oh…she taught me a trick to ward off the Shadows. It's temporary but keeps them from seeing us inside a building."

"What sort of trick?"

She shrugged. "It's kind of a Wiccan spell."

"Marie's a Celestial, not a Wiccan."

"Why can't she be both?"

There were numerous reasons but none that were truly logical. Alex stopped himself from voicing them. If Celestials truly were as old as his research said, then they were likely worshipped as Gods at one time and whatever gifts they had could be mistaken for spells or magick.

He sighed and shook his head. "Never mind. We need to figure out our next move. The Shadows know we're here. If they've infiltrated the local police then we're in bigger trouble than expected. And they most likely know about the lawyer."

She nodded. "You were right. We shouldn't have come here." She took a deep breath through her nose and let it out slowly. "Should we forget about all this and head home?"

It was tempting. They would be much safer on their own turf where they had the equipment to protect themselves from the Shadows and just about any form of attack. Here they were wide open. There was no place they could hide, not for long at least.

"Do you still have contacts here?" he asked.

"The EDC headquarters isn't far from here...if it's still operational, but...they may not accept us. Director White doesn't exactly like me. With what happened in Ottawa...I highly doubt she'll give us sanctuary."

That left them very few options other than to find and confront this lawyer. If it was a trap, they would have to deal with it. Alex was glad they hadn't booked a hotel yet. They may need to make a speedy retreat to their plane and leave as quickly as they arrived.

"Do you have the addresses for the skyscrapers Lucas allegedly owns?" he inquired as he stood up.

Her brows furrowed. "Yes?"

A smirk tugged at one corner of his mouth. "Then let's have a look at them." He offered her his hand. "Let's see if the Shadows are hanging around the building and the one the lawyer is supposedly located. Make sure everything is legit before we meet him."

Her lips pursed and nose wrinkled in deep thought. Then she shrugged, took his hand, and stood. "Why not? Better than waiting for them to catch us."

"Exactly...but first, that little spell or charm you did to hide us here...can you do that on a personal level? Maybe like a shield around us?"

She bit her lower lip, looking uncertain. Then, without a word, reached for his necklace and took the two small canisters that contained some of both Owen's and Lucas's ashes in it. She murmured the same words she had as they entered the café, so low that Alex could barely make them out. It caused a tingling sensation in Alex's right hand, a sign of the power she was pouring into the necklace. It lasted but a moment before settling. She did the same to her own necklace, a similar canister hung from it with some of Lucas's ashes.

Alex was hesitant, not happy that she chose to charm the ashes. Another part of him was almost relived that she had. In a way, it was as if Owen and Lucas were still protecting them. It was oddly comforting. He squeezed her hand, his thumb rubbing a gentle pattern across the back of it as he would when she was little.

He still doubted the existence of these skyscrapers and apartment buildings, but together they would get to the bottom of this mystery.

Chapter Four

They found the building that housed Tisdale and Associates, the lawyer claiming to be handling Lucas's Canadian will. It was only a few blocks from the café. According to the map Kyra pulled up on her smartphone, the skyscrapers weren't that far away either, only a kilometer south on Queen Quay West. Both were within walking distance. They went into the office building to confirm the lawyer office was in fact there and spoke with the receptionist. Neither one gave their real name. They merely asked about what sort of law the association specialized in, got their card, and booked an appointment for the following Friday. It was enough to prove that Tisdale and Associates was a real company. Whether or not it was dominated by Shadow-beings remained to be seen. Alex was still certain this was a trap.

They decided to stay in the five-star hotel directly across from the lawyer's office. Normally, to get into such a fancy hotel, they would need to book months in advance. However, Kyra changed their appearance once more. Now they looked like they were a high class, power duo of lawyers that came to Toronto at the last minute to meet with Tisdale and Associates. Kyra requested adjoining rooms for one or two nights. When they asked for a credit card, Kyra pulled a large envelope of cash from her bag and handed it to the desk clerk.

"There's more than enough in there to cover our expenses," she assured the young man. "We would like rooms on the twenty-first floor, facing south."

The clerk stared at the cash in disbelief before pulling out all the money and counting out the amount needed for the rooms for two nights, as well as the deposit fee. He handed the rest back to Kyra, taking her and Alex by surprise. Some people simply accepted the money without a word. He printed out keycards and handed them to Kyra and Alex.

"Take the central elevator up and follow the signs. There's a balcony connecting the two rooms," he informed them. "The restaurant is open until ten and bar until two. Room service is available."

Kyra gave a nod and thanked him, then led the way to the elevator. Once they were inside the carriage and alone, she visibly relaxed.

"I don't think we've been here before," she remarked. She sat her bag on the floor and rolled her shoulders.

Alex had to think for a moment. "No…usually we're closer to the ROM." A small laugh escaped him. "Lucas would try to get the penthouse suite every chance he could. He would be highly disappointed you didn't go for it here."

She laughed as well. "We're on a recognisance mission. Plus, we're paying cash. I only have a limited supply of it…and we're already nearing our budget. I don't want to hit the bank if we can help it. The moment we withdraw anything…the government is going to know exactly where we are."

"Yeah," he agreed with a nod.

He had no doubt the government was tracking their financial activity. When they moved into the mountains, they made it a point to take out as much money as he and Lucas could from their bank accounts and stashed it at the chalet. It was for a sense of security more than anything else. It wasn't as if anyone was going to steal from them way out in the mountains, but trekking into the nearest town sometimes meant cash was handier than a bank or credit card. Of course, there were a lot of places that no longer dealt with cash, such as most hotels. A credit card was needed to hold the room. They managed to get lucky this time. Or perhaps it was merely Kyra's power that had convinced the clerk to let them pay in cash.

"How's our Shadow situation?" he asked.

"I charmed the entrance, but it's hard to tell whether or not they'll enter another way," she reported. "So far, they're leaving us alone…but they're close. Twilight is coming. They'll be more powerful then."

"Then we'll stay here for the rest of the evening. You can charm the rooms and we'll order room service. The less exposed we are the better."

Kyra sighed, her heart obviously on something different, but she didn't object.

"We'll go to the CN Tower tomorrow for a late lunch," her father promised.

She nodded but didn't say anything.

A *ding* sound signaled they reached their floor. The wide double doors slid open to reveal a cream-coloured hallway with a beautiful floral pattern carpet, dark cherry wood accented walls and doors. Wooden signs with numbers painted in gold, directed them toward their rooms. They were at the end of the hall which turned out to be far larger and more elegant than Alex was anticipating. His room had a small living room/dinette with a work space. He passed through that to reach the bedroom and bathroom. Large floor to ceiling windows looked out over the city and gave a perfect view of the lawyer's offices. Kyra's room was identical.

"A real bed," Kyra sighed. She dropped her bag on the sofa and strolled toward the large bed, flopping face first onto it.

"You have a real bed at home," Alex reminded her.

"Yeah, well I'm sleeping on a cot at the Sanctuary," she countered. "You have no idea how much my back has been killing me."

"No one said you had to move there."

She gave him a sideways look that clearly said she didn't have much of a choice after the hybrids began showing up. She lived in the Sanctuary to care for them.

"Please tell me the tub is a jacuzzi," she murmured. She stretched out on her bed, as if she was ready to go to sleep already rather than spy of the lawyer.

"Those things are horrible in hotels," Alex advised. He took a peak in the bathroom for her, nonetheless. "Yep, one big noise echoing jacuzzi. If your back is bothering you that much, we could head to the whirlpool."

"That too…peoplely." She rolled onto her side. "I just want to soak for while…before bed, not right now."

Alex frowned in concern. In his mourning over Lucas, he had forgotten how much stress his daughter was under. Not only from losing her father, but also from becoming the leader of a group of young people. They may be hybrids, but most were young kids who either ran away from home once it became known what they were, or escaped government agents and Shadows that had been hunting them. Kyra was now in charge of not only housing and feeding dozens hybrids, but also protecting them. She didn't have nearly enough help to accomplish this. Those that worked with her were young adults as well, with the exception of himself, Marie, and the few remaining EDC.

"Go bathe in the jacuzzi," he instructed. "By the time you're done, dinner should be here."

"Are you sure?"

He nodded as he picked up the phone. "You need it. Go on."

A small smile lit her face as she got up.

"Thank you," she told him. She kissed his cheek before disappearing into the huge bathroom.

He ordered dinner for them both. Nothing too fancy, but something they would both enjoy and was far better than what Kyra had been eating the last few months in the Sanctuary. A nice thick steak with potatoes and vegetables and a bottle of wine would make them both feel better.

The sound of running water came from the bathroom followed by the loud hum of the jets of the jacuzzi a few minutes later. Alex shook his head in bemusement as he headed toward the balcony. The jacuzzi wasn't as loud as some but it was still an annoyance to him. Despite the cool weather, the balcony was enjoyable. There was a small bistro patio set that allowed him to sit back and relax as he looked out over the city. It was the perfect vantage point to spy on the lawyer's office, but it also allowed him to look past the other building toward Lake Ontario and the few skyscrapers that dotted the shore line. One of them was Lucas's. Their plan to scope it out had fallen short, but at least they knew how to get there. His mind travelled back to the numerous time he and Lucas had come to Toronto. Perhaps Lucas had said something about the properties, even if passing. There was one time, way back when they first officially became a couple that Lucas asked if Alex would ever consider moving to the city and perhaps live in an apartment or skyscraper. Alex had shot down the notion. He had just begun building his vineyard in Massey where he owned nearly a hundred acres of land. Why would he ever move to the city? Had Lucas been hinting at the property he owned? Had he subtly tried to tell him that he didn't want to live in the country but rather be in the city? Lucas had enjoyed the nightlife before they got together, often attending prominent events and parties. Guilt hit Alex like a punch to the gut. Lucas had sacrificed so much more than his life for him. He had given up everything he knew to be with Alex…and Alex had questioned their relationship earlier that day. It took quite a bit of love and devotion to upend one's life for someone else.

"Damn it, Lucas. Why didn't you tell me?" he muttered.

He ran a hand across his face. Lucas seemed so happy with their life, especially after adopting Kyra. He tended the vineyard, excelled at making homemade wine, even after they lost the original vineyard and winery. Was it all an act to appease Alex? Did he really want to be here instead?

He took Kyra's phone and tried calling Elizabeth again. She should have been in Toronto long ago. However, there was still answer.

"Hey…are you okay?" Kyra asked.

Alex jerked with a start. He hadn't noticed the jacuzzi stop running or the bathroom door open. His daughter stood in the doorway, wrapped in a luxurious white robe and slippers. She still wore her human disguise but looked exhausted. It wouldn't take long for her to fall asleep.

"I'm fine," Alex assured. He looked past her to the cart now in her room. The food had arrived without him noticing. "I'm sorry, I must have been daydreaming."

She nodded. "It's okay. I was getting out of the tub when I heard the knock. I paid for it."

He shook his head. "I should have…"

"It's alright. Do you want to eat out here or…"

"No…no. You're wet. We'll eat inside."

He stood and followed her back into her room. For the rest of the evening, they enjoyed a quiet dinner and took turns watching the lawyer's office. It was late by the time they closed and the last person left for the night. Well near midnight. No Shadows appeared, other than the natural ones. That didn't sit quite right with Alex. There were street lights everywhere, each shining brightly and creating shadows as vehicles and people passed below. It was the perfect environment for the Shadow-beings. It was a virtual breeding ground. Yet, he could not feel them. The world outside was quiet. Even Kyra was at ease, her senses not picking up anything out of the ordinary.

Unsure what else to do and not yet tired enough to sleep, Alex suggested they was a movie, something they had no done as a family in many years. Kyra's eye lit up with a childlike joy. They snuggled together on the sofa in her room and watched one of her childhood favourites that was available for rent. She only made it half way through before exhaustion finally took hold of her and the promise of a comfy bed was too much to ignore. She bid Alex goodnight, climbed into bed, and within minutes was sound asleep. Alex smiled softly as he covered her. She looked peaceful as she snuggled under the comforter. It reminded him of when she was little. He left the lights on, as he had since she was little. A small protection against the Shadow-beings despite her protective charms. She didn't even use a night mask. The light didn't bother her, only the dark.

Alex closed the shades then retreated to his room. He closed his own shades before going to the sofa in his room, completely foregoing the bed. He couldn't sleep in it. It was too large, meant for two, and Lucas was not there with him. He didn't bother to turn his lights off either. It was harder for him to sleep with the light on, not that he expected to get much sleep. Nonetheless, he had to try. Tomorrow was going to be a long day and he couldn't face it exhausted. He did that far too often for his liking.

He closed his eyes and tried to make his mind go blank so he could sleep, but nagging thoughts refused to go away. He kept thinking about the lawyer, the alleged properties, the Sanctuary, the hybrids, Elizabeth. Where was she? Why hasn't she shown up or at the very least return any of his calls? Was she alright? This wasn't like her.

With a groan, he sat up and turned on the television, keeping the volume low as to not wake up Kyra. There was very little of interest on and he was not in the mood to rent another movie. There were a few old comedies from his childhood, news, late night talk shows. He flipped through the channels, hoping something might catch his interest.

Go to bed, a familiar voice whispered told him. It whispered across his mind like a gentle caress.

He shrugged it off, believing it to be a figment of his imagination.

Go to bed, Alex, it said more firmly.

The door between his room and Kyra's suddenly closed, startling Alex. It wasn't loud enough to awaken his daughter but the sudden movement did not go unnoticed. Alex stood and looked around. All the lights were on. That didn't mean they were safe. Lights casts shadows meaning the Shadow-beings could move within them. Kyra's spell was all they had to ward them off. Nonetheless, that spell came from Marie and he was still not certain if they could trust her.

He cautiously moved to the door, fearful a Shadow may have made it into Kyra's room. Opening the door, he quietly slipped inside and checked every dark space, including under the bed, searching for movement, something darker than the average shadow. There was nothing out of the ordinary. Relieved, he went back to his room and searched it as well with the same result.

There must have been a breeze.

He glanced at the alarm clock next to the bed, tempted the call Elizabeth once more. It was nearly three in the morning. Wherever she was, she was likely asleep. He hated this. She should be here or at least call to tell she'd be delayed. It was unlike her. His stomach knotted in worry. What if…

There was no way he was getting any sleep until he heard from her. He sat back on the sofa and stared blankly at the television. Now what?

Alex…go to bed, that voice insisted.

He knew that voice. It was in his head and he was no going to acknowledge it. It would only prove he was losing his mind. Lucas was dead and gone. His past whispers were just that, in the past. Lucas was not coming back to him, no matter how much Alex wanted him to.

Turning off the television, he lay down on the sofa, his head resting on the spare pillow he had found in the closet. He closed his eyes and begged whatever deity above would bless him with sleep. It refused to come. He lay there, wide awake, first on his side, then on his back staring up at the ceiling. The sofa wasn't quite long enough for him to fit properly. Nor was it comfortable. Neither of those things mattered. It was only a matter of time before sleep would come.

Stop being so stubborn, the voice chastised him. *You're hurting your spine each time you sleep on the sofa. Go to bed.*

Alex rolled over and pressed his face in the pillow. He didn't want to listen to the voice. No one was there. It wasn't real.

"Go away," he pleaded. He *was* losing his mind.

Fingers carded through his hair. They were cool and soothing and regardless of his mental anguish, Alex relaxed under them. They felt real, even though he knew that was impossible. The fingers were replaced by warm lips to the back of his neck and scarred shoulder. Alex knew it was impossible, that this was all some sort of dream, but the tension in his shoulders slowly began to melt away until his body finally relaxed. Fingers kneaded his shoulders, pressing deep into the muscles like one of Lucas's deep tissue massages. It may all be a dream, but there was nothing wrong with indulging it. He could worry about Shadows and Elizabeth in the morning.

Go to bed, the voice urged once more.

This time, rather than dismissing the advice, Alex pulled himself off the sofa and padded over the to large bed. The plush pillows and silver comforter called to him, but he froze, unable to pull down the covers and climb in.

Stop being so stubborn.

He flexed his fingers. Then, hesitantly, he drew back the covers and climbed in. His body melted into the softness. No wonder Kyra fell asleep so quickly. It was the perfect mix of firm yet soft and the pillow supported his head and neck exactly as it should. The bed was simply divine, if not too large for one person.

He stared longingly at the other side where Lucas would normally be and the contentment he felt slipped away, replaced by cold loneliness.

Stop it, the voice chastised once more. The ghostly fingers brushed over his cheek, wiping away his tears. *You're not alone. You never were. You just need to quiet your mind.*

Alex blinked away a few stray tears and sniffled. "I miss you."

"I miss you, too."

Alex froze. This time the words were real, not just in his mind. As were the gentle touches. He rolled onto his back, a cry about to escape him, only to be silenced by firm lips pressing against his own. He grasped broad shoulders and shoved with all his might, ready to fight. How someone managed to get in his room was beyond him, but there was no way he was going to let them anywhere near his daughter.

His breath caught in his throat when he finally pushed the man off him.

"Lucas?"

On the edge of his bed, staring back at him with warm brown eyes was his husband. Lucas was there but not there, almost like a ghost or dream, made of light as if one of the many Guardians that protect the Sanctuary. Tears dotted the corners of Alex's eyes. A Guardian…his Lucas was a Guardian.

"Hi, babe," Lucas said with a note of teasing. He brushed away the new tears as they rolled down Alex's cheeks.

Alex shook his head, unable to believe what he was seeing. "You're real."

A delighted laugh escaped Lucas. "Of course I'm real."

Those warm lips pressed against Alex's once more, proving he was very much real. Alex hesitated before returning the affection. He let Lucas lower him back against the pillows, not pausing once from kissing one another. Large, familiar hands tugged at his boxers, pulling them down his hips then off. Alex groaned, moving with his beloved, turning his head to one side as Lucas peppered kisses along his jaw to his neck. The kisses continued as Lucas made his way downward, creating a fiery trail along Alex's chest and stomach, igniting a desire Alex feared he would never feel again.

The rough palm of Lucas's hand rubbed against Alex's inner thigh as the fingers of his other hand carded through his hair. Alex pressed himself against him, wanting more…needing it as much as he needed air to breath. He slipped a hand over Lucas's and moved it to where to where he really wanted the attention, on his hardening length. Lucas chuckled but didn't object. Instead, he moved his hand a little lower to knead Ales's testicles.

Alex's breath hitched for a moment before a soft mew slipped past his lips. His back arched. He spread his legs and braced his good foot against the mattress in anticipation. That adorable yet smug smirk lifted one corner of Lucas's mouth. He slid between Alex's legs without anymore encouragement. The hand that was in Alex's hair caressed a trail down the length of his body. His thumb dipped teasingly into the smaller man's naval.

A strange thought gave Alex pause. "I don't have any lube. I could…" He gave a grin. What he would do to wrap his lips around Lucas's hard, pulsing cock.

Lucas pressed a kiss to his brow. "Maybe another time, love. All I want is to pound that lovely ass of yours until you finally have a good night's sleep."

That made Alex laugh out loud. He clapped a hand over his mouth to muffle the sound, not wanting to wake Kyra. Lucas's eyes lit up, filled with mischief. He slid the index finger of his right hand into Alex's mouth, and, knowing what to do, Alex sucked and licked the digit, making it nice and wet. Another chuckle left Lucas as he pulled his finger free. He teasingly trail it down Alex's body, around his naval, past his aching manhood until he reached his lover's ass. Slowly, teasingly, he traced the ring of muscle around his opening before gently pushing the tip of his finger inside.

Alex gave a small his at the intrusion before relaxing his muscles. It had been months since the last time they had sex but it might as well have been a lifetime. It felt as if this was his first-time having sex. He was scared and excited at the same time. Scared this was all in his imagination and that he really was losing his mind. Excited because this this was Lucas and it was all worth it.

Discomfort turned to pleasure as Lucas expertly found Alex's prostate and began playing with the bundle of nerves like a finely tuned violin. His finger rubbed and stroked it, pressing against it in such a way that Alex would arch his back, moaning and whimpering for more. Alex was so hard his cock was dipping precum. He might burst if Lucas kept teasing him.

"Lucas..." he whined.

"My poor baby," Lucas teased.

The first slide of Lucas's long length into Alex hurt. Lucas had a sizeable girth and was wonderfully long. It stretched Alex's opening, forcing open muscles that had not been used in many months. Despite the initial pain, his length rubbed against Alex's sweet spot, bringing such pleasure that the smaller man was momentarily light headed. They took a moment to reacquaint themselves with one another's body, to get used to the feeling of filling and being filled.

Lucas stroked Alex's cheek. "Are you alright?"

Alex nodded, unable to trust his voice. He could fill every inch of Lucas inside him and it was marvelous.

Lucas held him by his hips, a small grin lifting his lips. It was a warning of sorts, that he was not going to take it easy on him. They had a dominate and submissive relationship. Lucas was always the Dom but he respected, loved, and cherished Alex. He would not do anything Alex was uncomfortable with, and would stop if told to. Alex didn't want him to stop. He wanted everything Lucas had to offer. He wanted Lucas to dominate his body. He wanted his body to ache with the memory of him.

The first thrust was hard and fast, drawing a little cry from Alex. He covered his mouth to keep the sound in. Lucas liked him being loud but they were in a hotel with their daughter next door. Loudness was not something they couldn't be right now. Lucas grinned and thrust hard again, enjoying Alex's struggle to be quiet. He found his pace, going deep and hard with each thrust. He let go of Alex's hips to pull his hands away from his mouth. Then, holding both Alex's hands in one of his above the younger's man's head, he grasped Alex's throat with the other. His thumb pressed firmly against Alex's windpipe, not enough to completely cut of his airway, but enough to show the power he still had. Alex wrapped his legs around Lucas's waist, his ankle and prosthetic crossing to hold on tight as his husband fucked him.

The pace became faster, Lucas's hips snapping back and forth like a well-oiled piston. Harder, deeper, pounding Alex into the bed. All the while they kept eye contact. Lucas hungry with desire, Alex daring him to use his body, to take everything he had to offer. It was the type of sex that made the body tremble and ached with the promise of bruised hips and tender insides for days to come. Alex arched and pushed back, wanting Lucas to go even deeper. It wasn't possible, he knew. Lucas was already slamming into him, balls deep. The wet slap of the older man's testicles against his bare ass and heavy grunts were audible, like a wild beast rutting into him. Alex took joy in the fact that he made Lucas make such sounds. He purred with desire, enjoying the predatory hunger in his lover's eyes. His fingers slowly wandered up Lucas's arm, teasing as his love had his way with him, until they made their way into Lucas's hair. His fingers knotted around dark locks. He gave a playful tug, telling Lucas what he wanted without words. Lucas's gaze softened. He let go of Alex's throat and let him pull him down. They kissed, their mouths molding together along with their bodies. They continued moving together, slower now, more leisurely until they finally came together. It wasn't an explosion of pleasure that left one seeing stars but rather a mutual and satisfying connection that was electrifying and left them both happily blissful.

Alex lay his head on Lucas's chest, listening to his heartbeat as his fingers idly carded through his thick chest hair. "Why didn't you tell me about the property here?"

Lucas shrugged. "You wouldn't have liked it here…and there never seemed to be enough time."

"Time is all I have," Alex responded.

Lucas pressed a kiss to his brow. "No, it's not."

* * *

Alex awoke with a small hum. His body felt as if it was pulsating in the way only a good night of sex would produce. He felt relaxed and happy, something he had not felt in ages. There were no aches or pains. He felt rested and refreshed. He gazed toward the large patio doors. Even with the blinds, it was easy to see it was a grey, wintery day outside. Snow was likely on the horizon. Fresh powder would make for a beautiful family walk in High Park. They haven't done that since Kyra was twelve or thirteen.

He rolled over, excited to tell Lucas his plans for the day, arm outstretched to pull him in for a snuggle. It landed on the bed. The other side of the bed was empty. Lucas wasn't there, nor was he anywhere in the room. The left side of the bed was untouched, the covers and pillow had no impressions from another person. They were as pristine as the night before.

Disappointment filled Alex, but it was short lived. He felt no anger or sorrow at the revelation. Lucas was gone. He was not coming back. All he was left with was a dream, and oh…what a wonderful dream it had been.

He allowed that to lull him back to sleep. The faint scent of his husband's cologne lingering in the air.

Chapter Five

They slept in the next morning, which was a first for Alex. He couldn't remember the last time he slept past seven in the morning without a monster size headache. It was shortly after nine but even Kyra wasn't out of bed yet. Alex begrudgingly went to the coffee maker to get it started then tried calling Elizabeth again with the same result as the previous day. He sighed and padded into Kyra's room in his bare feet. Normally he would knock but when Kyra was asleep she went into a deep sleep. He would have to give her a gentle but firm nudge to wake her. She groaned and mumbled for him to go away. She was far too comfortable to get up yet. She pulled the comforter over her head and tried to ignore him. This was something she had not done since her early teens. It was amusing and for a moment, Alex was tempted to let her be. She needed the extra rest. However, they had a job to do and he needed her. It took several minutes, but he finally got her out of bed. The allure of freshly perked coffee helped as that was the first thing she went for the moment her feet touched the floor. She held a mug in both hands and inhaled the aroma.

It was several hours before their appointment with the lawyer. They spent that time watching the office building and strategizing what they would do should it be a trap. There may not be any Shadow-being patrolling the building but that didn't mean there were no police or military stationed inside. Every part of the government and defence were under the Shadows control and they had regular humans doing their dirty work. Alex and Kyra needed to be prepared for anything. There was a beep from the smartphone, alerting them to a message. When Alex checked it, there was a simple message: *I had to go to Trenton. I won't make it. See you at the Sanctuary.*

Alex frowned but decided not to get too upset about it. Elizabeth still had a job to do. If she couldn't be with them there was little anyone could do about it. I would talk to her later about the lawyer and Lucas's properties. He was in too good of a mood to dwell on anything else. If only the good feelings could last.

"You've got to be kidding me," Alex grumbled. His good dress pants would not button up and were far too tight. "I've had this suit for nearly twenty years!"

"When is the last time you wore it?" Kyra asked. She was in her usual human form, her skin tone and hair matching Alex's in his youth, her eyes a deep dark blue. She wore a smart, crisp white pant suit that hugged her curves perfectly.

"I don't know. Five...ten years ago. I don't exactly dress up often."

"You're not built like you were in your twenties," she pointed out.

He shot her a glare. He was a little softer around the middle than he used to be, but they didn't need to acknowledge it.

"Just wear a pair of jeans with the shirt and jacket."

That was more his style. Kyra took her fashion sense from Lucas who could pull wearing a suit everyday if he so choose to. Alex was happy in causal clothing. Jeans and a t-shirt did him just fine, which was why he only owned two suits and rarely wore either of them. He grabbed a clean pair of jeans from his bag, happy to have brought a spare pair, and quickly dressed.

They ate a late breakfast in the hotel's restaurant, taking their time to enjoy the food as they continued to observe the building across the street. No one out the ordinary entered or left, at least from the main entrance. There was no telling who may have been entering the building from the back, or the underground parking. As the time for the meeting drew closer, Alex began to wish they were armed. He didn't like guns, hated them in fact, however he was well versed in using many assorted firearms, as was Kyra. Right now, a Glock would make him feel a whole lots safer. The Shadows couldn't be killed by such a weapon, but the human hosts could be, slowed for a matter on minutes. To truly kill someone possessed by a Shadow, they needed to be decapitated.

"How's your teleporting coming along?" he asked nonchalantly.

Kyra glanced away from the building to stare at him with wide eyes. She glanced around the restaurant but it was almost empty, most of the guest having already left to go about their day. There was no one to overhear their conversation.

"I'm still learning," she confessed. "The furthest I managed to go was Onaping Falls. I tried Sudbury a few times, but it's hard to hold the image of where I want to go in my mind. I don't know how Archer did it. He took us all the way from the Sanctuary to Ottawa as if it was nothing."

"He had years of practice. You're still new. You'll get the hang of it."

She nodded and looked back toward the building for a moment. "Why do you ask? Are you thinking of that as an escape route should things not go as planned."

"It'll be the fastest way out. Even if you only got us to Vaughan or Barrie…it will give us enough time to find a vehicle and head home. Or…if you're strong enough…hope from one location to another until we get home."

"I don't know."

Her shoulders slumped, doubt filling her. She was powerful, but that power was still new. Every hybrid and Celestial had their own gift, but without proper training, those gifts were left unchecked and could spiral out of control. Kyra limited herself on what she did due to that fear. Gaining Archer's powers didn't help. She now held the power of two people but not the knowledge. She was stuck learning how to control and manipulate Archer's gifts on her own.

She drummed her fingers on the table, an unconscious habit she had when she was nervous. "It's almost noon," she told him. Her gaze shifted back to him. "Perhaps we should go now. Show up early and may be catch them off guard if it is a trap."

He tilted his head slightly, watching her carefully. "Are you sure? Do you sense anything?"

"No." She shook her head. If was evident she was getting antsy. She wasn't good at staying in one place for long. She needed to move or be doing something, or her anxiety got the best of her.

"Alright," he agreed. He stood and offered her his hand. He left enough money on the table to cover their food and a generous tip. "I think we should rent a locker for our bags and just take what we need."

"Makes sense, but wouldn't we need to do that at Union Station?"

"No, they have lockers here," he assured.

They went to the front desk to inquire about a locker and within a few short minutes they had their bags stored away so they could see they lawyer without being weighed down by their overnight bags. All their carried were their wallets and in Kyra's case, one small purse that went with her outfit and completed the business fashionista look.

They waited for a lull in the traffic before crossing the street, then hurried into the office building. The place was a buzz of activity as people hustled to and from offices. No one paid them any attention as they strolled toward the elevator that would take them to the floor Tisdale and Associates was located. Nothing out of the ordinary happened. No one approached them. No one followed them. It was like any other building with multiple offices and businesses.

The elevator dinged, alerting them they had reached the twentieth floor. The large double doors opened into a large foyer and across from the elevator sat the receptionist they spoke to the day before at a large desk that wrapped in a semi circle. It could have accommodated two more people. She held up a hand as Alex and Kyra approached and spoke into a headset to someone on the phone.

Kyra folded her arms across her chest and sighed in annoyance.

"Relax," Alex encourage. He gave her arm a squeeze. "We don't need to do this. We can go home right now and forget all about it."

Her lips pursed in thought and another sigh escaped her. "We need to see him. If Papa did hire this lawyer, then we need to know why he kept us in the dark about these properties."

He gently tugged her toward until they faced one another. "No, we don't. Lucas had his secrets for a reason. They can sale the properties for all I care. I'm more concern about you."

She shook off his hand. "I'm fine." She turned her focus to the receptionist who was still chatting away. Her hands slapped down on the desk, surprising the dark-haired woman. "We're here regarding the Griffith estate. We want to speak with the lawyer handling it *now.*"

There was a ripple of power in her words.

The receptionist stared at her wide eyed. "I need to go," she told whoever was on the other line. Then, not asking for identification from either Kyra or Alex, she turned to her computer and pulled up the Griffith estate file and lawyer handling the case. "Barry Russell is handling the estate. His office is down that hall, fourth door to the left. He'll be leaving for lunch shortly."

Kyra gave a curt nod and began heading toward the office. The receptionist got up to follow but Alex raised a had to stop her. He was happy she didn't recognize them from yesterday.

"You don't want to get in her way," he warned. He hesitated a moment longer to thank the receptionist then jogged after his daughter. "Calm down," he told her once he caught up. "We're trying to keep a low profile."

"I know."

"So, what's wrong?"

She glanced at him. "I don't know. I'm just…I need to know what's going on. I need to know why Papa kept this a secret."

He sighed softly and gave a nod. "I know. Come on."

He took her by the elbow and led her the rest of the way to the office. Barry Russell was at his desk, his phone pressed to ear. No doubt the receptionist called to warn him they were headed his way. He glanced up when Alex knocked on the door frame, the office door wide open, thanked the receptionist, then hung up.

"Come in, come in," he said.

He stood and gestured them toward the leather armchairs in front of his desk. The office was huge, a corner unit with floor to ceiling windows on two sides. Expensive décor decorated the room, including a wet bar, solid oak bookshelves that took up the entirety of one wall, and a sofa with coffee and end tables under one set of windows. It said money and oddly reminded Alex of how Lucas was when they first met.

"Doctor Jackson," the lawyer gushed. He held out his hand to shake Alex's. "I've heard so many great things about you. I swear, you were all Lucas ever spoke of. You and your lovely daughter. Kyra, I presume?"

She hesitated before shaking his hand.

"I wish we could say the same," Alex told him. He sat down and took in the office. "Lucas never mentioned having a local lawyer."

"In all honesty, most of my dealings with Mr. Griffith transpired almost twenty years ago. We met once or twice after his brother died and just about every transaction afterward was done over the phone or through the property managers." Russell opened a folder and began flipping through the pages. "The last time I spoke to him in person was shortly after Kyra became part of your family. He called to update his will to include her."

"How did you find out he died?"

"I received a call from Captain Elizabeth Monroe."

Alex frowned. "Of course," he muttered. She couldn't be bothered to give him a heads up.

"Once we verified his…passing…we contacted the property managers and began the paperwork to transfer everything into both your names. Mr. Griffith had acquired quite a small fortune and…"

"We don't want them," Alex interrupted.

"Beg pardon?" Russell asked. He looked up from his papers in confusion.

"The properties," Alex clarified. "I want them sold. We have neither the time nor interest in them."

"You won't need to do anything. The property managers will continue as they have for years. The company they work for handles everything from repairs to renovations. Your husband had a special account the rent and skyscraper fees went into that cover all necessary repairs and fees."

Kyra placed her hand over Alex's. "Dad, maybe we should just leave things as they are. There are people living there. If we sale, they may lose their homes. With the housing market as it is, they may not be able to find new ones."

Russell nodded in agreement. "A lot of the people living in the apartments have been there for years. Their rent is geared to income and has barely changed in the last ten years. Finding a safe place to live for the cost they currently pay would be next to impossible."

Alex glanced at his daughter than back to the lawyer. They could have used that money to help the hybrids…but Kyra was right; they could potentially hurt other people by selling the buildings.

"Fine," he agreed.

"Now that's the properties he own," Russell continued. He put those pages aside. "If you do decide to sale them, their combined value comes in at $154,673,901. However, Mr. Griffith has other assists. His bank accounts, not including the maintenance account, currently stands at $28,976,420. He also has a penthouse in the south-west skyscraper valued at $2.5 million. Value of the artifacts within the skyscraper, as well as personal jewellery, and miscellaneous items come in at another $3.1 million. Two Town cars equalling $125,000. There is also a housekeeper and a driver still on payroll, both receiving a rather healthy pay despite having not worked directly with Mr. Griffith in a number of years." Russell hummed softly in thought. "Would you like me to call driver? He can take you anywhere you want while you're in the city."

"No," Kyra answered. "We're fine. We're heading home this evening."

The lawyer shrugged. "Suit yourself. I would have thought you would have wanted to visit the penthouse to collect any personal items you may want."

Alex leaned back in his seat and pressed his fingers against his forehead. "No…he's right. We need to go through these 'artifacts' and catalogue them. If they were collected before Lucas and I got together then they need to be returned to the countries they originated from."

Before Alex and Lucas became a couple, Lucas was an Archeologist for hire. He would locate treasures and artifacts all around the world and sell them to the highest bidder. It was how he accumulated a lot of his wealth in his early days. He often kept the ones he prized most. This was not what Alex planned for today, but it may give him the answers he needed as to why Lucas kept all of this a secret.

Russell handed him a set of keys and an old business card that belonged to Lucas. It had the address and a local phone number. Alex's stomach knotted at the sight of it. This secret life of Lucas Griffith became all the more real.

"Would you like some time to read over the will before you sign the transferal papers? Everything, the buildings, the money, the cars, and penthouse...they all belong to you now," the lawyer said. He handed the documents to Alex to review.

Alex nodded, his body feeling numb.

"I'll give you some privacy." Russell stood and left the room, closing the door behind him.

His hands shaking, Alex handed the document to Kyra. "I need a drink," he told her.

He stood and went to the wet bar to pour himself a Whiskey. He didn't care if he had permission or not. His head was spinning and hands shaking. He needed a moment to collect himself.

Kyra crossed one leg over the other as she read over the papers in her hands. "I'm not a law major, but everything seems legit. The apartments and skyscrapers...the penthouse...shit! Papa really did come from an upper-class family." She held up a photo of the penthouse. "He must have had an interior designer. I can't see him or Uncle Owen doing this on their own."

"I kept telling him not to spend so much on the winery when we began. I was worried he would bankrupt himself if it didn't work out. I thought he might have after the fire destroyed everything, and here he was...with all these investment properties, taking care of gods know how many people...and he never told me. Not once." He drank down the

Whiskey in one shot then refilled his glass and sat down. "So, now what? Do we take the money and stock up on supplies for the Sanctuary or leave it?"

She shook her head, unsure. "The accounts are probably being watched. Even if all this is ours, we can't touch it. We can't touch any of it until the Shadows are defeated. We touch so much as a penny and we'll have every police department and military unit on us. They can track any withdrawal."

"It doesn't matter what we do, we're not getting ahead." He strolled the few feet between them, took the document, and signed it. "It may not help us now, but once we defeat the Shadows, we're going to need the money to care for the hybrids and maybe find them a safer place to live."

He gave the document back to Kyra to sign then went to the door to let Russell know they were done. It was time to get out of there... after a quick visit to Lucas's penthouse.

Chapter Six

Elevator music was perhaps one of the most annoying sounds Alex had ever heard. It seemed as if it was always the same music no matter where in the world he travelled. He wasn't quite sure when he began disliking it, or if it was simply the situation they were in. Either way, he was anxious to get their inspection of Lucas's penthouse over with and head home. He would have the lawyer hire someone to clear it out after he and Kyra took inventory of the artifacts Lucas had collected, with clear instructions on where each artifact needed to be sent to. After that, he was washing his hands of the whole ordeal. The most he hoped to find was a reason Lucas had kept all this secret from him.

He groaned when the elevator doors opened to a brightly lit foyer.

"Are you kidding me?" Kyra said in awe.

The foyer was large and opened to a huge living room that hosted floor to ceiling windows with a fantastic view of Lake Ontario. The furniture was high quality and expensive that distinctly showed Lucas's taste. It was far more elegant than what they had in either their chalet in the mountains or their previous home in Massey.

"We should have brought our bags," Kyra exclaimed. She kicked off her boots and threw her coat on the entrance table.

Alex cringed at the sight. If Lucas was with them, he would have reprimanded her and told her to hang the coat in the closet and put the boots on the mat. Alex absently did so, placing both his and Kyra's winter coats in the closet and boots next to the door.

"We're not staying," he reminded her.

"Forget dinner at the CN Tower, I'll gladly have it eat. Look at this view!"

"Kyra..."

Alex sighed as he entered the living room. The view was lovely and not obstructed by a lot of furniture. In fact, the room was rather sparsely furnished, with only two sofas facing one another in a conversational setting, and a low glass coffee table between them. There was no television – not that Lucas watched television often – and what few shelves there were, were along the wall to the foyer. They were decorated with books and small artifacts, not the center pieces Alex expected to find.

"I tell you what," he told Kyra as he stood next to her to admire the view as well. "You can order whatever you want for dinner as long as we get everything catalogued. I don't want to stay here any longer than we need to."

She glanced at him with a small smile and tilt of her head. "Party pooper. Man, why didn't Papa bring us here when we came to the city?"

He snorted. "If you figure out the answer, let me know. I'm going to find whatever he stole from all those archeological digs he did before we got together and catalogue them. You should do the same."

"Dad, you need to relax. Even the lawyer said, this place was purchased back when Uncle Owen was still alive *before* you and Papa got together." She turned to face him fully. "Besides, you're a small-town person. Papa was more..."

"Upper-class?"

"Not what I was going to say, but…maybe. He was always more comfortable when we visited the city than you were. He's always been better with people…you have to admit that."

He fought back a smile. "No, I don't. Get moving. Find and check the bedrooms. There should also be an office and library around here somewhere."

"Sure," she pressed a kiss to his cheek. "Try to relax a little. This is Papa's place, there should be a wine cellar hidden here somewhere." She said the last part in a sing-song voice as she headed toward the kitchen.

"I'm serious, Kyra! Find a pen and paper and start taking notes."

She waved back at him, disappearing into the other side of the penthouse. Alex pinched the bridge of her nose. He should have known Kyra would be enthralled by the penthouse. It was like nothing either of them had been to before, far more elegant than even the fanciest hotel Lucas had taken them to over the years. It was probably like going to Wonderland, a new place to explore and discover hidden secrets. However, Kyra was right, Lucas probably had a good stash of wine, and Alex sorely needed some. Finding the wine cellar was easy enough, it was inside a large pantry next to the kitchen. The kitchen itself was large, a true chef's kitchen, and the pantry matched with a cozy coffee nook. There was no food, not that he expected to find any. It was obvious no one had lived there in ages, despite how clean it was. The wine selection, however, was immense. There were wine shelves filled with bottles of wine from all over the world. Surprisingly, there was a large selection of Canadian Wines, many from Niagara Falls, lots of which were their prized Ice Wine. Alex slowly reviewed each bottle until he came upon a familiar label. A small smile lit his face. Jackson Vineyard Merlot. Lucas brought wine from their old vineyard in Massey. There was more than a dozen in the four or five flavours they used to create. They still had a small vineyard in the mountains, but it was not nearly as large as their original one. The process of turning it to wine took much longer as well. Seeing bottles of their original wine was a rare treat. He took the Merlot, found two glasses, and went back to the kitchen.

"Kyra?" he called.

He looked in the direction he had last seen her. Maybe she couldn't hear him. It was a big place and he had no intention of yelling for her. Instead, he poured himself a glass of wine and set the bottle aside for her, letting it breath and knowing that sooner or later his daughter would fine it and pour herself a glass. He took his and began exploring the penthouse in search of the office or library, knowing either would not be far from the main living area. The hallway that separated the living area from the rest of the house was decorated with large mirrors that helped reflect the natural light from the living room, making the need to turn on the lights during the day obsolete. Whomever the interior designer was knew how to use the lightening to its upmost advantage. Alex sipped at his wine as he paused to look at the various photographs that lined the walls between the mirrors. Some were from Lucas's and Owen's time in the British military. He had seen a few before but it had been a long time before his home and winery had burned down nearly thirteen years ago. These were different. Lucas was younger, as was Owen, perhaps in their early twenties. In one photo, Lucas sat on the nose of tank while Owen stood next to him, one arm on his brother's shoulder. It was very different from how Alex remembered them. The grin on both their faces brought a pang to Alex's chest, but he smiled longingly as he slowly walked down the short hall, taking his time to admire each photo. He brushed away the moisture pooling at the corners of his eyes. A part of him wished he had known them both back then. Of course, there was a bit of an age gap between him and the Griffith brothers. He was ten years younger than Lucas.

The library was at the end of the hall and turned out to be larger than the living room and kitchen combined. Shelves lined the left and right walls all the way up to the high ceilings, requiring thin ladders on tracks to reach the upper shelves. Display tables dotted the room with glass enclosed artifacts. Yet, they weren't the type Alex was expecting to find. He thought he would find Egyptian or Sumerian, or any number of treasures for long lost civilizations. These pieces were from Celestial temples. Statues and pieces of temples, alters, stone gears, and jewels. Detailed information about them was written on planks attached to each, as if they were meant to be showcased in a museum or he was going to host a gala to show them off. The library wasn't quite big enough, nor set up for that. At the end of the library, in front of the vast windows, was a desk. It was large and made of solid oak, stained a deep ebony. A matching office chair sat behind it. The library and office were combined.

More photos sat on the desk in expensive silver frames. Alex rounded the desk, expecting to find more images of Lucas and Owen in their youth. Instead, he found family images. Alex's breath caught in his throat. Without thinking, he put his wine glass on the desk and sat down in the large chair.

"Oh Lucas…" he whispered.

He picked up a group picture of himself and Lucas, with Kyra in front of them. She was only seven or eight. He remembered when the picture was taken. Elizabeth had taken it to commemorate Kyra's adoption being finalized and celebrate their new home. There were other photos. Some of Alex and Lucas when they first became a couple. Alex laughing at some silly antic. Kyra throughout the years. There were a mix of traditional silver frames and several digital ones. It would seem that regardless of keeping this part of his life secret, Lucas always had his family with him. All the anger Alex felt drained away with that knowledge.

In front the photos was an old leather journal. Alex immediately recognized it as one of Lucas's. He had created a rather large and detailed collection of them over the years. Each neatly dated along the side and featured Lucas's handwritten script, far neater than Alex's own, with sketches and diagrams of his findings. This particular journal was at least six or seven years old and should have been safely catalogued and on a shelf, not left on the desk as if it had recently been written in.

Alex curiously flipped through it, surprised to find the back half left empty. Lucas never left blank pages. He would use a journal until it was filled then begin a new one. His journals traveled everywhere with him until they were filled and he moved on to the next. This one was different. There were diagrams of the temples they had researched or encountered. Drawings of Celestials and mythological beings, Gods and Faeries, and creatures that did not exist. Alex sat forward as he read Lucas's notes. He had been drawing connections between what was believed to be myth and what they had learned about the Celestials and Shadow beings, as if they were possibly the same thing. It was an argument they had many years ago, when Alex first brought up the possibility and Lucas argued it was impossible. Here their roles were reversed with Lucas believing there may be a connection and Alex…Alex didn't know what he felt with this revelation. Why would Lucas keep such a thing from him? Why would he not want to work side by side to find the truth?

"How's it going?"

Kyra smiled at Liam's greeting to her video-call. She leaned against the large window and gazed out over the lake, marveling at the open water in the middle of winter. "It's been weird."

"Yeah? So, the penthouse is real?"

"It's real…it's huge." Her gaze travelled over the room. Owen's room. It was the first time she had been in close proximity to anything her uncle's that proved he once existed.

"Penthouses tend to be. At least that's what I heard."

She laughed. "I wouldn't know, but I'm pretty sure we can fit half the camp here."

That brought a laugh from him as well. "Don't let my mom hear that. She'd insist we take the whole building over to accommodate everyone."

"After what happened in Ottawa? Let's not move everyone to a skyscraper. It make too convenient of a target."

He nodded. "Noted. Underground safe, skyscrapers not."

She tried not to laugh. She liked Liam. A lot. "So, how are things there?"

Liam looked around, or at least made it seem as if he did. He was blind but liked to act as if he wasn't. "Don't tell your dad, but we may have made figured out the Void."

"Well, that is why I left you and Winston in charge."

"I know...but you're dad may be right. I don't want to send anyone through and I sure as hell don't want to let any Shadows in." He paused to collect himself. "So, I was talking with Elizabeth. She may be able to get us some drones to go it and investigate. Winston wants to replicate the technology being used for the shield. That way, eventually we can go back and forth but the Shadows can't."

She hummed in thought. "It's worth a shot," she agreed. "It would keep them from following us, no matter where the Void takes us."

"My thoughts exactly."

"Okay, tell him I approve."

"Thanks." He fell silent for a moment and Kyra thought he was about to say good-bye. Instead, he asked something she hadn't thought he would. "Have you told Alex about us?"

"Oh...uh...no, not yet," she confessed. "He's suffering through Lucas's loss. I can't have him worrying about us any more than he already does."

His expression fell, obviously not happy with her response.

"I'm sorry."

He shook his head. "No, I get it. He's going through a lot. Right now, isn't the best time."

"Maybe when we get home."

"Sure."

"I'm sorry."

"No...no...no...no..." he said quickly. "Don't be. You're family has been through so much. We all have. We don't need to tell anyone anything yet. I mean, we just started to...can it even be called dating?"

A laugh escaped her at his innocent, confused expression. "Yes, we can call it dating."

"Okay." His entire face lit up with relief and happiness to finally have a label on their relationship. "So, when are you coming home?"

"Tonight. Dad wants to get out of here as soon as possible."

"I can't blame him. Finding out your husband has a secret penthouse is a little much. What's next? A secret family?"

"And now I need to go."

"Sorry."

She sighed and looked out over Lake Ontario toward the Toronto City Airport where her plane was still parked. She could barely make out hers. Nonetheless, it was amusing to think she could see it from the penthouse. Most people couldn't even see their car from their window. It was reassuring. "It's okay. It's not as if we haven't been wondering the same thing."

"I'm still sorry."

"I know. Hey…be careful if…when you open the Void. It might be best to wait until Elizabeth is there and the shield is set up. I don't want anything to happen to…you or anyone else," she told him, feeling a little nervous not being there to protect everyone.

"We will. You take care of your dad," he responded before quickly adding. "Love you."

She stared at his image, taken back by the sentiment. It was the first time one of them told the other they loved them. She blinked away the sudden moisture in her eyes, her chest swelling with an emotion she was not accustomed to. "Love you, too."

She let out a long breath when he hung up. Her insides felt shaky, like a bird frantically trying to escape a cage. The idea of being emotionally invested in someone who was not a family was a little scary. She had never felt the way she did for Liam for anyone else before. They connected in a way that wasn't sexual but still very much love. Fearing her legs may give out, she sat on the edge of the bed and stared at the screen of the phone. How was she going to explain their relationship to her dad? He hated Liam's mom. She was a Celestial, the very beings they were at war with. Well, one of them. They were the creators of the Shadows and hybrids alike. It didn't matter that the Celestials were having a civil war or that many of them sided with the humans and chose to live among them. The trauma Alex had suffered at their hands – albeit only one Celestial who fed on humans and a cult that worshipped it – had tainted any possible friendship that he and Marie could have formed. It wasn't for lack of trying on Marie's part. She adored Alex and was an avid fan of his work with the temples. She was one of the Celestials who had blended in amongst humans so well that she considered herself one of them and forsaken her heritage and birthright. None of that mattered to Alex. Once he knew what she was, he kept clear of her, fearful that she would betray them at the first chance. Kyra knew that fear had been there with General Caldwell…or rather Admerial Caldwell. Of course, the situation with her was a little different. Cadwell was a Celestial who infiltrated the military and worked her way through the ranks without anyone knowing who or what she truly was. Not only that, but she also killed Kyra's parents to "protect the human race," and removed Kyra's uterus when she was still a baby. Then put her into a deep sleep in a cryogenics tube where she would still be if the Shadows had not attacked the old NORAD base in North Bay. Caldwell kept the truth about that and Kyra being a human born pure-blood Celestial a secret right until the day she died. A lie the severed any chance of Alex or anyone else trusting her. Had Kyra's not unintentionally killed her when her powers suddenly expanded and lashed out, Alex probably would have ended the admiral himself.

Marie was different though. Where Caldwell was cold and calculating, Marie was warm and kind and wanted to be there to help. She was honest and told it as it was, no embellishing or lying. She would tell Kyra to be honest with Alex about her feelings for Liam, as well as her plans to use the Void to find the hybrids a new home. That was something she couldn't do. Alex wanted the Void sealed. He was better off not knowing what Liam and Winston were doing until she was certain it was safe and there was a place to take the hybrids. She had to do what was right for her people, regardless what her father said or thought.

Guilt hit her hard in the stomach. She glanced toward the corner of the room. Whispers could be faintly heard. A deep rumbling voice that both consoled her and scolded her. In her mind's eye she could almost make out the shape of a tall, muscular man, the ghost of her father but it vanished nearly as quickly as it appeared. With a sigh, she nodded to herself. The spirit followed her, attached to her like a ghost. He, like Marie, would not want her to keep secrets from Alex. With a sigh, she stood. It time her and Alex had a nice long talk. Lucas wasn't the only one with secrets that needed to come to light.

"Dad!" she called. She got to her feet and strolled into the hallway. "Dad?"

"Back here," Alex called back. His voice sounded faraway, another reminder of just how large the penthouse was.

She headed in the direction she believed his voice came from and eventually found her way into a large library. She gave a low whistle as she overlooked the artifacts set up on marble pillars and wooden stands throughout the room.

"Is this Celestial?" she asked. She stood in front of a glassed display case that held a stone carving. "Or Samarian? It looks like both."

He nodded, his attention going back to the journal in his hands. "A lot of cultures have similarities like that. Probably due to their gods all being Celestials who've stolen a human as their vessel."

"Bitter?" she asked, one brow risen.

He glanced at her again, unsure if she was joking. "Fact." He waved at the artifacts. "What humans once believed were gods were in fact Celestials. Think about it. Every culture shares a similar origin story for their gods. They come down from heaven in glorious light, do similar miracles, breed with humans, cause wars and chaos…it's all the same, no matter where you go…and it repeats itself, just as it is now."

She opened her mouth to argue but stopped herself. "So, what are you reading?" she asked. She strolled across the room to the large desk.

A sigh escaped him and he handed the journal to her. "A theory Lucas and I came up with years ago. More fairy tales created by the Celestials."

She glanced at the page he left open. "Literally, fairy tales?"

"In some countries, there's a strong belief that faeries, elves, and other mythological beings exist. Some call them the 'wee people' or sorcerers and witches. I don't remember how Lucas and I got caught up in the discussion but I theorized that beings like the Sidhe could be real and merely hidden."

"The Sidhe, faeries hidden unground…oh, because of the temples and how some of the locations flourish underground like a whole other reality."

"Exactly," Alex agreed, becoming more animate. "Just like the gods stories, very culture has stories about supernatural beings so I thought maybe they were all related and possibly Celestials or hybrids in other forms. Lucas thought I was overthinking it and eventually I dropped the subject. Apparently, he didn't."

Kyra took a seat in front of the desk and scanned through the journal. "This isn't something Papa would normally research. He hates fairy tales and mythology. Everything had to be logical and provable. That's why he was an archeological, to prove the facts in history existed. Fairy tales were only good for bedtime stories."

"I know."

She tossed the journal back on the desk. "It's papa's penmanship, but it doesn't feel like him. Maybe he was planning a novel. With everything you've been through, it could have made a great fantasy series."

Alex laughed, a smile lifting his face and brightening his eyes. "Perhaps." He pulled the journal back to him. "It wouldn't explain why he would hide it, or any of this, from us."

"Maybe he was embarrassed," she responded with a shrug.

"Maybe." Amusement filled his face and he visibly relaxed. "Let's order some dinner then finish cataloguing everything. Some of this can come home with us." He tapped the journal on the edge of the desk as he stood.

"What about the rest?"

"I don't know. When we get home, I'll contact the lawyer about an estate sale. We don't have room for it and I can't see any of it being of use at the temple." He reached over and squeezed her hand. "If there's anything you want to take, I'm sure there are bags around here someplace."

There were a number of items Kyra wanted, namely photographs and books. Anything that may have been sentimental to either Lucas or Owen that should be kept in the family. "What about Chinese or Korean for tonight?"

He kissed the back of her hand. "Whatever you want, love."

Ordering food was a rare delight and Kyra cherished the moment as she strolled in front of the massive windows and placed the order. She was used to one of her fathers cooking, or she herself cooking, so their meal plan was rather repetitive, especially now that they were also caring for refugee hybrids. Sometimes it was nice to try something new and having someone else cook it was a blessing. She gazed out the windows as she spoke with a woman on the phone. The sun had set and it was now dark out, making Lake Ontario look almost like a black void with twinkling stars shining above. There were lights coming from several of the small islands, including the airport. In the distance were more lights, almost like flames dancing across the night sky.

She tilted her head to one side, watching them as if transfixed. They were different from the rest and growing larger as she watched, as if moving rapidly toward them. Her breath hitched in sudden understanding.

"Dad!" she yelled.

She darted away from the window and into the kitchen where Alex was pouring himself a fresh glass of wine. He turned toward her in surprise, his eyes growing wide as the windows were suddenly blown inward. He grabbed the journal, his movement automatic as Kyra threw her weight against him. Her power surged to life as the heat of an explosion moved toward them both, the penthouse suddenly consumed in fire. It happened too quickly to register. One moment everything around them was being destroyed, the next they hit the hard asphalt of the airport, Kyra teleporting them away from the danger. They lay on the ground in the cool winter air and stared back toward the skyscraper as the top floor exploded into flames.

"What the hell?" Alex breathed, disbelief dripping from every word.

Kyra shook her head, confusion filling her as well. She still clenched her phone in one hand and without thinking, hung up on the restaurant she had been ordering from. "We need to get out of here."

Except, they were not alone. The screeching of tires caught their attention as military vehicles and soldiers surrounded them. Kyra helped Alex to his feet then raised her hands as automatic weapons were aimed at their heads.

"Don't move! Don't move!" soldiers yelled.

It was impossible to tell who was talking. Flood lights blinded Kyra and Alex, casting long shadows around the soldiers. The Shadows twisted and weaved, not all human. The sound of more running feet and the clang of weapons told of even more soldiers racing toward them.

"Kyra...teleport us somewhere else," Alex said in a harsh whisper.

"Where? I can't see anything," she retorted.

"Get on the ground!" someone ordered. "Face down!"

"Kyra..."

The butt of a gun jabbed her in the back. Anger raged within her as did the power she had used only moments ago. It lashed out, throwing everyone except Alex back with it's force as she shifted from her human form to her Celestial one. She used it to throw men, women, and machinery away from them in order to have enough room to create a proper portal to teleport her and Alex home. It took more concentration than fleeing the penthouse. The mountain range was over five hundreds of kilometers away, further than she had ever teleported before. It required a portal that only she could hold open. It also ran the risk of allowing a Shadow to pass through which was why she reverted to her Celestial form. The light her body produced kept the creatures at bay.

82

She knew it worked the moment she felt Liam and Winston on the other side, both confused and surprised by the portal's sudden appearance within the Sanctuary.

"Go," she told Alex.

She backed toward it, her focus on the soldiers and Shadows before her. It left her flank open. Before she could cover it, a shot range out and searing pain erupted in her right shoulder, tearing through flesh, and crushing bone.

"Kyra!" Alex screamed.

She looked at him in confusion, unsure what had just happened. Her vision blurred, becoming double then cloudy. She saw him run toward her.

"Dad?" she whispered.

Her grabbed her arms, stared at her with wide, blue eyes. Then, before she could say anything else, he shoved her backwards, into the portal. It closed around her, leaving him behind as she crashed to the Sanctuary floor. The journal he had been carrying was now in her hands as consciousness faded and Liam's cries filled her ears.

Chapter Seven

Since losing his eyesight in an attack by the Shadows, Liam learned how to "see" through his other senses. While he couldn't see a person's physical appearance, he could see their aura, the energy they produced and that moved through them. Every person was different, which made it easier to tell who was who until eventually he was able to move and interact with people as he has when he had his sight. There were still difficulties, of course. Navigating his way around the sanctuary was not an easy task without the use of a staff in order not to trip or walk into something. It was annoying to say the least. It was also why he stuck close to Winston when Kyra wasn't around. He hated the way the others would rush to assist him, as if he was unable to care for himself. Winston and Kyra didn't. They may call out the odd direction, but they let him find his way himself, knowing that if he needed them, he would ask.

"Any word from Elizabeth?" he asked.

He sat on one of the stone slabs as Winston tinkered with the altar, an alien artifact that somehow controlled the Void. They were in the Vault, the one place Alex forbad them from going. Kyra, however, wanted Winston to learn everything he could about it and had even smuggled some of her fathers' journals to assist them. Naomi served as their look out, telepathically contacting them whenever someone entered the Sanctuary, specifically Alex. They understood that he had been through a lot with the Celestials and the Shadows. Entering the Vault was forbidden, but the hybrids were running out of resources and could not keep hiding forever. They needed to find a better and safer place to live. Somewhere where they weren't under constant threat by a government that should be protecting them. There was no other way to do so without being discovered by the Shadows or the military.

Winston stretched, causing an audible cracking sound when he twisted to the right. "She should be landing soon. Smuggling a shield converter out of Trenton isn't exactly an easy task. It's not like she can fit it in her back pocket. Not to mention downloading the schematics…but she does that directly to her phone so…it shouldn't be much longer. She had to skip out on Alex and Kyra to get it."

It would be easier if they didn't have to rely on the Void to move everyone.

Liam opened his mouth to respond but paused, his brows furrowing. "Kyra?" he whispered.

"What?" Winston asked.

Liam stood. He could feel her. There was shock, pain, and confusion. It was moving rapidly toward them. He felt a surge of power unlike anything he had felt before. It tore through the fabric of space and time like a fiery vortex.

"Holy shit!" Winston cursed.

"Kyra!" Liam cried.

Her aura filled his senses as a portal suddenly opened. She tumbled through a portal and land hard on the ground with a painful cry. The portal closed with a snap behind her. Liam fell to his knees next to her.

"Kyra? What happened? Where's Alex?"

She struggled to get to sit up. Another painful cry escaped her. She grasped her right shoulder and fell to her side, dropping a leather journal she had been holding.

"I've got to go back," she insisted. She tried to get to her feet but fell. That didn't stop her from trying again. The result was the same.

"Winston, get my mom," Liam said urgently. "Kyra, lay down. Tell me what happened. Where's Alex?"

Winston hurried off but Kyra refused to lay down. She stopped struggling to stand and instead sat on the marble floor with a humph of annoyance. Her breathing was laboured, laced with pain, fear, and anxiety. It reflected in her aura, showing her emotions better than any facial expression. What Liam saw made his blood run cold with fear.

"We were ambushed. They knew I would teleport us to the airfield when they destroyed the penthouse. It was all a trap." She shook her head, the energy within her pulsing and fluctuating with her emotions. "Dad said it was a trap. I should have listened. They have him… It's all my fault…"

Her words turned into a painful groan. She grasped her shoulder and leaned toward it, as if trying to curl herself around the injury. The energy around the injury pulsed red, bright, and fiery, far more than he was used to seeing from her. However, it was not as disconcerting as the growing blackness in its center. Liam reached out to her, gently grasping her upper arms as to not cause her anymore pain. She didn't fight him as he guided her to the ground until she lay flat on her back.

"You were shot," he stated, surprised she had not told him.

"I'm fine." The pain in her voice said elsewise.

"No…you're not." He tore her shirt open over the injured shoulder. The blackness was growing, moving within her. "What is this?"

"What is what?" she asked.

He shook his head. "I don't know. I've never seen anything like it. Okay, let's…uh…let's just rest. Winston is getting my mom. She'll know what to do."

"No…I have to go back. I need to save my dad."

She managed to get to her feet and raised her right hand as if to open another portal. The energy swirled for a moment, her power focusing on what she intended to do. It last mere moments before another scream tore from her lips and she collapsed on the ground, clenching her shoulder. That didn't stop her from trying again and again until Marie arrived to stop her. By then, Kyra was frantic, and in utter agony. She was unable to stop the older woman from putting her on a stretcher that was handled by Winston and one of the new hybrids, Luke. She struggled for a moment then relaxed when Marie placed a hand on her forehead. It had a calming affect that Kyra needed at that moment.

"We need to get her away from the Void. Take her to the infirmary," Marie ordered, her voice stern and leaving no room for questions. She strapped Kyra down then walked next to her as they left the temple. Liam walked on the other side, his hand grasping Kyra's.

Whatever was in Kyra's shoulder was serious. Liam had never seen anything like it before. It was growing and with it, the darkness slowly began to take over Kyra's shoulder. It looked like a living parasite. He picked up the journal Kyra had dropped and stuffed it in his back pocket.

"What's in her shoulder," he asked his mother, knowing she likely saw what he did.

"We'll discuss it later," she told him, leaving no room for discussion.

Liam wasn't dissuaded. "It's moving within her and causing her temperature to drop drastically."

"Not now," Marie insisted. "Let's get her to the infirmary where we can remove it."

There was a warning in her voice, one that clearly said she did not want to discuss this in front of others. Liam couldn't stop staring at Kyra's shoulder. He watched helplessly as the darkness spread and her upper arm slowly began to turn black.

"It's a Shadow…" he suddenly gasped, understanding dawning on him.

"What?" Winston snapped, almost dropping his end of the stretcher.

Marie's shoulders tensed and hands balled into fists. "We will discuss it in the infirmary, not in public. Kyra needs to be placed in a light chamber so we can remove and destroy it. I would prefer to do that before it takes over her arm and we have to amputate it…or worse."

"That's impossible," Kyra insisted. She tried to sit up but the restraints kept her securely vertical on the stretcher. "Shadows can't possess hybrids or Celestials. Our light…"

"They can't," Marie confirmed. She took Kyra's free hand. "But they can kill us. Sometimes all it takes is a little piece of them to make their way inside us and they can begin destroying our body like a cancer. It uses our tissue like a shield to protect itself from our natural light. So…we need more light, something they can't hide from, and cut it out. Once it's out, it will deteriorate in the chamber. However, if we try to do it out here…it could try to activate the Void and bring more of its kind here."

"Let me get this straight," Winston piped in. "As long as that thing is in Kyra, we're safe, but it could kill her."

"Will kill her."

"If we take it out…it can wipe us all out."

"In essence…yes," Marie confirmed.

"We're getting it out of her," Liam told Winston firmly. "We get rid of that thing, then we find Alex."

They were careful carrying Kyra out of the temple and down the long staircase to the village. The infirmary wasn't far but having Kyra strapped down to a stretcher made a lot of people stop and look. Naomi, who was helping some of the newer hybrids, immediately ushered them away, ensuring a clear path to the infirmary. Marie shooed the EDC medics out of the way and had Kyra taken directly into the light chamber. Transferring her from the stretcher to the gurney was tricky without causing her more pain. Liam waited until Winston and Luke were out of the way before going inside the light chamber with Kyra and his mother.

"What can I do?" he asked. He didn't want to leave Kyra. She needed him and he had promised to support her no matter what.

"Stay outside," his mother told him.

One of the medics went into the chamber to assist her. Liam hesitated for a moment before following them inside. Regardless what his mother said, Kyra was his priority and he would stay by her side no matter what. He stayed out of their way and stood next to Kyra's feet, giving plenty of space for his mother and the medic plenty of space to work.

"I'm not leaving her," he said firmly. His hands shook. He could feel Kyra's pain and see how much the thing in her shoulder was hurting her.

Marie scowled at him. "Alright, just stay out of the way."

Every inch of the chamber was lit up. The light was UV, mimicking natural sunlight. There were so many sources of light that no shadows existed within the chamber. There was no place for a Shadow being to hide. The light would also help Kyra heal. Celestials naturally absorbed sunlight. Being underground was not natural for them.

"Kyra, honey," Marie said. She stroked Kyra's cheek, trying to calm her as the young woman writhed in pain. "We need to cut open your shoulder to get to the Shadow. We'll do it as quickly as possible."

"Do it," Kyra said between clenched teeth.

The medic pulled out a diamond tip blade, one of the few tools strong enough to cut through Kyra's flesh, regardless which form she was in. "I'm ready," the man said, the blade posed over the injury.

"Kyra, when I say to, change fully into your Celestial form," Marie instructed.

Kyra nodded without a word. She hissed a moment later as the blade cut into her.

Liam placed a reassuring hand on her right leg as the medic worked. He watched the way her energy moved and fluctuated. The Shadow creature moved in her shoulder, long tentacles waving about as if trying to escape the medic. It was impossible for them to simply remove it with a scalpel. The creature had no corporal form. It hid within the darkness of the human body.

Marie moved around Kyra as she instructed the medic to stand back. She placed her hand over the wound, her own energy shifting as her arm changed from human flesh to ethereal blue energy, which she directed into Kyra. The younger woman screamed, her body arching away from Marie. All that kept Kyra to the bed were the straps to the gurney otherwise she may have fallen off.

"Change forms," Marie ordered.

"It burns!" Kyra objected.

"Do it now!"

Liam had seen Kyra changed forms only once before. It was not a smooth or graceful transformation. It was violent, her true form bursting from her human one as if an alien tearing it's way out of flesh.

90

Not even the straps could hold her. She was pure energy encased in what many may assume to be crystal. It pulsed and shifted, floating mere inches above the gurney. The Shadow that had been within her was utterly obliterated, shredder into nothing. Whether from Marie's blast of energy or Kyra's transformation, it was unclear. Regardless, Kyra's energy levels returned to normal.

Letting out the breath he was holding, Liam sat on the edge of the bed. His heart raced, blood pounding in his ears. That was close. Fear still had a tight hold on his heart as his mind spun with what might have happened had his mother not been able to help Kyra in time. She could have died...or worse...been possessed. Even if Celestials and hybrids allegedly couldn't be possessed by a Shadow, it could have done awful things to her from the inside. The creatures weren't looking to capture them anymore...they were going to annihilate them. There was no negotiating, or trying to find a peaceful solution. They had to stop the Shadows any way possible...but how do you defeat something that quite literally took over every branch of the government? The hybrids weren't soldiers. Most didn't even know they had powers let alone how to control them. They were on the defensive with no way to protect themselves. At least, not from here. The Sanctuary was only that, a sanctuary. It could only protect them for so long. They had no choice but to move. The Void was their only safe exit. With or without Elizabeth and the shield, it was time for them to find a new home.

He was hesitant to leave Kyra to relay these orders to Winston. His friend was standing just outside the chamber, watching them with a worried frown. His mother and the medic were still fussing over Kyra. He had time. Nonetheless, letting go of Kyra was near impossible. He afraid if he did, the Shadow may return. It was foolish, he knew, be he couldn't shake the fear. If they had been able to do this to Kyra, who knew what they were doing to Alex.

He mentally sent that message to Winston. It felt weird exchanging thoughts with someone else. Kyra claimed the hybrids had a hive mind, but that was the furthest from the truth. The shared thoughts, feelings, but they were each their own person. Most simply spoke to one another as anyone else would. Still, being able to tell Winston what was going on and what he wanted him to do psychically was convenient. Winston gave Kyra one last worried look then was on his way. With luck, Elizabeth would arrive soon to help him.

Marie placed a comforting hand on his shoulder as the medic exited the chamber. "We should let her rest. Did she say where Alex was?"

"My guess is Toronto," he answered. "She said they were ambushed. The portal she used…it opened only for a split second."

"We'll assume he was captured." A low sigh escaped her. "This isn't good. He knows everything there is to know about the Sanctuary and how to get passed the security. When they break him…"

"*If* they break him," Liam interrupted.

"My love, there is no 'if.' They will break him. No matter how strong Alex is, they will do inhuman things to him. Find his deepest, darkest fears and desires and use them against him," she warned. "What they did to Kyra will be mild compared to what they will do to him. They don't want him dead. They will make him into a weapon that not even we can defeat…" She glanced at Kyra's unconscious form still floating inches off the gurney. "…nor her. We need to find a safe haven before that happens."

Liam hesitated for a moment then pulled the journal Kyra was carrying out of his back pocket. "She had this when she came through the portal. I don't know what it is but it looks important."

Marie took it and quickly flipped through several pages before stopping. "She had this?"

Liam nodded. "What is it?"

"Possible help." She was silent for a she slipped through several more pages. "When Kyra's strong enough, we need to have a meeting. I'll radio Elizabeth and find out how far out she is."

"What about Alex?"

The silence that met him made his heart sink.

"I don't know," she answered honestly.

That meant they weren't going to rescue him. It would be too risky. One Shadow had already made it in with Kyra. There was no telling how many more might try to use Alex as a vessel to get inside the Sanctuary. Marie squeezed his hand before finally leaving the chamber. He pulled the only chair in the small room next to the bed. It would be a while before Kyra awoke. In her Celestial form, she would absorb the UV from the lights in order to heal what damage the Shadow creature had done to her shoulder. It may be hours before she returned to her human form and longer still before she awoke and they had answers as to what happened.

Liam pulled a chair from the corner of the room to the bed and sat down. There wasn't much he could do. He wasn't a healer like his mom or the medics, however, he was Kyra's mate, even if they have yet to make it official. He was still new to his powers. He could make things move with just a thought, float in the air or change forms. Back when he had his sight and lived a relatively normal life, he used that gift in the short films he produced for high school. He would claim they were special effects or computer-generated images. He did study that and did created a large number of CGI characters and effects that his power could not produce, but it felt more natural when he did it through his powers. Back then, he thought he came from a Wiccan heritage, not knowing what he truly was, or at least not one hundred percent certain of. Not until he met Kyra. She opened him to a whole new world. Even after losing his eye sight, he still felt more complete next to her than he ever did alone. With her, the world felt right, even under the not so ideal circumstances they currently faced.

He reached out and took the hand closest to him. He could feel her energy move throughout her body. It pulsed and beat in time with her heart and moved through her to him. The change wasn't unexpected. He felt his human form shift to one of energy and light, his body responding to her. It happened before when they shared energy. Even unconscious, she called to him, needing his touch and energy to heal. It was an unusual feeling to share one's energy with another, yet right at the same time. Kyra would let him know in her own way when she no longer needed him. It could take all night but it didn't matter. She was his Queen and he would do anything to protect her.

Word of Kyra's abrupt return travelled quickly throughout the Sanctuary. With it came panic. Now that Kyra had returned to her human form and was resting peacefully, Liam felt it was his duty to help his mother calm everyone down. Everyone had a right to be scared. Kyra was the strongest among them, their Queen. If the Shadows managed to infect her then it wouldn't be long before the beings found a way to infect them. The circumstances of what happened didn't seem to matter, only that it was now a very real possibility. Having to explain all this to Elizabeth when she finally arrived was even more tedious. She stood before the mess hall, nervous energy coursing through her body, utterly confused before anger began to set in.

"He didn't come through with her?" she demanded, as if it was somehow Liam's fault.

He shook his head, unsure what else to do. "The portal opened and closed too quickly. It was almost as if she was pushed through. I only sensed Alex for the briefest of moments."

"That son of a bitch!" she cursed.

There was a loud bang, as if she punched something close to her. Liam could see the natural energy that flowed through humans, but it was not nearly as easy to read as it was in the hybrids or Kyra. He watched her carefully, wishing he had his natural sight in order to interpret her motions better. She was harder to read than most. Her energy was darker, almost sluggish in a sense. He attributed it to her coming in out of the cold. The cold did odd things to people's bodies and affected everyone differently. Personally, Liam hated the cold and how sluggish it made him feel.

Elizabeth grumbled under her breath before sighing. "And Kyra's still asleep?"

"She will be for maybe another hour or so. Mom's not entirely sure." He shifted from his left to right foot then back again. "Mom wanted to wait until she's awake to hold an emergency meeting, but it can still be a while and people are getting antsy. They want to know their Queen is safe and well. We're pretty sure we know where they were attacked but we thought you might have a better idea of where Alex was taken. If they're using the military or police…"

Elizabeth ran a hand through her hair. "It's hard to say. They could still be in Toronto or on their way to Ottawa, or Trenton. I don't know. Without Kyra, it will be next to impossible to track him down."

Liam nodded. He expected as much. Kyra and Alex were tied together in a way that was unlike most father and daughter relationships. They shared a psychic link that sometimes allowed one to view what the other was seeing or feeling. It was similar to the bond Liam shared with Kyra but ran deeper. There was no telling how Kyra's injury affected Alex, or how his possible injuries may affect her.

"There's something else," he began. He rubbed the back of his neck, feeling uncertain. "Kyra had a journal on her. It looked like someone had shoved it in her hands just as she entered the portal. My guess is Alex wanted to make sure it was protected along with Kyra."

"A journal?"

"Whatever is in it, it has mom spooked."

She was silent for a moment then let out a deep breath. "Lucas…" she whispered. "It must be his. I can't see Alex taking extraordinary steps to protecting anything other than his daughter and Lucas's notes…whatever they may be." She rubbed her face, clearly tired and worried. "Alright, let's lock everything down and go on high alert. I'll radio the patrol team and let them know what's going on."

"What about the chalet? Will you lock that down as well?"

The security for the chalet was world class. It may look like a normal A-frame style home but it was heavily armoured. The roof was made of thick metal with sections that slide over windows and doors, barricading it from the outside and reinforced by an energy shield similar to the one that surrounded the perimeter.

"No...not yet. With Alex missing and Kyra injured, there's no one there that needs protecting. Let's focus on securing the Sanctuary. I brought the portable shield Winston asked for." She hesitated a moment, one hand on the large duffle bag she was carrying. "You're certain this will keep anything from coming through the Void?"

"Winston is," he assured. "Kyra and I trust him."

There was another moment of hesitation before she handed Liam the bag. "Then I'm trusting the three of you to be right about this."

"Thank you."

He hoisted the bag to his shoulder, a little surprised she had given it to him rather than waiting to hand it off to Winston at the meeting. Elizabeth was one of the few that did not treat his blindness as a disability. He appreciated it more than he could ever express.

"We should go inside." He gestured at the mess hall. "Mom wants to figure out our next move."

"Yeah," the former general agreed.

Liam took a deep breath as she passed him. This was not going to be good. Elizabeth and Alex were best friends, almost as close as siblings. She would be expecting to lead a rescue team to find Alex, not what Marie had planned. He wasn't even certain if what his mother's plan would work, but they needed to give it a try. He hoped Elizabeth agreed. They needed her, especially with Alex gone.

The hall was full. Every member of the EDC within the Sanctuary, as well as every hybrid that had complete control of their powers and served as part of their defense were there. All the tables were pushed against the walls, next to cots that served as beds for the overflowing amount of refugees. The chairs and benches were arranged in a circle around the large glass woodstove that heated the large stone building. Children played along the outer edges, too young to understand what was going on. Marie was pacing in the middle. Nervous energy raced through her. The journal was open as she read through it. Liam followed Elizabeth to her. The two greeted each other with a small hug and kind words, both concerned about Kyra and Alex.

"Can everyone be seated?" Marie called out. Her voice resounded throughout the room much as it used to at their old bookstore when she would announce a guest author doing a signing or reading. She waited while everyone took their seats. Liam set the duffle beg on the ground and took a seat next to her. Elizabeth sat on his other side. "As many of you may have heard, Doctor Jackson is missing."

Murmurs filled the hall. For most, Alex was the first person they met before they entered the Sanctuary. They knew that if he was missing it was serious.

"He and Kyra were attacked while in Toronto," she continued after a moment of silence. "Kyra was returned to us, however, I fear the Shadows have taken Doctor Jackson." She paused, letting that sink it. "Worse, with him, the Shadows now have the key to the Void…every Void hidden within every remaining temple. Which means…they now have a way to by-pass all our defenses and get in here."

"Provided they have access to temple with an active Vault," Elizabeth interrupted.

"Which, they no doubt do," Marie agreed. "That means we don't have much time. We need to move, to find a new safe haven."

"How?" Naomi asked. She stood. Several youths nodded around her. "If they have access to the Void then how to we escape through ours? They can trap us in it or…or send an army here through it."

"That won't happen," Marie insisted.

"You don't know that."

There were grumbles of agreement as fear began to set in.

Elizabeth stood. "Listen!" she snapped. She took a step next to Marie in support. "Our only options are the Void or going top side and walking out of here. My plane isn't large enough to take all of us and if we walk…the moment we get past that shield the Shadows will be on us. They know we're here and they have Alex. It's only a matter of time before they have us as well." She took a deep breath. "Kyra may be injured but your Queen is still with us and will awaken soon. We need to start packing. Only the essentials. There won't be much time when we begin moving."

Marie nodded. "Those of you who can control your powers will join the EDC. If push comes to shove, we need to be able to fight the Shadows. The EDC will train you with their weapons as well as help you direct your powers. Remember, bullets can not kill anyone possessed by a Shadow. They're already dead. We need to remove their heads. Those of you that can, will be trained with weapons that can accomplish this." She paused to let that sink in. It was a horrible reality they all had to face. It was why some of the EDC agents had taken to forging swords and hunting knives. Anything that could separate a Shadow's head from their body. "All lights are to remain on. We need every inch of the Sanctuary lit…inside and out. Naomi, Liam, and Winton, I need you to stay. The rest of you, start packing."

Naomi and Winston made their way to Liam as Elizabeth pulled one of the tables away from the wall. She unrolled a large paper world map and held it down on the table with several tin cups.

"We're sitting ducks here," Naomi muttered as she looked the map over. "How exactly is that supposed to help us?"

"It's a map of the Earth's Ley Lines," Elizabeth answered.

"So? Can't we just pull that up on the computer?"

"We're going radio silent from here on out," Elizabeth told her sternly. "Our internet is satellite, which means the government – if they're watching – will know everything we're doing. With a paper map, we're blind them."

"Which means we can search for other temples without them trying to stop us right away," Liam threw in.

"One problem though," Winston pointed out. "How are we going to use the drones if we can't access the satellites? We need them for the remote control. If the Void takes them too far, we won't be able to see anything. The link will be severed."

Liam frowned. Winston was right. They needed the link up to the satellite in order to control and see what the drones saw. Everything they had was military issued. "We'll need to reprogram them," he said. "Instead of using the satellites. Can we create a direct link to a laptop? Maybe through Bluetooth?"

It was hard enough negotiating the Sanctuary without proper sight, but something like the Void? It would be near impossible. They need the drones.

"That's why we have the map," Elizabeth reminded him. "This is how Alex and Lucas originally searched for the temples. They followed the Ley Lines."

"Okay…" Naomi began.

"Shh…" Marie abolished.

Elizabeth traced out several of the lines. "They're like roads, linking one temple to the next. If we subtract the temples that have been destroyed we should be able to locate a functioning one."

Liam perked up at that. He had always been fascinated with Ley Lines. It was something his mother spoke of often when he was a child. He had always thought it had to do with her love of the occult and Wicca, now he knew it was more about their race.

"We know where the major temples were located." Elizabeth taped the map to indicate the numerous places. "We even found many of the secondary ones. So, we know where just about every ruin is. Those underwater are no assessable. That leaves us only a handful of places to investigate."

"And we're not just looking for temples," Marie added. She laid the journal on top of the map and opened it to a page she had book marked. "We also looking for mounds, underground kingdoms."

Liam's head lifted in surprise. That was new. "What do you mean?"

He felt a nervous energy come from his mother as she struggled with her next words. "Alright…look, there's a few things I may have left out about the Celestials and hybrids."

"Such as?" Elizabeth inquired, her tone suspicious of whatever secret Marie was withholding.

"Okay…as you may know the Great Rebellion happened over twelve thousand years ago which forced the Celestials underground."

"Yes?"

"It also forced the hybrids into hiding."

"Which makes sense."

"Now think of every legend and myth throughout the entire world. Gods, mythical creatures, supernatural beings…" Marie asked.

There was a long moment of silence before Elizabeth answered. "Celestials posed as gods?"

"Some. Others posed as what many would call angels." There was a pause. "When the rebellion first occurred, many of us fled. We left the planet, not wanting to risk destruction, but many stayed and after a few centuries, created new roles for themselves. Some became 'gods' and 'angel' that would descend to Earth from time to time. Others preferred to stay underground, building themselves entire new worlds away from mankind. A place where they could protect their offspring, especially as humans continued to advance and their weapons became more deadly. I thought they went extinct but it seems Lucas may have found them…or at least a lead to finding them."

"Wait…what are you saying?" Naomi asked, obviously confused.

"You don't really believe this is the first-time hybrids have been part of the world?" Marie asked in a teasing voice.

Naomi stumbled for an answer then shrugged.

"There have always been hybrids. Most go unseen and have no gifts. They can mingle amongst humans and never know that they are not one of them, but others, like yourself, are far too powerful to go unnoticed. In some cultures, they were known as demi-gods, but in places like Ireland, those choosing to hide were given another name…the Sidhe, the remnants of the ancient city of Tuatha De Danann, one of the first Celestial temples."

Liam scratched the back of his neck. "Wait…you're saying that faeries are real and they're actually hybrids like us?"

"They were the first."

"And what happened to them?" Winston asked, his interest peaked.

"They were hunted down like us," Naomi grumbled. "That's why no one believes in them any more. They went extinct and became fairy tales."

"Not necessarily," Marie interjected. "Unlike the temples, the fae mounds are usually located at minor Ley Line junctions. They avoid cities and would completely move the entrance to their realm should any sort of human development begin near them."

"Realms?" Winston asked.

"They've learned to manipulate the Void and created a pocket realm within the Earth. A world within a world if you may."

Realization hit Liam. "This is what you wanted to talk to Alex about! You weren't planning to use the Void for travel but to create our own realm."

His mother nodded. "Yes." She tapped an image in the journal. "Lucas appeared to think the same think. There have always been realms within realms, but creating one is not going to be easy. It will take more power than most of us have..."

"Most?" Elizabeth asked, intrigued.

Marie hesitated. "It's difficult to explain...and with Alex captured...it's no longer safe to attempt here. We need to find a new location...but, with access to an active orb...I should be able to create it."

"Fine, let's figure out where to begin our search. Winston, go set up the shield for the Void. We're going to have to set the coordinates manually. Naomi, help keep the little ones calm, and not a word of this to anyone," instructed Elizabeth. "Liam, with Kyra unconscious, you're going to have to serve as our guide."

He gestured to himself. "I'm blind. The most I can do is read energy."

"Exactly. You'll be able to detect whether or not there is an active orb the moment the portal opens. If there isn't one, we move on without sending anyone in."

It made a strange sort of sense.

Elizabeth picked up the journal and flipped through the pages. "This is Lucas's journal but the theories are Alex's."

"Excuse me?" Marie asked in surprise.

"After they adopted Kyra, Alex began theorizing how human history and mythology made more sense with the discovery of hybrids." She sat down and set the journal aside. "Everything you just said about the gods, angels, and faeries…he said the same thing…that everything we thought about religion and mythology…the Celestials created it. They were the gods man worshipped…the angels that 'blessed' us…the faeries and magickal beings of lore. All of it was them either trying to control us…or hide from us. Look where it led us…holy wars, religious cults, one man trying to hold his religion over another when it's all the same beings. My ancestors worshipped the Sky People for generations. It wasn't some story…they were real. Everything Alex theorized was real…Lucas just needed to prove it to himself."

"Okay…but how did the journal end up in Toronto?" Liam asked, clearly confused. He only knew Lucas for a short time, but from what Kyra told him, the penthouse had been untouched for years with only a skeleton crew maintaining it. It seemed unlikely that Lucas would have left a journal with such important research there, especially pertaining to the Celestials.

"I wish I knew."

"Wish you knew what?" a tired voice asked from behind Liam.

Joy filled Liam as he felt Kyra's energy move toward him. She placed a hand on his lower back, a gentle gesture to let him know she was there, then stood next to him. Her energy burned brightly. It moved within her and around her, like a chaotic storm, hiding her emotions from the outside world. Nonetheless, Liam could feel the biting fear it concealed. She was hiding it well though.

"Kyra!" Elizabeth gasped. She wrapped her arms around the young woman and drew her close. "Thank god you're safe."

Kyra returned her embrace. "I don't think any of us are safe. Where's Dad?"

Silence met her.

She looked from Elizabeth to Marie to Liam and then back. "Aunt Beth...what happened to my Dad?"

"Oh, honey...we don't know," Elizabeth answered honestly. "You were the only one that came through the portal."

"You're Dad saved you," Marie added.

Kyra was quiet for a moment. She stepped away from Elizabeth, fear radiating from her. "What happened?"

"We were hoping you could tell us," Marie told her. "All we know is you were the only one to come through the portal...with this." She showed her the journal. "That's all you had with you."

Kyra stared at it for a moment but didn't touch it. "Can it help?"

"I think so."

"Good. I need to go back and find my Dad. I'm not losing him, too." She turned to leave but Liam caught her hand.

"Don't," he said, his voice deep and commanding. It didn't feel quite like his own despite his words. "They have Alex and tried to kill you. That means they want him alive. Whatever the reason...he's safe for now. We need to focus on finding a safe place to evacuate to. The Sanctuary is compromised as long as the Shadows have him."

"That's why I need to find him," Kyra argued.

"They could have taken him anywhere," Elizabeth pointed out. "Kyra...we'll get him back, but right now, we need to protect everyone here."

"As our Queen…" Marie began.

Kyra raised her hand. "I get it…but I'm not abandoning him. Aunt Beth…can you monitor the government channels…listen for any chatter than may tell us where he is? They set all this up for a reason. I want to know what it is."

"You've got it," Elizabeth agreed.

"I'm going to try to connect with him. Maybe we can figure out their game plan and head them off.

"You can use my hut." Liam offered without a second thought.

He and Winston roomed together. Everyone was doubling, even tripling up in the huts. There was a limited number of them. Others lived in tents. Thankfully, the Sanctuary was well heated…for now at least.

She nodded without hesitation. "Thank you."

She wrapped an arm around his waist. Whether it was for his comfort or her own, it was hard to tell. He held her as well, happy she was safe, and shaving her worry for her dad. She was still recovering from losing Lucas. She may not say anything, but he caught her on crying on more than one occasion. They left Marie and Elizabeth to figure out their next move.

"You should be resting," he told Kyra once they were alone.

She shook her head. "I don't have time to rest," she objected. She sighed. "I can feel him. He's in trouble. I didn't want to say anything in front of your mom or Elizabeth, but…I may be able to use it to find him. I just need someplace quiet to focus."

"Winston is working on the drones. We've got the whole place to ourselves," he assured.

A small, tired smile tugged at least at her lips. She sat on his bed and crossed her legs under her. She rested her hands on her knees, closed her eyes, and shifted into her Celestial forms. Her pearl white hair float around her as she went into a trance, her mind reaching out to find Alex.

Chapter Eight

"Uh…" Alex groaned.

His head hurt. Someone had punched him so hard in the gut he blacked out. Pain radiated from his stomach to his chest and shoulders. His arms were tied behind his back, the rough rope chafing his wrists, and pressure pulling against his shoulders. It was normal to feel pressure when your arms in such a position. What wasn't normal was the feel of ropes criss-crossing his body, the odd position of his good leg – which was also tied – or the fact that he was naked and prosthetic leg missing. He didn't need to open his eyes to know that. The position he was tied in was reminiscent of the time he and Lucas used bondage in their old sex dungeon. It was a long time ago but his body remembered certain things…the feel of the rope, the cool air against his naked body, hanging from the ceiling unable to move or stretched. The total and complete lack of control. Such a thing under Lucas's control would be thrilling…but he had no idea who had done this to him or why. Fear filled him as memories of being kidnapped and raped forced his eyes opened.

He looked around the room. It was only twelve by fifteen feet, if that, completely padded, making it soundproof, and dimly lit from above. The ceiling and floor were both stone, the later showcasing dark brown stains that he could only assume were blood. A few feet from him was a woman in a gray skirt suit with matching pumps. She looked like a government official despite the out of place setting. She smiled brightly when he looked at her.

"Welcome back, Doctor Jackson," she greeted him, her voice upbeat.

It hurt his neck to look at her for long. The position he was end was slanted to the point he was practically facing the floor. He hung his head for a moment to relieve the pressure to his neck and shoulders.

"Where am I?" he demanded.

She clicked her tongue disapprovingly. "Where's my manners? My name is Acantha. Let me help you and then I can explain what's happening."

Any hope of her letting him go was quickly abolished when she pulled one of the ropes, forcing him into a more upright position. Pain flared through his shoulders and chest, but other than a small grunt, he kept the discomfort to himself.

"I have to admit, you look more distinguished than the last time we met," she told him, her voice like a soft purr. One of her hands brushed over his stomach. "Not quite as tone as I remember."

"Am I supposed to know you?"

Her dark brown eyes met his. "No, we were never formally introduced. It must have been fifteen…sixteen years ago. You were young…vibrant…and served our master well."

His brows furrowed in confusion. "Master?" His eyes widened. "You're a Shadow."

He should have known that. His mind was still foggy. On the far edges, he could sense Kyra searching for him. Their bond was incredibly powerful but for once, he did not want his daughter to know where he was or what was going on. Not just yet. He was in a horrible position, with a Shadow no less, and if his guess was right, things were about to get a lot worse before they got better. There was no need for her to experience that along with him. He shielded his mind, creating an imaginary barrier around it that she could not enter.

He almost missed what the Shadow was saying.

"You don't remember our master?" she asked. She looked slightly disappointed.

He stared at her for a moment then gave a slight nod. He remembered being possessed by the Celestial. It was a memory he fought hard to forget, yet it tormented him almost on a daily basis. "I remember."

"Tell me what you remember. Tell me about the things he showed you."

"Like what?"

She stepped away from him and shook her head. "I'm not sure if you're playing dumb or truly don't remember," she mused. "When a Celestial possesses a host, memories of their past hosts are often shared with them."

She sat on a stool next to the lone small metal table in the room and began fiddling with some of the tools on it. Now that Alex was upright, he could see there were vials of some sort of liquid, likely drugs, as well as syringes, and – strangely enough – sexual toys such as various size rods and dildos, even a strap-on. It was obvious what she intended to do to him.

"Why did you attack my daughter and I?" he asked, trying to distract her. The longer he could keep her talking the better his chances of escaping without her assaulting him.

She hummed softly to herself as she filled one of the syringes from a blue vial. "I'm sure you know by now that hybrids have existed as long as humankind has."

"I assumed as much."

"My child was a hybrid."

His eyes widened slightly in surprise but he said nothing in response.

"Beautiful little boy. I served as one of our master's many consorts, letting him take me whenever he wanted. I had no choice really. It was that or be fed upon." She shrugged as if it was no big deal. "I served him well. Gave him a strong son. You would think I'd be rewarded and granted a chance to give him a second...but no. He got what he wanted and when next he bedded me...he ripped out my heart and ate it in front of my dying eyes, cursing me to be one of his Shadow-beings. Untouchable...unlovable. Damned to watch my son grow and become a monster like his father. My child...he enslaved entire nations and destroyed any that would not bowed to him. And what could I, his mother do to stop him? Nothing. All I could do was served him, like I served his father."

She stared off into the distance. Her long fingers brushed against one check, brushing away moisture. She looked at her fingers for a long time in wonder. "I haven't cried in thousands of years. Shadows can't cry." A small hollow laugh escaped her as she turned back to face Alex. "Did you know the Shadows were once human? Each and every one of us. We were slaves forced to serve the Celestials in life and death. They bred us like cattle then bond us to them for eternity."

"They don't control you anymore," he pointed out.

She nodded. "No, thanks to you. You freed us..."

"Then we're on the same side," he pointed out. "We can stop the Celestials together."

Her laugh was musical but there was no joy in it. "The Celestials are dying. They only came to Earth to save their race. They created the hybrids to be the perfect beings, but they are just as infallible and dangerous as their predecessors... However, if we control the narrative…if we control who they breed with, then we control the next generation of hybrids. We can ensure there is no Queen."

"Hybrids cannot be possessed by Shadows," Alex reminded her.

"No, but we can control them. We can decide what ones are bred." She traced a hand along his severed leg. "Imagine, Alex…no more wars. No more infighting. No more countries. It will all be one world, not controlled by Celestials or greedy humans, or hybrids posing as Gods. We can create the perfect society free of oppression…free of Celestials."

Her fingers moved upwards, skirting over his lower stomach, up to his chest to one nipple. She began rubbing her thumb over it, as if in awe. Lord only knew how long it had been since she had been with another human. Alex ignored the tingle of arousal that filled him.

"You're talking mass genocide," he pointed out. "You want to kill humans and hybrids alike."

"The hybrids for now…humans will eventually kill one another. All they need is the right…push." To demonstrate, she gave him a small shove that sent him swinging from his binds. "As we speak, the Shadows are already infiltrating every country's government and taking it over. Even all those Sanctuary countries that have agreed to protect the hybrids. Soon, they too will be hunting them down. Hybrids may be hard to kill but they do die. They always die in the end. Even your precious Kyra. Of course, she's not a hybrid, is she? She's a human-born Celestial. All the powers and abilities of a Celestial in a human shell." She laughed. "And that was her undoing…the human shell. It took the Celestials centuries to figure how to make the perfect being, two Celestials within two separate hosts had to mate one another. Still, that little bit of humanness is all it takes to kill them. I'll be sure to find and end her mate as well…not that either of them could reproduce anyway. I suppose they would have died out eventually but why wait?"

"You're not making a lot of sense," Alex told her. He needed to learn what she did to Kyra. His daughter was alive, he could sense her. What was this Shadow planning?

That laugh returned and it turned his stomach. "Live as a Shadow for twelve thousand years and tell me your sanity survived," she challenged.

He tried to flex his shoulders, his neck cramping painfully. "Look, I'm sorry for what the Celestials have done to you, and your people. None of you deserved that…but it's not the hybrids' fault. They are victims as much as you are. These people you're both using as hosts…they have families and lives. Taking them makes you no better than the Celestials."

She hummed softly. "And what about your victims?"

Alex inhaled deeply and closed his eyes. He did not want to get into *that* discussion.

"You hosted our master for how long? Months? How many people did you feed upon and kill?" Her voice was a purr. She pushed on his good knee, causing him to spin in a circle from the rope. "How many did you fuck before ripping out their hearts and feasting upon it as they died, either with you still inside them…or they inside you?"

"I had no control," he retorted. "I was possessed…just like this woman you possessed."

"Really? Yet, our master did not feast upon your loved ones. He primarily followed your sexual orientation. How many women did you seduce? One…maybe two. The rest were men, were they not?"

"I don't know. I wasn't always conscious of what the Celestial was doing."

Her lips brushed against his ear. "I think you were…otherwise Lucas and Elizabeth would have died right at the beginning. He would have fucked them endlessly then…"

"Shut up!" He threw his weight as best he could at her but it had no affect.

She merely laughed. "I see why he liked you. Feisty! He must have enjoyed having men pound into you. I bet you enjoyed it just as much."

His hands flexed into fists. "What do you want? You kept me alive for a reason and I highly doubt it was for the commentary. Or do you bore all your victims with endless chatter?"

"Oh…catty, are we?" she shot back. "Truth be told, you're the first surviving host I've meet. The rest usually die or go insane. So, this is a rare gift."

"Get to the point."

She pouted. "I thought we were having fun." She shrugged and took the syringe filled with the blue liquid. "Fine. I need access to your precious Sanctuary. We're going to put down those hybrids and use the Void to find the rest and kill them all. Then we'll do the same to the Celestials. No one will every suffer because of them again."

"And you think drugging me will make me help you?"

She knelt before him, far too close to his genitals for his liking. He tried to struggle…to kick her with the stump of his bad leg, but it did no good. She looked up the length of his body with a cruel grin. "No…this is just to heighten the sensations you're about to feel. I plan to break you in every way a man can be broken."

She took his manhood in both hands and kissed the tip. Her tongue delved into the foreskin to lick at the slit. A low growl of irritation escaped him as she began pumping his length. He shifted his hips, tried to pull away, but in the end there was nothing he could do to stop her. What she did felt good but was unwanted. Nonetheless, after a few minutes, his length began to swell in her hand.

"There we go," she purred.

Alex cried out as she plunged the needle of the syringe into a fat vein on the underside of his length. The liquid burned as it was forced into him. It made the organ feel larger and heavier than it was. Any erection he had quickly vanished as his body began to feel as if it was on fire. That didn't deter his captor. She grasped his parted thighs and pulled him toward her. Then, with a twisted grin, she took his length in her mouth and began to suck. It wasn't playful like a lover, it was hungry, as if she wanted to eat him whole. Her teeth scraped the sensitive organ as she swallowed his length deep into her throat and seemed to try to take his balls as well. He struggled and yelled. It hurt more than anything he could remember. More than the shock of losing his leg. Every struggle and yell was met with a hard warning bite, as if she was not afraid to bite his cock off. Her fingers moved from his hips to his ass, teasing his puckered hole of things to come until finally the pain began to subside and pleasure took it's place. His length pulsed as if with a mind of it's own. White hot pleasure replaced agonizing pain until his body was trembling with need and his vision blurred. Whether he wanted to or not, he was forced to come, his juices shooting down her hot throat. She didn't stop once he emptied, she kept sucking, renewing the burning pain until he was shouting for her to stop as his length hardened once more.

"The fun's just beginning, love," she promised. She stood and picked up one of the ribbed rods. Her fingers ran playfully over the length. "Did you ever wonder what happened to the people you murdered? If they were bound only to the Celestial or perhaps…you as well?"

Alex's body shock in a mix of pleasure and pain. What was she going on about? He tried his best not to remember those horrible events. They were dead. The Celestial murdered them. He had only learned what the Shadows really were from her. Why would he think of how they were bound to the Celestial? Wait…did she say bound to him? That wasn't possible. How could they be bound to him?

"No…" he breathed as the door opened.

114

Men and women began filed in. Only a handful, but he could almost sense each one. Not quite like the hive mind of the hybrids but something darker. Shadows but darker, angrier, vengeful. He almost forgot about Acantha as his gaze met one of them. He was larger than the rest and while it's host's body was not the same as it's original, the presence it held was just as dark and fearsome as it had been in life. No matter what the other's did to him, it was nothing compared to what this creature could. The nightmares and horror he suffered years ago came rushing back to him. It took all his strength not to have a full-on panic attack. His chest burned as his heart pounded in a mix of fear and anxiety. He feared being raped but this would be far worse. In life Kirill Drago had kidnapped him, used his body like a toy. Raped him, tortured him, pierced parts of his body without consent, and inserted toys that were far too large for him into his body. When the Celestial killed Drago and cult, Alex thought that was it, he was free. He never considered they would become Shadows. Now they were back for revenge. There were others in the group, those killed during the time the Celestial control him, but they did not frighten him nearly as much as Drago.

"I've waited a long time for this…" the Shadow purred, his thick Russian accent unmistakeable. The large man wrapped one hand around Alex's throat and lifted him until they were face to face. It wasn't enough to choke him but it did hurt. Drago's thumb rubbed along Alex's Adam's apple. "I'm going to enjoy making you scream."

Alex's eyes narrowed, a mask of indifference sliding over his features. "You released the Celestial and used me as a sacrifice. What did you think was going to happen? You thought a god was going to thank you and make you his right-hand man?" He burst out laughing, certain he was losing his mind. "The fact he made you and your little cult into Shadows ought to be enough to show your worth to them. You were nothing but a sadist then, you're nothing but a sadist now. You're nothing…and this…this doesn't change that."

He expected the backhand. It landed across his right cheek and made his ear ring. He grunted in pain but it was temporary. The punch in the gut was far worse. Drago's huge fist landed two…three…four times against his bare stomach and side until something cracked. Alex's breath hitched as he felt a rib fracture…possibly break under the onslaught. It reduced him to a bundle of pain and agony, hanging from the ceiling, unable to curl around the injury to protect himself.

"That smart mouth is better at other things than talking," the Shadow sneered.

Alex bared his teeth. "Try it and I'll bite the fucking thing off this time," he warned.

He fully expected Drago to try shoving his cock down his throat. He'd done it before, tearing his throat raw. The man took what he wanted, regardless what other's thought. It would be no different now.

His head was yanked back as Drago's large fingers knotted in his hair, the Shadow now behind him. Alex felt the tip of his cock push against his rim. There was no more foreplay. What little there was, came from Acantha, who watched with a satisfied grin. Despite his fear and anger, Alex forced his body to relax as best he could. There was no escaping this and the more he fought, the more it would hurt, and the more Drago would take pleasure in it. He was not going to give Drago that. He was not going to give any of them that. They could do whatever they wanted to his body…but they were not going to break him.

"Gentle, Kirill," Acantha tsked. She knelt before Alex once more. Slowly, she inserted the ribbed rod into his urethra. Alex hissed at the sensation of it filling him. "There are a lot of us who want to spend 'quality' time with the dear Doctor."

Drago grunted, but her words didn't stop the burning agony that took hold of Alex as Drago all but shoved his length into him. Alex held back a scream as the much larger man slammed into him, shoving every inch of his fat cock as deep as possible before taking up a brutal pace meant to deliver the upmost pain. His hand still knotted in Alex hair, he forced his head up so all can watch as he was defiled and hear every cry and whimper that escaped him. It wasn't long before the other Shadows approached him. They stroked and caressed him, some even kneeling between his legs to suck his cock, rod and all, while the others took turns fucking him. Alex had no control. No matter how much he tried to separate his mind from his body, it proved impossible as pain and pleasure washed over him in waves until he was shaking and begging for them to stop. He was no longer able to shield himself from the torment...only for it to begin all over again.

"No!" Kyra cried.

She fell from her floating position over Liam's bed, no longer able to focus as Alex's pain rushed over her. She could feel everything...every person that touched her father...everything that entered him. It left her shaking and horrified. When she first reached out to him, he had immediately blocked her, put up a mental wall so she could not see what was happening. Something had shattered it and all his fear and suffering slammed into her like a tidal wave she could not escape from.

Liam rushed to her. His hands grasped her shoulders. "Kyra?"

"No!" she gasped. She pushed him back. "Don't...don't touch me. Give me a minute."

She could feel all those people touching Alex as if they were touching her. It was disgusting. How could someone do such things to someone else? How could anyone treat another like that? She hugged herself and sat on the stone floor, her back against Liam's bed. When her father told her all the things he had suffered through in the past, she never thought it was as horrifying as what she felt. Her parents had always been very sexual and done some crazy stuff together. A part of her thought Alex had described something similar, not...this. She felt as if she was going to be sick.

"Do you want me to get Mom or Elizabeth?" Liam asked. He sat on the floor across from her, within arm's distance if she needed him.

Kyra shook her head. "No…no… I need to find my Dad. We need to get him back before…before anything else happens to him."

"But Mom said…"

"It doesn't mater what she said."

She took a deep breath. Tears lingers at the corner of her eyes. Her Dad was in trouble. She couldn't leave him to whatever fate the Shadows had in store for him. She needed to get to him, regardless where he was. It was likely a trap, but it didn't matter. One way or another, she had to find him, but she needed help. The Shadows already proved they could hurt her. If only she could open a portal directly to him. Get him and get out with the least amount of conflict. Her power wasn't strong enough. It was still new to her…she needed someone who knew more about portals than she did…someone who had worked directly with them before.

Her gaze met Liam's sightless one. "Where's Naomi?"

"Helping the others pack."

"Alright," she said. She used the edge of the bed to get to her feet then hesitantly helped him up as well. Touching another person felt wrong. It made her skin crawl. She could still feel what Alex was going through, even if the psychic connection was broken. "Let's find her and prep the infirmary for incoming. There's no telling how bad of shape Dad will be in once we find him."

"And how exactly are we going to do that?" Liam asked. He followed her outside. "I'm supposed to be helping Winston navigate the Void."

"You're not coming with me," she told him pointedly. "You're staying here and I'm going to find my Dad. We'll only have minutes…maybe hours…after we free him before the Shadows attack. They can't get past the shield but that doesn't mean they won't to pry the codes for it out of him." She paused and looked at him. "I need you to

118

find us a safe haven. I'll put him in the light chamber the moment we get back…the cryochamber if I have to…I don't know. All I do know is I'm not leaving him behind."

"Kyra…" he tried to object.

"Go…help Winston." She stepped up to him and pressed her lips against his. It wasn't their normal passionate kiss that hid promises of something more. It was a desperate, 'please trust me' kiss that begged he do as she asked without further questions.

He sighed and nodded. "Be careful."

Chapter Nine

Kyra's hands shook as she approached Naomi. The younger woman was watching a group of children play near the communal garden. Despite Naomi's sass, she was great with kids, having had younger siblings of her own. The dark-skinned woman was trying to keep an air of calm and normalcy. However, Kyra could see the anxiety and stress that pinched the corners of her mouth and created dark circles under her eyes. Despite the smile, her lips were pressed together, showing it was forced and hid her true feelings.

"You okay?" Kyra asked, her voice low for only her friend to here.

Naomi glanced at her then inhaled deeply, hiding a small sniffle. "I don't know," she said honestly. She ran a hand over her tightly braided hair. "Every time I think things might actually be looking up, something else happens. I'm tired of hiding. I've spent my entire life hiding. First my parents, then bigots like them, now these Shadows. I'm tired. I want to fight."

"I know," Kyra agreed.

Naomi fought hard to be accepted for who she was rather than who her parents thought she should be. It meant running away from home at a young age and leaving her siblings to fend for themselves. She used her power of manipulation to make people see her the way she did. It allowed her to go back to school under a new name and preferred

120

gender. Had the Shadows not attacked, she and Liam would be graduating this spring.

She nodded and looked Kyra over. "Are *you* alright?"

Kyra hesitated then shook her head. "I managed to connect with my Dad. He's…they're…torturing him."

She couldn't bring herself to say what she knew was happening to him. Rape was a touchy subject. Both she and Naomi had experienced it. In very different ways from what she sensed was happening to Alex. They were manipulated and minds psychically invaded by Archer, tricking them into following him. What was happening to Alex was far worse. Archer they were able to defeat. Shadows were another thing. In a host body or not, they could escape into the natural shadows and evade them, only to strike again later. It was impossible to destroy them, hence the need for light rooms, and why most hybrids slept with their lights on. It wasn't much, but it was a form of defense. Some argued that using light only created more shadows for the beings to hide and move about, being counterproductive. In some ways it may be, but that was why there was a perimeter shield. With the exception of the light room, leaving the light on at night was more of a safety blanket.

Naomi read her expression and almost instantly understood. Without saying a word, she wrapped her arms around Kyra and drew her into a hug. "It's okay. We'll find him."

Kyra's shoulders fell. She leaned into Naomi and let the other woman embrace her, her own arms wrapping around the other's waist. "I can't lose him. Losing Lucas…it nearly broke me, but Alex…"

"I know." Naomi gently pushed her back. Her hands held Kyra's upper arms. "We'll get him back…even if I have to hitch hike all the way to Toronto and get him back for you."

That made Kyra laugh. Naomi would do that, just for her. It wasn't a line. They had come to love each other like sisters and would do anything to help the other.

121

"Do you still have that contact in Toronto?" Naomi asked. "Director White or whatever?"

Kyra nodded. "Director White…yeah, I was supposed to call her while we were there."

"Do you think she might be able to help?"

"Maybe. I'll have to go to the chalet to call her…after we meet up with Liam and Winston. We need to figure out navigating the Void. Something tells me we don't have much time. There's no telling what they'll get out of my Dad if they break him…"

"I get it."

Naomi warned the kids to stay away from the underground waterfall and river. While it was flowing due to the warmth underground, the water was frigid and moved quickly. It was very dangerous. To be safe, she waved down one of the EDC as they approached the temple to keep an eye on the children. There was no power struggle. Despite Naomi's age, she was well respected by all and the agent did as requested without complaint.

They made the long climb up the steps of the temple, then the long trek down to the Void at it's base. If there was a secret entrance from the ground level, they had yet to find it. Kyra could simply portal them to the vast chamber, she was still recovering and the walk helped ease the stress she felt. After all, she had spent most of her childhood exploring the temple with his fathers. It held many happy memories for her. She ran one hand along the wall as she and Naomi made their way down to the Vault, the alien ship that housed the Void. The ship was dead. No power ran to it despite the volcano buried deep below the mountain. It was inactive, therefore not supplying the power the Vault needed to work. This made it safe for the hybrids to live underground but may not provide the power needed to open the Void. With luck, the electricity Winston had been siphoning from the solar panels outside would do the trick.

Liam and Winston were waiting for them at the control panel for the Void, a large altar like device that had hieroglyphics craved into what appeared to be a mix of metal and stone. Winston tried tinkering with the intricate lock with little success. It could only be opened by a matching key…or Alex, who's right hand just happened to be a key. It had been horribly scarred by an artifact years ago and tied him not only to the temples but also the Celestials, like an early warning system when he was close to one. For some reason, it was also able to open the Void which it shouldn't. Despite being scarred, a human hand did not have the right dimensions or shape to fit the lock. The groves and bumps on the key were larger than the palm of Alex's hand. Yet, somehow it worked. He could open the Void without so much as an incantations. He had been able to long before being possessed by the Celestial, which meant his connection to them surpassed that one event. It was almost as if he was branded for no other purpose than to be a conduit for them. Thankfully, Kyra had one of the artifacts that served as a key ready to use in his stead.

"Give me good news," Kyra said. She walked up to Winston as the tech whiz tinkered with one of the drones.

"Well…good news, I've managed to connect the drones via Bluetooth to my VR set. So, I'll have better control of them once they enter the Void. I'll be able to read heat signatures, radiation levels, and pin point the location on the map," Winston reported. He tapped the refurbished head set sitting on the altar.

"And the bad news?"

Liam let out a low sigh. "We can't open the Void."

"What do you mean? I gave you the artifact." She stared at him in disbelief. "Is it broken? Is there a gem missing?"

Winston shook his head. "It's in perfect condition. No chips or cracks. Every gem is where it should be."

"Then what's the problem?" Kyra mused. She picked up the artifact and inspected it, expecting to find something Winston may have missed, but there was nothing. It was exactly as it should be. "Is the altar getting enough power?"

"Yep, there should be more than enough. I don't get it."

Frowning, she placed the artifact into the lock and infused it with her own energy. If power was flowing into the altar, perhaps all it needed was a boost. The sound of gears moving and engine powering up should have filled the Vault as it came alive, but neither happened. The only light was from the fixtures the military installed long ago. She waited, letting her energy flow into the artifact and down into the altar, but still, nothing happened. It was dead, not responding as it should. The Void remained unchanged. The Void was literally that, a big black wall of darkness that took up one entire wall the length of a football field. No one knew where it led or dared touch it. The darkness was like a thick fog and ice cold to the touch. Things froze solid the moment they met it. When it opened, it was like a tear through space and time, the fog parting to allow the beings on the other side through. How it worked was a complete mystery.

"Maybe Marie knows what to do," Naomi suggested. She tried on the VR set only for Winston to take it from her. She glared at him but said nothing in retort.

"Is that wise?" Liam asked, surprising everyone. "Alex said he didn't want her to open the Void. He was downright livid at the very idea. Maybe he has good reason."

"Maybe he sabotaged it to keep us from leaving," Naomi mused. It earned her a dirty look from each of the others. "I'm just saying…he was scared, and given what happened…the fact that the Shadows now have him…maybe he was right."

"That's my Mom," Liam reminded her.

"I know."

Kyra shook her head. "There has to be a way to open it. Regardless what my Dad thinks…it's our only chance of finding a safe haven for everyone. It's not like we can just fly everyone out of here and go off into the great beyond."

"Well, if we can't open it then we're trapped here," Winston concluded with a shrug. He kicked a pebble into the darkness.

He was right. They were all trapped here. There was no way they could pack everyone on a plane. First, they didn't have one large enough. Second, the airspace around the mountain was constantly patrolled. Yes, they could trick their computers but a large plane – if the could find one large enough and safely land it and take off again – would attract a lot of unwanted attention. Kyra could open a portal but that was also limited. She was unsure where to take everyone, how long she could hold it open, and how many times she could to it. However, if they couldn't activate the Void then what else could they do? She needed to talk to someone who knew the Void intimately. Marie didn't. She had been amongst humans for too long…but she wasn't the only Celestial Kyra knew.

She ran a hand through her hair. She needed to contact Director White either way. The Celestial would help find Alex. Helping them open the Void was another question. It was a subject most Earth-bound Celestials avoided.

"I need to head to the house," she announced with a sigh.

She didn't want to talk with White. After everything that happened with rescuing hybrids in Toronto less than a year ago, and how White treated her like a child despite her plan – or lack there of – working. It left a bad taste in Kyra's mouth and she very much didn't want to interact with her again. It was why she was stalling as long as possible. Unfortunately, her Dad didn't have time for her to stall, neither the hybrids.

"Do you want me to come with you?" Liam asked.

Naomi gave her an expectant look as well, silently offering the same thing.

Kyra hesitated. She wanted to spend more time with Liam but if White could help them locate Alex, she would have to leave immediately, either by plane or portal. Given the fact that the Shadows most likely thought she was dead or in a coma, and the government had planes patrolling their airspace, portal may be the best bet. After all, she succeeded in opening one to get back to the Sanctuary. Opening one to White's base of operations shouldn't be too hard. It wasn't far from the airport. Perhaps even close enough to wherever Alex was being kept. However, she did need backup. Someone able to fight and with a skill set that could help them get into places she normally couldn't.

"We've discussed this...I need you here, Liam," she reminded him. "Whether or not we get the Void open, we still need to get everyone moved. Tell your Mom what's going on. She may be able to help...or at least figure out what's going on."

His lips pressed into a hard line, not happy with her decision.

She placed a hand on his shoulder. "Hey, I trust you to lead and protect our people. Naomi has my back in a battle."

"I have your back," he argued.

"I know..."

He shook his head, clearly angry that she still refused to take him with her, especially now that the Void was not working. It changed nothing. If the Shadows got their hands on both of her and Liam there was no stopping them. They would have all the hybrids. As Celestial-born, she and Liam all but ruled the hybrids. Capturing one of them could be devastating to them and destroy the hive mind the hybrids shared. Capturing both could give the Shadows control of it. With Naomi by her side, Kyra could reach into people's minds, find Alex's exact location, and manipulate them to do as they wanted. Right now, that was more beneficial than some of the powers other hybrids had, including Liam. Most of the hybrids were not fighters and have never had to fight a Shadow or another of their kind. Naomi had. She was the best person for this job.

"As soon as I have news on how to fix the Void, I'll contact you," she told Liam. "We're going to make this work. We have to."

His lips tightened into a frown but finally he nodded in agreement. "I'll see if Mom can fix it. It's probably a stupid crossed wire somewhere."

"Hey!" Winston objected. He didn't like people questioning his work.

Liam shrugged, unsure what else to say.

"Are we going to portal to the house?" Naomi asked. She pulled her braids back into a make-shift bun.

Kyra thought about it for a moment. "No," she answered. "We're going to portal directly to warehouse."

Naomi's brows furrowed in questioning. "Warehouse?"

"It's an EDC hideout. Let's just hope the Shadows haven't found it."

Much as the Void ripped through the fabric of space and time, so did Kyra. The only difference was she could travel anywhere, not a set destination ruled by the Ley Lines. She gave Liam and Winston one final look before offering her hand to Naomi. Together, they crossed over and back into Toronto.

Alex groaned in pain as he was shoved into the hard, unforgiving wooden chair. Everything hurt. There were multiple "toys" within him, both he ass and his penis. They pressed and rubbed in ways that would normally be pleasurable but instead stabbed and hurt in ways he could not fully articulate. Mixed with the beating he took, his body was bruised and battered, with several ribs likely broken by the Shadows that

127

gracefully decided not to rape him, he was in utter agony. Hanging from the ceiling was almost better than sitting. He didn't fight or struggle as Drago tied his arms behind the back of the chair. His shoulders already ached but the position was much better than before.

"If you choose to kill him, I want to be here to watch," Drago told Acantha. He grabbed Alex's chin, his thumb rubbing circles into his cheek. "I want to be inside him when the light fades from his eyes."

Alex glared at him. He hurt, but disgust overrode logical thinking. He turned his face toward the larger man's thumb and bit it with all his might, breaking skin and separately the digit from the rest of the hand. Drago howled in a mix of pain and rage as Alex spit the thumb onto the ground. The pain surprised Alex. The human host the Shadow possessed was supposed to be dead. How did Drago feel pain? He wasn't given much time to think about it. Drago punched him across the jaw with his good hand, knocking Alex and the chair onto the ground.

"I'm going to enjoy watching you die," the Shadow growled. "I'm going to make you choke to death with my cock so deep in your throat, it'll be your last memory."

Alex gave a snort of laughter. "And I'll bite it off as well."

A hard kick to his lower stomach knocked to air out of his lungs and left Alex gasping.

"After all that, you're still as feisty as ever." The Shade yanked him and the chair back into position. "On second thought, don't kill him. He's far from broken." He grabbed Alex's manhood, a thick rod still deep inside, and gave it a hard squeeze until the smaller man cried out. "Just like the last time I played with him." He ran his fingers from Alex's groin to his throat and gave it a hard squeeze as well. "And I have the tools to keep your mouth wide open while I fill your throat…don't I, Alex?"

He did. Alex remembered he past experience with Drago all too well. He may be a Shadow now but there was no denying the horrible things he could and will do, regardless of the body he possessed. He didn't let the threat cow him. He glared at Drago once more and spat in his face. He didn't get slapped this time, instead Drago grinned at him.

"Clean yourself up," Acantha instructed. "He's not going anywhere, and we have a lot to discuss."

"I have nothing to say to you," Alex retorted only to have Drago laugh at him.

"I do wish I could stay and watch," the Shadow purred. He glanced at his right hand with the missing thumb. "We'll have our fun later."

He left, his injured hand dangling at his side, blood dripping onto the floor. Despite it hurting, he was not afraid of blood loss. The Shadow would likely find another host rather than worry about the damage to the body he currently inhabited.

Alex's shoulders sagged just a little once Drago was gone. He hated to admit it, but he still feared the man. Having him come back from the dead as a Shadow did nothing to quell that fear. Of all the people to come back from the dead…why Drago? Why not Lucas. No, he didn't want Lucas to come back as a Shadow, but he would have preferred Lucas to Drago any day.

Once the door was closed, he turned his focus to Acantha. "Whatever you think you're going to do to break me isn't going to work. I'm a masochist, I like sex and pain. What your friends did…it turned me on." That was a partial truth. Pain did turn him on, but he had his limits. He hoped it would cause her to rethink her plans and maybe buy him some time.

It didn't.

"Oh, I know," she purred. Her hands stroked inside his thighs. "I also know you don't like women, not that I care. I still plan to ride this lovely cock of yours…but that won't break you. You've been inside women before…even if only due to the Celestial." Her hands moved to his right leg, stroking gently down the length and to the scarred stump. She caressed the mangled and twisted flesh where his lower leg was ripped from his body. "Does it still hurt? Do you still get phantom pains after all these years?"

She rested it on her knee as she examined it.

"What are you doing?" he demanded.

He tried to pull it free, but her grip was like a vice. She placed one hand firmly on his knee to keep it in place as she reached for her tools on the table next to her. She drew a long stainless-steel needle and held it up for him to see.

Understanding dawned on him as she began humming.

"No…" he pleaded.

He tried to pull free once more, but she was inhumanly strong. He could not break her grip. He bit back a cry as she slowly pushed the needle past the scar tissue and into his stump. It was only a few inches, but it burned like fire. It took a few moments to catch his breath and work past the pain, but just as he thought he could handle it, another needle was pushed into his leg, this one going in deeper. Then another, going in deeper yet. Followed by another and another until it felt as it they were going directly into his bones and knee. He wasn't sure when he began screaming but it echoed throughout the room. All that time, Acantha continued to hum and continued to deposit needles into him leg until she had no more. She waited until Alex gained control of himself before ever so carefully, placing his stumped on the seat she had been occupying.

With shuddered breath, Alex looked down as his mangled leg. "Take them out," he begged.

"Why?" she asked. She straddle his lap, taking his still hard length deep inside her.

Alex cursed the rod filling his cock, and the ring around the base. Both kept him hard despite the agony he was suffering. A whimper escaped him as she began to rock. Her added weight forced the dildo in his ass to press against his prostate, sending an unwanted surge of pleasure to mix with the pain. She was wet, hot, and tight, her insides squeezing his length with each downward thrust, her rear slapping against his naked thighs. The sound of wet flesh hitting wet flesh filled his ears. He hated it while another part of him loved it.

"I thought pain turned you on," Acantha purred, her lips a breath away from his own.

Her movements made the needles dig in further, his broken ribs pulsate, the toys within him rub. It hurt, tingled, and pulsed, pain and pleasure battling for supremacy. Being bound to the chair only heightened all of it, triggering something deep inside him that both hated and enjoyed every moment of it. He was not lying about being a masochist, he just never thought his body would betray him in such a way to actually like what was happening to him. His mind whirled with unanswered questions only to be drown out by the sensations filling him.

"Don't worry…we have all the time in the world to figure out just how much pain you like," she whispered. She ran her tongue over his lower lip before nipping the top one. "Don't worry about Drago…I won't let him kill you." Her lips brushed against his good ear. "I enjoy watching the others have their way with you."

She began rocking harder and added a little bounce as her insides clamped down hard on his manhood. Alex mentally fought against the rapidly increasing sensations that rocked his body until it became all consuming. His vision exploded into white as his body teetered at the edge of orgasm, only to be denied by the rod in his urethra. Pleasure quickly melted into a new type of agony as Acantha continued to ride his length, over sensitizing his body, and bringing him on the verge of orgasm again and again until she finally came. Her juices covered his thighs. She pressed her lips to his temple before finally getting off him, leaving him panting and drenched in sweat.

"Catch your breath, darling," she whispered. "I have twelve thousand years of reacquainting myself with the pleasures of the flesh."

Alex looked at his stump. The needles were clearly visible and now that they were no longer having sex, the pain was quickly coming back. If they weren't removed soon, they would do even more damage than they already had, perhaps crippling him to the point of further amputation…provided he lived that long.

Chapter Ten

The portal opened into a vast warehouse. EDC agents, hybrids, and the few Celestials who worked with them manning computers and working on vehicles glanced up from their work at the sudden arrivals but didn't seem surprised. It proved that those here were part of the same hive mind as those at the Sanctuary. Kyra took several deep breaths to orient herself. She was dizzy after that jump, proof she needed more time to recover. Time was one thing she didn't have. She would have to push though her fatigue if she hoped to save her Dad and her people. Squaring her shoulders, she headed toward the stairs leading to the office on the next floor. It overlooked the entire warehouse. As she reached the landing, she noticed the back of the building was converted into a camp of sorts, with nearly as many hybrids sleeping on cots and caring for one another as there was at the Sanctuary.

"How many do you think there are?" Naomi asked. A worried frown tugged at her lips.

"A hundred, maybe more," Kyra answered. "They're not going to be able to sustain them all at this rate. They're having the same problem we are."

"At least they have stores and places to get supplies quickly if needed."

Kyra sighed and looked at her friend. "It also makes them a bigger target," she pointed out. "The Shadows have more cover here...more people to possess and track them down. They're no better off than we are."

Naomi shrugged, clearly not convinced.

Taking a deep breath, Kyra opened the door to the "War Room." It had only been a few short months since she was last in this room but it still sent a shiver down her spine. When she left, she had sworn she would never come back, never work with this group again. Yet, here she was, about to ask them for help.

Director White, a tall thin woman with striking white hair and a sickly pale completion, looked up from the table she and other EDC members were bent over. She gave Kyra a hard glare before standing to her full height.

"It certainly took you long enough," she snapped.

Kyra folded her arms under her breasts and glared back at her. "I'm sorry, am I missing something?"

"Doctor Jackson has been..."

"I know, I was there."

"Then you willingly walked into a trap?"

"What?" Kyra all but yelled. "No!" She bite her bottom lip to keep from snapping further. "I made a mistake. You can't help us."

She turned to leave but Naomi caught her arm. "Kyra...we need them. Not just to find your Dad but also the Void."

"What are you talking about?" White asked, surprising both women. She rounded the table, the agents in the meeting moving out of her way. "The Void was destroyed years ago. What are you trying to do?"

Kyra froze and turned back to her. "What to you mean 'destroyed?'"

White studied her for a moment, her lips pressed into a thin line. It slowly softened. "You don't remember, do you?" She sighed, her shouldering slumping ever so slightly. "You were merely a child then. So much happened…you probably pushed it to the far reaches of your mind. To save you and Alex…Lucas destroyed the Void. He took a bomb into it, destroying the very fabric that held it together. It cannot be opened. If it could…we would no be dealing with the issues we are. We would have found a safe haven for the hybrids ages ago."

"Why didn't they tell me?"

Sympathy replaced the usual hardness that covered White's face. It was unnerving and almost made her look human…how her host must have looked normally, like a caring grandmother. "I assumed you remembered, as they must have."

Kyra shook her head. "No, I mean Alex. Why didn't he tell us when we began looking at it as an option to move our people? He knew we were trying to root power to the altar to open the Void. He told us not to try opening the Void, not that it was gone."

"He may have feared a part of it still existed," the older woman explained. She gestured to a chair in front of the table for Kyra to sit in.

Reluctantly, she did so, her mind racing with what she just learned.

The Director tapped the table, a large computer with a touch screen monitor that posed as a table. A three-dimensional image of the Void and the numerous temples it connected to appeared above the table. "The Void is a tangled network that webs it's way throughout space and time, but it is fragile. Break one thread and the entire network begins to fall apart until eventually it's no more. No key can reawaken it, not even Alex, trapping Celestials, Shadows, and hybrids to this realm."

"Then why take him?"

"Because he is one of the very humans to have been possessed by a Celestial and then freed. He was not sentenced to a life in servitude, only a few short months and lived to tell the tale. He was given a gift the Shadows never were. He's an enigma, a mystery that they want to figure out. They can possess humans but their coldness kills their host in a matter of hours or days. They have never found one they could wholly inhabit like us. They can never truly feel human touch...something many of them long for. They want what we have, to live, to breed, to be human once more."

Kyra's eyes narrowed as she looked at the older woman. "You were never human."

White's brows furrowed in annoyance. "No, but if I chose to find a mate, have a family, I could. The Shadows can not. They were slaves and acolytes. Once they served their purpose in life, they were cast into the darkness to continue serving us. Now they want their turn in the light. Metaphorically speaking."

Kyra leaned her elbows on the table and covered her face, completely at a lost. She had been looking for answers and advice, now she had more questions and absolutely no answers. White was in the same situation she was. As was everyone else trying to provide refuge for hybrids. The only bright side was that no new Celestials or Shadows could come through the Void.

"What about that laser that took down the lab in Ottawa?" Naomi asked.

The question surprised everyone in the room.

"We've located the source to a satellite orbiting the planet," one of the EDC agents responded. He glanced at White who nodded in approval. "It wasn't alien in origin. It was manmade. We believe a Shadow possessed whoever fired it, but it's impossible to verify."

Kyra perked up. "So, it wasn't the Celestials?"

"Why would we fire on our own?" White asked.

It was a fair question. Kyra opened her mouth to answer then promptly shut it. She and Alex were under the impression the Celestials destroyed the lab and hybrids inside because they were either impure or expendable. A Shadow possessing a human and doing it made far more sense. Not only did they wipe out a large number of hybrids, but it made it look as if the Earth was under attack by the Celestials and that the hybrids were dangerous. The Shadows played everyone.

Naomi placed a hand on her shoulder before hugging her from behind. "We'll figure this out," she promised.

"There may be a way," Director White announced.

Kyra placed a hand over Naomi's and looked up. "What do you mean?"

The image on the table changed to a fancy castle. Kyra instantly recognized it as one of the ones in Toronto. Did that mean Alex was still in the city?

"There's a gala this evening," White explained. She took a seat corner-wise from Kyra. "The guest list is rather intriguing. Normally these functions are for the upper-class, celebrities, those with big names and the power that goes with them. This one...it's a little different. Our sources report this event will primarily be military personal and government officials...as well as some very influential people. If Alex is anywhere, it's likely there."

"You have the guest list?" Kyra asked. She straightened in her seat as Naomi let her go.

"We do." White nodded to one of the EDC agents.

He produced the list and handed it to Kyra.

Her brows furrowed as she read through it then looked back at White. "Karen White? You're on the list?"

"Several of our EDC agents are," the older woman confirmed with a slight nod. "As well as a number of Celestials in hiding."

"It's obviously a trap."

"Obviously...but if we have any chance of finding and saving Doctor Jackson, then this is where we should begin." White stood from the table and nodded to one of the agents. "We'll get you put on the list."

"How?" asked Naomi. She leaned against the edge of the table and folded her arms across her chest. "Wouldn't they be curious about us suddenly being added?"

"Leave that to us," White insisted. "We have a few hours before the event. Ethan, show them where the gowns and suits are. And get our Queen properly armed." A smirk lifted the corner of her mouth at the surprise on both Kyra's and Naomi's faces. "You didn't think we were going in unarmed, did you?"

Kyra was at a lost for words. A small smile slowly lit her face. Even though she had Naomi by her side, she felt she would be alone in rescuing her Dad, that White would turn them away, banish her as she had before. Perhaps it was because of what Alex meant to the Celestials and hybrids, his connection between their realm and the humans. Or perhaps White had her own agenda. She often did. Whatever the case, Kyra now had a small army to help her. Once he was free, they could figure out how to move the hybrids to a safe place...or at the very least, how to defend their home better.

She needed to inform Liam and Winston about the state of the Void. There was no point of them continuing to transfer energy to the altar if they could no longer access the portal. How they were going to get everyone to a safe place was anyone's guess. This was not going to be an easy conversation.

"Son of a bitch!" Liam cursed.

He fought back the urge to throw the satellite phone. Instead, he paced back and forth. He couldn't believe it. They spent months trying to pump energy into the altar in order to activate the Void and for what? The Void didn't even exist anymore! It was gone, destroyed well over a decade ago and no one bothered to tell them? Alex couldn't be bothered to tell them, instead leaving them with a false sense of hope? As much as he liked Alex, he couldn't help but curse him. All their hard work for nothing!

His hands clenched and unclenched into fists. Now what? There had to be another way. The only thing he could think of was Kyra's portal. She was powerful. All she needed was to learn to control that power in order to open it anywhere and teleport everyone someplace safe. It was the only alternative. No one else had gifts like hers. Not even him, her supposed mate and equal. He felt useless.

He scuffed his foot against the marble of the temple floor.

"We'll find another way," Winston insisted. He leaned against one wall, clearly not happy with the news but not knowing what else to do either. He sighed. "We might as well wait until they come back."

"And do what?" Liam snapped. "Reinforce the shields? Keep hiding underground until the end of our days?" He pulled at his hair. "This is insane."

"I know," Winston agreed. "But there's nothing we can do. If the Void's dead then it's gone. We need to accept that and come up with something else."

"Like what?"

"I don't know."

"Don't know what?" Elizabeth asked, surprising both men. "Is everything alright?"

She mounted the last few steps to the top of the temple, slightly out of breath from the long climb. She took a moment to collect herself once she reached them than gave a small smile. "There's a reason I don't come up here very often. I have no idea how Alex makes the climb every day."

"He hasn't been here in the last few months," Liam pointed out, thankful for the distraction. "I think he's been avoiding it since all of us moved in. Or because of Lucas."

"Lucas, most likely," Elizabeth agreed. "He's having trouble coping with his lost. We had the same issue when his father and our research team died. He'll come around when he's ready and not a moment before."

Liam nodded. He had never experienced anything close to what Alex had, but he did know grief took time to process and move through. The stages weren't the same for everyone. Losing his eyesight took Liam a long time to adjust to. Being able to read energy wasn't the same. He would never see a sunrise again or enjoy the stars at night. He missed those thing as Alex missed Lucas, but the grief was different. It was a different sort of loss.

"So, what's going on? I've never seen you two so stressed," the older woman inquired.

Liam rubbed his face. With a sigh, he told her everything Kyra had told him, stressing the seriousness of the situation. He began pacing again as he spoke, a nervous habit to keep himself busy. "So, we're effectively trapped here, waiting for the Shadows to come and kill us all."

"That's not going to happen," Winston objected.

Liam turned on his friend. "They have Alex! It's not a matter on if they'll break him, it's a matter of when!"

"Kyra will find him before that happens."

"What if she doesn't?"

"Whoa…" Elizabeth interjected. She stepped between them with her hands raised. She looked back and forth between them with surprised, wide eyes. "Look…I get it. The situation isn't ideal. The Void is gone. Alex may not have known. He may have thought the explosion didn't completely destroy it because he never attempted to open it again and assumed it could still be opened. Whatever the case, it's gone. We need to fine another way to get everyone safely out of here. Have we located a new Sanctuary?"

Liam threw up his hands in frustration. "Same problem. Without the Void we can't even look for one."

She was silent for a moment, deep in thought. "We do have a list of known destroyed temples. Let's go through it again. Once we eliminate them and the countries hostile to hybrids, then we'll have a likely location of a suitable Sanctuary."

"Yeah, but that still leaves us with one problem…how do we get everyone there safely?"

Winston nodded in agreement. "There are jets patrolling the ridge. Even if we took people in shifts on your plane, they'll figure it out quickly enough and shoot us out of the air. I can distract them...but not for long."

Elizabeth worried her lower lip then glanced over her shoulder toward the flowing river in the distance. "There may be another way. Come with me."

Liam and Winston shared a look. They had already looked at all the Ley Line maps. What else could Elizabeth have to show them? They didn't know her very well. She came to the Sanctuary every few weeks and usually only stayed a few hours, sometimes a day or two. She usually stayed close to Alex and Kyra as they were part of her family. Sometimes she hung out with Liam's mother, but rarely spoke with him unless in the presence of one of them. However, Alex and Kyra were not there. As Kyra's mate, Liam was her proxy. It made sense that Elizabeth would turn to him in her stead. As such, he had to entertain any possible idea that may save their people.

He and Winston followed Elizabeth down the long staircase and into the village. A few people greeted Liam much as they would Kyra, like some sort of royalty that he felt was misplaced. The majority went about their business, paying them no mind. Liam focused on following Elizabeth. Her energy was that of a human, not nearly as vibrant as the hybrids and nearly invisible with only the odd swirl of blue and purple that was hard to follow. He was forced to rely on his hearing to track her and was thankful she kept talking along the way. Winston stayed by his side but knew better than to touch him if he went astray, instead telling him left or right in order to correct course.

"There's a part of the Sanctuary no one is allowed in, including Alex and Kyra," Elizabeth explained. They followed the river toward the very back of the cavern, hundreds of feet from the temple and village. "It's part of the military compound no longer in use. In fact, very few people have been back here since the base was shut down. However,..."

The sudden grinding of gears pierced Liam's ears, making him cringe at the horrid sound. It was followed by metal scratching against metal as a large, heavy door opened outward. The familiar clicking of lights turning on came a moment later, as did the cool crisp blast of fresh winter air. The sound of rushing water was near ear crushing, singling they were behind one of the many waterfalls that cascaded down the mountain.

"Whoa..." Winston cried out.

"Are we outside?" Liam asked, having to yell to be heard over the rushing water. He didn't pull away when Elizabeth took his arm and lead him over what felt like a large lip in the floor. The door shut behind them, keeping the cold air from entering the cavern.

"No quite," she told him.

"We have jets?" Winston asked excitedly.

"What?" Liam asked, unsure if he heard his friend correctly.

"We have jets!" Winston exclaimed.

Liam turned toward Elizabeth, his brows raised in questioning.

"When the military abandoned the base, the air force left a number of fighter jets behind," she explained.

Confusion and excitement filled Liam. He knew the Sanctuary existed beneath an old military base but was given very little detail about it. It was once used for research and experiments meant to figure out what the temple was, but Liam knew very little else. Jets seemed unusual to hide within the mountain.

Liam raised a hand as they walked underneath on, letting his fingers glide over one wing. "They just left them here?"

"Yep."

"Sabre...Sabre...Avro CF-103... Oh my god! Liam, they have an Arrow! They have a fucking Avro Arrow!" Winston yelled from somewhere further in the chamber. "I thought all of these were destroyed?"

"I guess not," Elizabeth laughed, clearly amused by his enthusiasm.

Liam's shoulders fell. He wished he could see the plane. He heard stories about the Avro Arrow and how the development of it and the

142

Iroquois engines used within them ceased development and were destroyed. At least that was what the government claimed. It put Avro, the company developing the jet, out of business and caused the loss of multiple other jets developed solely for the Canadian Air Force. Liam missed his eyesight now more than ever.

"They've been here a long time," he mused. The metal was ice cold with ice accumulating over the wings from the spray of the waterfall. "We'll have to divert power to here to thaw the ice build up. Winston, check the engines and see how much work they need, if any." He moved around the jet he was next to, his hand never leaving the cold metal. "The other issue is fuel. If these have been sitting here all this time, it's unlikely the fuel will be any good. It's probably separated by now."

"Jet fuel can last forever if the sump tank was built properly and no water got into it," Winston pointed out.

Liam gestured toward the waterfall. "We're surrounded by water."

"The water is out there, not in here. If the sump was dug deep enough into the rock and properly insulated, it will keep the water out and fuel pure." There was a clang as he closed the hood of one of the planes. "Not only that, but most jet fuel is made from kerosene, something we have a lot of. All of our generators use it and Elizabeth just brought in a new shipment, so..."

"You can get us in the air," Liam finished. A small sense of hope flitted to the surface.

"Yep...once I get these engines cleaned up. Give me a few hours. I can use a few extra pairs of hands." Winston paused. "This tech, though...it goes beyond what I know about the Iroquois engines. The markings are similar to those on the altar. You don't think the military tried to fuse their tech with the Celestials?"

"It's possible. I'll find you some help," Elizabeth told them. She patted Liam on the back. "You've got this. We'll get everyone out of here."

Liam nodded. They had a chance now, as small as it was. He hoped Winston was right, that the planes were salvageable and fuel good enough to use. They would need everything they had to keep the air force from discovering what they were doing and keep them from shooting down Elizabeth's plane as she flew people out of there. Now to break the news to his mother and Kyra. He wasn't sure which would be more upset but they were running out of options and Liam had to make the hard decisions they could not.

It wasn't long before members of the EDC filled the cavern, each just as awed by the discovery of the planes as Liam and Winston. They immediately went to work, following Winston's instructions as they began cleaning and rebuilding the engines. Excitement filled the room. The worry Liam felt slowly began to melt away as they worked toward a common goal. He stayed out of their way, unable to help. Instead, he stayed to the side as Elizabeth and his mother reviewed the maps to plot out a flight path that would suit them. Since they were unable to use the Void, it meant they would have to fly to a to either Greenland or Iceland as temporary refuge, refuel, then either bounce from country to country, following the Ley Lines, until they found Sanctuary, or find a ship large enough to transport everyone. It wasn't ideal but it was better than nothing. He wanted to make sure the plan was solid before telling Kyra. After losing the Void, they needed a plan that was sure to work. He didn't know how long it would take to prepare the jets to fly after so many years being dormant...if they could even fly.

"We need access to a satellite...maybe a few," Elizabeth told them after going checking off every known destroyed temple. "If we can find the radiation signature of an orb, then we'll know exactly where to go."

"Can you connect to one?" Marie asked, a hint of desperation in her voice.

"Maybe. I'll need to go to the chalet and reprogram our dish. It'll let me talk to the satellite and possibly set it into search mode...and request a second transport plane. Finding a large enough one to meet our needs and can land safely on a half-frozen lake was a tall order."

"Do it," Liam said with a nod. If a satellite could find an active orb then the that meant there was an oasis that could sustain them. Confidence began seeping in. This might work. It might really work.

Chapter Eleven

Kyra stared at herself in the full-size mirror. The dress she wore was almost exactly like the one she pointed out to her fathers years earlier when she expressed her desire to go to school with other children and experience prom and other social events. It was a royal blue princess cut ball gown that showed off her arms and shoulders and reached all the way to the ground. An impressive feat given her height. Lucas was willing to buy the dress she wanted all those years ago – he would buy her almost anything she wanted – but would not let her attend school. They worried about her control over her gifts and feared what would happen if someone discovered who and what she really was. At the time, it hurt to not be able to attend such things but in hindsight, they were right. Had she not spent her life training with them, she could have been one of the many hybrids kidnapped and killed rather than fighting for their survival.

"You look amazing," Naomi gushed. She came to stand next to Kyra in a long red number with a pencil line skirt and corset that was slightly too large for her frame. She frowned at her image but said nothing.

"You look great," Kyra assured her. She turned away from the mirror and began removing the gown. "This isn't practical."

"What do you mean?"

She hung it back on the hook and looked at the other outfits. "I need to be able to move and fight. A frilly gown with a tight corset is not going to work."

"Think of all the weapons you can hide up that skirt?" Naomi teased.

Kyra burst out laughing, not expecting such a response. "But then how to I kick butt if my legs are tangled?"

Namoi made a thoughtful face. "True enough. How about something with a slit?" She showed off the one on her gown that allowed a generous portion of her leg to be shown, right up to mid thigh.

"Yeah, I'd rather not have anyone hitting on me."

The other woman laughed then turned to the mirror to pick at the top of her corset. "I really wish I had been able to get top surgery before all this happed."

"You're gorgeous," Kyra reminded her. "Besides, you can manipulate people's minds. You can have any chest size you want."

Naomi sighed and changed her focus to her hair. "It's not the same."

"I know."

There were quite a few outfits to choose from. Only a few of the dresses were Kyra's size but each one proved to have the same problem, full length ball gowns that allowed little movement should there be a fight. She could always cut the skirt if needed but that would take precious time they may not have. Her fingers glided over the fabric until she founds a gold tuxedo jacket. Pulling it out, she checked the size and cut. It was actually a one-piece jumpsuit with jacket. There was a shimmer to it that was almost mesmerizing. The fabric was soft as well, not scratchy as one would expect. She slid it on, half expecting it to either be too tight or too short and was taken back when it fit perfectly. She found a matching pair of low chunky heel boots to go with it then slid them on as well as the jacket.

"Now that is an outfit fit for a queen," Naomi said with a low whistle. She came up behind Kyra and lifted her long hair into a loose bun with sweeping long strains haphazardly falling along her shoulders. "All you're missing is a crown."

Kyra smiled at her image. As much as she loved the princess gown, this did suit her much better. The blouse was low cut, showing a generous amount of cleavage, even with the jacket buttoned up, but it wasn't enough to expose her breasts. It was a small tease. With her hair up, it showed off the long column of her neck. It looked a little bare but Kyra was not one for necklaces and such things could get in her way in a battle. That was what this whole operation was about. It wasn't dressing up and going to a fancy ball, it was rescuing her father. She was going into battle.

The door opened, causing Kyra to turn and take a defensive step in front of Naomi. Director White entered with several of her agents, some already dressed for the event while others looked as if they had just gotten their hair and makeup done. White studied both Kyra and Naomi for a moment, the permanent frown tugging at her lips. Her gaze lingered disapprovingly over Naomi for a moment longer.

"Should you not be in a suit?" she asked, clearly mistaking her gender.

Naomi stepped forward to explain herself as she had many times in the past but Kyra bet her to it.

"She's dressed exactly as she should be," Kyra answered.

White glanced at her. "She?"

"Yes."

White looked from Kyra to Naomi and back again. One of the agents went up to her and whispered in her ear. The look on her face went from confused to understanding. She gave a nod and dropped the subject without another word.

"When you're ready, we have a stylist that will do your hair and makeup," she told them. She went to the rack of clothing and pulled out the outfit she would be wearing that night. "Getting weapons past security will to be a challenge. If they don't do a pat down then they'll have scanners."

"So, they'll know we're hybrids?" Naomi asked.

A small laugh escaped White. "That won't matter. They purposely invited hybrids and Celestials, likely to expose us." She glanced at Naomi, shrugged, then began changing into her evening gown. "The scanners I'm talking about are metal detectors. They'll expect us to be armed. That means conventional weapons are out. Not that they work very well against the Shadows. Regular humans serving them…"

"It's not as if we can simply hide a sword anyway," Kyra pointed out. She stayed still as Naomi began pinning her air up, earning another frown from White for not going to get her hair and makeup professionally done. Kyra didn't wear makeup or wore fancy hairdos. The most she would do was a ponytail or bun. Naomi knew that and would tweak it just enough to give her hair a touch of class. "I take it you have an alternative for the weapons? Someone to smuggle them in through the back?"

The first real smile lifted White's face. "We've got something much better planned."

One of the agents zipped up the back of her gown, a shimmery white full length, pencil cut dress, similar to the red one Naomi wore, that complimented her snow-white hair. Another handed her some diamond jewelry: glittery bracelets and matching choker. She could have passed for royalty. Of course, she was a Celestial and once upon a time she likely was considered royalty.

Another agent walked up to Kyra and handed her what appeared to be two long, leather handles, almost the length of her forearm. There was a small bump on the end of each one. She rubbed her thumb over one then gently pressed it. To her surprise, a long blade shot out of it in sections until it formed a three-foot-long sword. Kyra blinked in surprise. "What the hell?"

"It's like one of those toy swords I had as a kid," Naomi mused. She cautiously touched the blade. "It's sharp."

"It's metal," Kyra reminded White.

"Actually, it's carbon fibre," the agent who gave them to Kyra said. "As strong and sharp as steel but compactible. No one will know what they are until it's too late.

"Hmm... Stand back," Kyra told everyone. Once the immediate area was clear, she activated the second sword and took a few practice swings. She twisted and moved within them, not only testing the blades but also the range of motion her outfit allowed. Once satisfied, she pressed the small button once more, retracking both swords. "They have a good weight."

"We tried making them smaller, but that would have meant no hand guard," the agent explained. He presented her with a leather harness. "You can carry them in this. No one will notice under the jacket."

Kyra nodded. "Thank you."

She took off the tuxedo jacket and put on the harness then slid the two hilts into place. Despite their weight, they didn't get in her way or hamper her movements. In fact, it would be easy to forget they were even there. Pulling the jacket back on, Kyra took a deep breath and let it out slowly.

"Alright, let's go to this gala and find my Dad," she said. She straightened her shoulders and turned back to Director White. "Do we need anything else?"

The Celestial shook her head. "No. There is a limo waiting outside for us."

Naomi got excited and all but jumped on Kyra. "I've never been in a limo! I wanted to rent one for graduation. Archer promised me one and…" She stepped back, a blush filling her cheeks in embarrassment. "Sorry…I didn't think."

Momentary anger filled Kyra but she brushed it off. "It's fine."

White didn't look impressed by Naomi's enthusiasm but said nothing. Instead, she lead their group through the warehouse to the waiting limousine outside. It was an extra long luxury SUV, pearl white in colour and perhaps the most posh vehicle Kyra had ever seen. Naomi's excited grew at the sight of it, but she held herself in check, biting her lower lip and trying not to smile ear-to-ear. The driver was another agent. He was dressed in all in black, but despite being an agent, acted his role by holding the limo's door open and speaking formally to them, as if someone was watching them from the shadows. Given the situation, it was more than likely. Kyra wasn't worried. No one knew what she truly looked like. She was able to change her appearance whenever she wished. Right now, she sported long black hair in an up-do and would be seen as any other hybrid. It was unlikely the Shadows were expecting her to crash their gala.

She did her best to ignore the feeling of being watched and slid into the limo and as far on the side bench as possible. Naomi, still a bubbling ball of energy, bounced on the bench next to her. The two agents and White took the back bench. A few moments later the limo pulled away from the warehouse and onto the main street. They were quite for a while. White silently read a tablet, presumably getting more information from her spies. Kyra watched her, hoping it was news on Alex. Perhaps even a layout of the castle…anything that would help her find her Dad and get him out safely.

"They have guards at every entrance and exit, on every level," White reported. "As well as a number of what appears to be sensitive locations. Given that the Prime Minister will also be in attendance, it makes sense. We don't know if the Shadows have taken hold of him yet, or how much of his cabinet. We have to assume he's one of them and treat him as a threat."

"What if he hasn't?" Naomi asked, surprising the older woman. "What if he's still human? He could help us…he would be a great assist and could help us get the rest of the hybrids out of the country."

Kyra shook her head. "It wouldn't matter. His caucus is compromised. He may help us but that would mean getting him away from his handlers. There will be Shadows all around him. This is their chance to take complete control…if they haven't already."

Naomi wasn't deterred. "More reason to separate him from them."

White frowned and opened her mouth to argue but one of the agents spoke first. "We'll find him and see if he's still untouched. If he is…we'll get him out of there."

"Kidnapping for a good cause," the other agent mused.

Kyra fought back a grin while White rolled her eyes in annoyance. Nonetheless, Naomi was satisfied and smiled brightly at the notion that they may be able to somehow save the leader of the Canadian government therefore saving Canada from the Shadows. No one wanted to break the news to her that it was too late.

A small pang of guilt filled her. If Alex and Lucas had not felt the need to save her as a child, the Void would still be active today and none of this would be happening to the hybrids. The Celestials would still control the Shades and the hybrids would be free to be themselves. She sat silently, deep in thought as they drove across town. There was no telling what shape Alex would be in once she found him. She knew that he was tortured and raped. She had felt it even though he had tried to block her. Their bond was far stronger than what she shared with any of the hybrids, including Liam. She kept her mental shields locked tight to withstand the torture he was still enduring, otherwise she would be lost in his agony, unable to help him or anyone else.

"Kyra," Director White called to her, pulling Kyra from her thoughts. "I know you want to go directly to Alex, but we mustn't bring attention to ourselves. I need you to exercise patience. You will know when the time is right to find him."

"I can't…"

"You can," the Director snapped before Kyra could finish objecting. "You are our Queen and must protect us as well." White inhaled deeply before sighing. "Kyra, we can not help you if you rush in. I need you to play the role of a guest. Be gracious, mingle but stay close to the group. You will know when the time is right. If we go in guns blazing, we risk potential harm to the other hybrids and Celestials. They won't kill Alex. They need him. If they didn't, they would have killed him when they tried to kill you. Patience…you'll have him back soon."

Kyra bit her tongue to keep from retorting. White was right; she couldn't storm the place and expect to find Alex. She needed to be patient. She idly picked at the fabric of her slacks as she listened to White give instructions to her agents, only now learning their names were Ethan and Andrew. The thirty-minute drive felt as if it took a life time. Kyra was on the verge of tearing her hair out. Her stress level was at an all time high. She wasn't sure if she could keep herself from running into the castle and taking down anyone who got in her way.

A cool, soothing hand covered hers. She glanced at Naomi, momentarily forgetting her friend was next to her. Naomi gave her a small comforting smile and squeezed her hand, silently reminding her she was there and would remain at her side no matter what happened. It allowed Kyra to relax, if only a little. She squeezed Naomi's hand back.

"We're approaching the castle," the driver reported. "There's a line. We may be here a while."

Kyra's shoulders stiffened and a curse escaped her. Naomi squeezed her hand once more as White reminded her to be patient. Kyra took several deep breaths as the limo came to a stand still. Waits were normal, she told herself. She just needed to relax. Her Dad will be okay. He was strong and had gone through stuff like this before. He told her as much. That didn't make things any better. She felt his pain, his fear, and anger. It left a copper taste in her mouth, like blood. Like her, he was still holding a psychic wall between them but it wasn't as strong anymore. There were cracks developing and it was only a matter of time before it fell completely. When it did, it would hit Kyra like a tidal wave. She wasn't sure if she could handle that much anguish and pain, let alone function well enough to save him.

She jumped in surprise when the door suddenly opened.

"Our turn," Naomi told her. She patted Kyra's knee before standing and following White and the agents out of the limo.

Kyra took a moment longer to calm her racing heart and mind.

"Stay calm," she whispered to herself. She couldn't afford to lose her cool now. Alex was counting on her. Everyone was counting on her.

She stayed close to her group as they mounted the stairs to the main entrance of the castle, pass metal detectors and security guards who did little more than nod them through to the next check point where they gave their names to the doorman reviewing the guest list. Getting inside was much quicker than Kyra anticipated. No one questioned or challenged them. They were welcomed with open arms.

They moved through the large foyer to a huge ball room filled with bright lights and music. People mingled while others danced. There was champagne and wine. Silver trays of hors d'oeuvres were carried around by smartly dressed waiters. Namoi took two glasses of champagne and passed one to Naomi.

"Relax and blend in," she reminded her. "We need to act as if we belong here."

Kyra nodded. She took a sip of the champagne, waited a moment, then drank down the rest in one gulp. She placed the flute on the next tray that passed them and grabbed a fresh one. Naomi raised a brow as she downed that one as well. Kyra licked her lips and took the other girl's proffered hand as they made their way to the dance floor with dozens of other people. The music was loud, base pounding, and people bouncing to it. They were not the actions Kyra was accustomed to when it came to the Shadows, and many of them were indeed Shadow possessed. Kyra could feel them but whether or not they sensed her she was uncertain. They did not react to her and Naomi. They were more interested in their new found freedom than those around them. Kyra watched them as she danced, curious of their actions. She had never seen one of the Shadows seemingly at peace or enjoying themselves. She had always seen them as a threat, fought them in order to survive. Even as a child, they were hunting her. This felt wrong in ways she could not express. Not because they inhabited another's body, but because something deep inside her felt it was a personal betrayal.

She shook her head. Those were not her thoughts, nor the thoughts of any of the hybrids. It was older...the thoughts of the Celestials within the room. Those who felt what was occurring now blurred the line between master and servant. Anger, rage, and hatred radiated through them in dangerous proportions. The shock of such thoughts and emotions brought Kyra to a standstill.

"I need to use the powder room," she whispered to Naomi.

"Do you know where it is?"

A small laugh escaped Kyra. "Surprisingly enough...yeah. I came here a few times as a kid for a tour." She lowered her voice further as she leaned in close to her friend. "We need to find my Dad."

The younger woman looked at her in confusion. "White hasn't given us the sign yet."

"Doesn't matter." Kyra looked around. She spotted Director White with a group of other Celestials. They were talking in hush voices but she could feel the hatred coming from her as well. The Celestials were planning something. "Come on."

Naomi gave a small pout, clearly enjoying herself, but she quickly became serious, remembering their mission and the one they were there to save. "Okay," she agreed.

They slowly made their way to a side door and nodded to the guard that was there. Naomi jumped into action, her powers pulsing as she entered the man's mind.

"My friend needs to use the rest room," she cooed in a seductive voice.

She got in close and actively flirted with him. She ran her teeth over her bottom lip and glanced at Kyra to verify whether the man was human or Shadow. Kyra nodded. This one was 100% human meaning Naomi could manipulate his mind.

"Can we go some place private?" she whispered in his ear. "I like a man in uniform. I'm sure a big strong guy like you can show us a real good time." She ran her tongue along his earlobe.

It had the reaction she wanted. The guard looked around before opening the door for them. Naomi and Kyra followed him out into a long hallway. Naomi kept control of him, whispering commands until he led them to a stairwell where they encountered more guards. These ones weren't so easy for Naomi to manipulate.

"You're not supposed to be here," one of the guards told them. He stepped in their way while his partner fingered her sidearm. "Turn around and go back to the party."

"Why would we do that?" Naomi purred. She glanced at Kyra. "Looks like the party's right here. What do you think?"

What she was asking was whether or not the two guards were humans or Shadows, a question they both knew the answer to. Luckily, this was a quiet section of the castle, far away from the party and potential interruption. Kyra tilted her head, smiled gently at the two and hummed softly. "I believe you're right. I've got these two. Maybe you should take your new friend and take a little walk?"

A grin lit Naomi's face. "Be gentle," she teased. She looped her arm through her guard's and led him away.

Kyra watched them for a moment turning back to the two Shadow guards. Realization dawned on them as Kyra drew the swords from their harness. She dodged to the right as the male guard lunged at her with a taser. A quick twist and upward swipe took the female guard's head before she had a chance to draw her weapon. Her body toppled over, head rolling along the marble floor. Kyra put her foot on it to keep it from rolling too far away. The male guard turned back to continue the fight but froze when he saw his partner. His eyes widened in horror, his gaze moving to the blood-soaked blades in Kyra's hands. She opened one hand and gestured for him to take his best shot. He hesitated a moment, clearly weighing his odds, before attacking her once more.

He anticipated her swing and came in low, plowing into her. He lifted her off her feet and threw her off balance. Kyra cursed. She retracted her swords and instead slammed her elbows into the space between his shoulder blades. He was a big man and no amount of hitting seemed to work. Instead, he slammed her into a wall, knocking the air of her lungs and painfully bruising her ribs. Her head bounced against the bottom of the steps leading to the next floor. Her vision swam and the previous injury to her shoulder stung along with her ribs. He used her moment of disorientation against her, landing two hard punches to her ribs and stomach before she managed to kick him away.

"Where are they keeping Jackson?" she demanded. She reactivated the swords and took a defensive stance, ready for his next attack.

"Missing your Daddy, sweetheart?" the man taunted. Blue electricity sizzled between the two prongs of the taser. "Don't worry, I'll happily discipline you. You're a girl who likes it rough, aren't you?"

"Oh darling, you can't handle a girl like me," Kyra retorted.

She braced herself as he charged her once more. There was no room to swing either sword. She gave a grunt as he slammed into her again, this time using his whole body to pin her against the wall. Pain radiated through her as his weight pressed against her injuries, but that wasn't the only thing pressing against her. He was aroused by their confrontation. He pressed his erection firmly against her inner thigh and wrapped one large hand around her throat.

"You're much more feisty than him, you know that?" he whispered in her ear. "He tries to fight...he always does...but in the end he screams...begs us...me...to stop. This may be a new body, but his insides always feel the same. Tighter...quivering...begging to be fucked." He pressed harder against her. "I bet you're just like him. Like father, like daughter."

"Drago," Kyra breathed, understanding and disgust filling her. This was the man she felt assaulting Alex.

He purred, as if her knowing his name was the most sexually pleasing thing he had ever heard. He shifted position until he was firmly between her legs then gave a hard thrust against her core. It hurt and had there been no clothing between them, he likely would have torn her trying to get inside. It disgusted her all the more. Even alive, this man was not human. He was worse than an animal. He was a monster in every sense of the word.

However, in this form he was much smaller than he was in his previous life and though he had the upper hand, he was not strong enough to keep her there. She wrapped her legs around his waist and held him so tightly that he had to release his grip on her throat to try and use both hands to try and break free. Kyra didn't let go. She tightened her grip even more, digging her knees into his ribs and leaned back. He looked at her with frustration, his finger digging into her thighs. It did no good. She would not let go. Instead, she gave a little wave, reminding him of the swords she still held, then swung. It was like cutting through butter.

His eyes widened in surprise, not yet understanding what happened. Then his head separated from the rest of his body, rolling away much as his partner's had before his body finally collapsed, falling to the ground with Kyra still holding on.

Kyra groaned as she detangled herself from Drago's body. Anger still filled her from the knowledge of what the Shadow did to her parents in his previous life. He may have taunted her about Alex, but he had abused Lucas as well. She had learned as much from reading Lucas's journals, ones he thought were safely stored away at home. She kicked the body, hoping it would ease her anger but it did nothing. The Shadow had already fled, likely looking for a new host and alerting the others of her presence. They didn't have much time. Nonetheless, Kyra took a little satisfaction when she approached Drago's head. It had rolled toward the staircase. It's sightless eyes stared up at her. She gave it a small kick, rolling it on it's side before stepping on it. She dug her heel against its temple, making sure it would not roll any further, then put her entire weight down on it. The sound of bones cracking was oddly therapeutic. It slowly began to break and the wet sound of grey matter being squished as the skull was crush filled her with a strange sort of glee. There were other body parts that deserved the same treatment but this was only a host, not the real Drago. His body had been discarded ages ago.

"Having fun?" Naomi asked when she returned with her guard.

Kyra hummed softly as she kicked aside the remains of the skull. "Working through some family drama," she answered, rather pleased with herself.

"I see that."

The guard she had seduced looked horrified. "What have you done?" he all but screamed.

"The same thing that I'll do to you if you don't take us to my Dad immediately," Kyra told him. Her voice was casual but the threat was real. She was done playing games.

The man stared at her with wide eyes. Naomi shook her read and stepped in front of him, forcing his gaze onto her. "There's no need for that. You'll take us to Doctor Alexander Jackson, won't you? You know where they keep 'guests' don't you? All castles have a Keep."

He blinked a few times before nodding. "This way," he answered.

He cautiously stepped around the bodies to the staircase and led the way down into the depths of the castle. While the castle was modern in terms, just over a hundred years old, it was built similar to many others, expect where there would be dungeons there was a gift shop, café, swimming pool, wine cellar, and a tunnel to a coach-house and the stables. Kyra was surprised when they entered the tunnel. She glanced at Naomi, but the woman had a firm hold on the guard. He came to a stop nearly a hundred meters down the tunnel and turned to the left. He grasped one of the now electric scones attached to the wall and pulled it toward him.

"Here," was all he said.

The stone wall opened, sliding aside to reveal a large metal room. The rank smell of blood, sweat, and sex slammed into them like a wall. Kyra fought back the urge to throw up while Naomi and the guard gagged at the smell. Nevertheless, Naomi went inside without hesitation before Kyra could stop her, taking the taller woman by surprise.

"Oh, hell no!" Naomi cursed.

Kyra hurried inside, terrified at what she may find. What she found was worse than she imagined. Alex was tied to a chair, his amputated leg up and strapped to a stool. Long metal spikes stuck out of the stump, some so deep they broke the skin near his knee and up into his thigh, mangling his leg even worse than the explosion that had torn off his foot in the first place. His other leg was tied to the chair, giving him no mobility whatsoever. Blood seeped onto the floor, forming a pool under him, meaning there were even more injuries. Despite that, there was a woman happily settled on his lap, slowly rocking, and bouncing as she rode him. His legs were opened enough to see his cock was buried deep within her. The sound of wet flesh hitting wet flesh was unmistakable, as were the moans and grunts of two people having sex. However, it was clear Alex was doing this unwillingly. His grunts echoed the agony he was in. The woman didn't even bother looking up as they entered, lost in her own world and the pleasure she must be taking from him.

Kyra sidestepped around them to get a better view of Alex. His face was buried against her chest, allowing for a clear shot. Without a word of warning, Kyra swung her swords, slicing the Shadow's head cleanly from its host's body. The body didn't stop moving until Naomi pushed it off Alex. It landed in a heap next to the chair but the movement caused Alex to cry out in pain. It was clear to see why. Not only did his leg have spikes in it, but his penis was now pierced in numerous places. Little silver bar bells line the underside and at the tip was a ring that attached to a thick rod that was shoved deep into his urethra, making him stay hard. The bard bells also pierced his nipples and a chain ran from them to a leather strap wrapped tightly around his balls. The woman wanted to make sure he stayed hard. Lord only knew for how long. Deep cuts along his arms and thighs looked to be from a whip of some sort rather than a knife. Ropes criss-crossed his body, tying him to the chair.

"Dad?" Kyra whispered, afraid to talk too loudly and scare him.

He said nothing, his eyes closed as if he fainted. Kyra wasn't sure what to do, where to start. There were so many things in him that needed to be removed before they could even get him out of the room. It wouldn't be long before the other Shadows arrived. Her hands shook as she untied him.

Naomi caught her wrist. "Just open the portal and transport him like this. We can remove everything in the infirmary. It'll be better if he's laying down."

She was right, but Kyra knew Alex. He wouldn't want anyone to see him like this. She had to at least remove the piercings and rod.

He would want her to, but she didn't know how to do so without hurting him further."

"Leave him," a silky voice said, catching them off guard.

Kyra turned, swords ready but it was not a human, it was the Shadow that had possessed the female host moments ago. Kyra took a protective step in front of her father, ready to change to her Celestial form. Power raced up her arms, crackling with a blue energy along the swords.

"Bastard," she cursed. She desperately wanted to kill this creature.

If it was possible, the Shadow pouted. "Aw…so sweet protecting your Daddy. He's mine now. Every inch of him belongs to us and we will play with him how we see it."

"Think again."

"You would never understand. You've never been possessed by a Celestial. You've never been torn and remade by them. He has…I have. All the Shadows have. He can give us what we long for…he belongs to us," the Shadow insisted. There was a small sounds of desperation in its voice.

Still firmly grasping her swords, Kyra raised one hand behind her, opening a portal. It was risky with a Shadow in their midst but Naomi was right; they needed to get Alex back to the Sanctuary immediately, regardless of his present condition. The portal open directly behind Alex.

"Naomi, take him and the chair," she instructed. She looked at the guard, certain he was 100% human. "Help her."

The man, utterly confused by what was going on and sickened by the sight of Alex, hurried to help Naomi. He carefully lifted the chair with Alex still in it while Naomi took the stool to help balance his leg. The simple movement caused Alex to scream, momentarily awaken and thrash about. Naomi reacted quickly and used her power to put him into a deep sleep. They managed to get him into the portal with no interference.

Kyra pointed a sword at the Shadow as it moved toward the portal to stop them. "Don't even think it," she warned. She walked backward the few steps to the portal. "You and I...we're going to meet again and when we do...there will be no more Shadows."

"Are you sure?" the being taunted. "He's not your only loved one we've touched. One of ours is among you already."

Kyra was inside the portal now as it began to close. She stared back at the Shadow in shock and confusion.

"What?" she demanded, but it was too late.

The portal closed and she was back in the safety of the Sanctuary with her Dad, Naomi, the guard...and a Shadow posing as someone she cared very deeply for.

Chapter Twelve

Medics raced into the Light Room as Kyra lay Alex onto one of the gurneys. He was quickly strapped down for his own safety. Kyra was careful to extract the dildo out of his rectum and throw it in the trash before laying him down. It was for his own comfort rather than some sense of protecting his privacy. They were beyond that. He was naked with piercings, rods, and spikes in so many places that it would take an entire team to extract them all without causing further damage. First they had to get his core temperature back to normal. He was ice cold, his body trembling. He was on the verge of going into shock which would make what they had to do much harder.

A mask was placed over his face and nitrous oxide administered. He struggled for a moment, clearly not wanting to be tied down or gassed, but his fight didn't last long. He was already in a weakened state in which mere movement hurt. The doctors and nurses waited for the gas to take full affect and turned up the temperature in the small room. Light filled every inch of the room to keep any possible Shadows that may have hitched a ride with Alex at bay. Every human working in the room wore protective dark tinted glasses to protect against the harsh light. This wasn't an easy healing session like most times the light room was used. They were likely to be there for hours.

"Alright, there's a lot to deal with," Doctor Dobre mused. She looked over Alex's body, assessing the damage and deciding where to begin. "Let's focus on his leg. Depending on the damage we may need to amputate it further. Let's hope it doesn't come to that."

Kyra nodded, her worry the same. His leg looked completely mangled, with so many spikes in varying depths that it was hard to be certain how many were inside his leg. Dobre removed them by hand, taking them out one at a time and handing the blood-soaked metal to the nurse at her side. Each was a different length and width, some an inch thick while other thin as a needle. They ranged in length from a few inches to nearly a foot long, some of which dug into bone and nerves along the knee, others broke through the skin above the knee. Once they were removed, the scarred flesh looked more like rare meat. There was a steady flow of blood from numerous wounds. Dobre slowly waved a portable scanner over his right leg to make certain there were no more spikes hidden inside him. Once she was satisfied, she cleaned and disinfected the stump, then wrapped it in clean linen. If it needed further amputation, it would have to wait until after they removed the rod and piercings, some of which could be just as dangerous to his health depending on how long they've been inside him.

A small blush tinted Dobre's cheeks as she began removing the piercings along the underside of his penis. She held his manhood gently, careful not to hurt him further. They too were collected into the same metal pan as the spikes. Once all the piercings were removed, including those one his nipples, her focus moved to the thick rod that kept his length erect and hard. It was harder to remove. Opening the hoop that attached it to the lip of his cock was hard to open. It was a "clicker" that made it smooth and able to turn. Finding the razer thin lines that indicated the opening was almost impossible to find. Almost five minutes passed before she discovered it and finally open it enough to remove the hoop. Next came the rod itself. It was thicker than the average sound used for urethra play. Ribbed, long, and with a curve meant to press against his prostrate, it was a monster of a device meant for a much larger man.

"Okay," Dobre breathed. She shook out her hands, trying to relieve some of the stress she must be feeling. "Let's clean him up and then do a full x-ray. I need a good look at his leg."

"What do you want me to do?" Kyra asked. Despite Alex being home safe, her anxiety was still at an all time high. She gave her Dad's hand a gentle squeeze.

"Just keep doing what you're doing. He needs as much comfort as possible right now," the doctor instructed.

Kyra felt useless at the moment. She needed to talk to Liam and let him know there may be a Shadow among them. There were only a few people it could possess, maybe one of a dozen human EDC agents that worked in the Sanctuary. Most had been with them for several months. She had an inkling who it most likely was, but she refused to let her mind dwell on that…not until she was certain. For now, her Dad needed her. She only let go of his hand when it was time for the x-rays. Dobre was thorough. She took as many images of Alex's leg from as many angles as she could.

A knock to the window startled Kyra. She looked up to see Winston standing excitedly outside, a large grin lifting his lips.

"It's going to take me a while to review all images," Dobre informed Kyra. She glanced out the window as well and smiled softly. "We should let him sleep. If we need to proceed with the amputation, I'll let you know…and I'll call you the moment he wakes up."

Kyra hesitated a moment, fearful what may happen if she left him again. With a sigh, she nodded. "Please do."

She pressed her lips to Alex's temple then reluctantly left the light room. Winston met her at the door. There was a bounce to his step that took her by surprise.

"You're not going to believe what we've found," he gushed.

166

Normally his excitement would make her curious but this time Kyra was annoyed. "Show me later. I need to talk to Elizabeth."

Winston's brows furrowed, not used to her lack of enthusiasm. He quickly brushed it aside given the circumstances. "She's in the hanger with the others."

"The hanger?"

He grinned at her confusion. "That's what I was trying to tell you. There's more to this place than we were told. We may have a way to defend ourselves and escape."

Kyra didn't understand. She explored every inch of the Sanctuary as a child and never seen nor heard of a hidden hanger. Considering they were under an old military base, it would make sense that certain facilities were hidden underground along with the Sanctuary, but as a member of EDC why wasn't she told about it until now? By Winston no less?

"Take me to it," she ordered, already on the move.

He nodded and led her through the village, chattering all the way. She barely heard his words, only making out that there were jets in the hanger that were fully operational and plenty of kerosene to fuel them.

"Kerosene?" she gasped. She stopped walking and stared at him wide-eyed. "There is jet fuel here? We're sitting on top of a fucking volcano!"

"An inactive volcano," he reminded her.

"There are still vaults not running beneath us. All it takes is hitting one to cause an explosion large enough to destroy the entire Sanctuary and everyone here."

She inhaled sharply, her eyes growing wide. What if that was the plan? What if a Shadow possessed Elizabeth and was planning to ignite the kerosene? She broke into a run, desperate to find Elizabeth before anything happened. There simply wasn't enough time to evacuate everyone. There were too many people and nowhere to go. Depending on how much fuel there was, a large enough explosion could take down half the mountain.

Winston chased after her, trying to assure her everything was fine. She found the hanger. It was hard to miss a large open rock wall near the river, or the people hurrying in and out with various tools. She followed them inside, dodging around people in her search of her aunt, and stumbling to a stop at what met her.

"Oh my God..." she breathed.

When Winston said there were jets, she didn't really bad it any mind, she was more concerned about the kerosene. Now she saw what he was talking about. Four Canadian Air Force jets and a legendary Avro Arrow. She only heard stories of the delta-winged interceptor and seen images in museums. This was history come to life.

"How..." she breathed. "I thought the replica was in Edenvale."

"That's not a replica...it's the real deal," Elizabeth announced from her perch on the ladder leading to the cockpit. "Diefenbaker couldn't kill them all. Best of all, the government has no clue it's here...at least not this government. They all think she's in the bottom of Lake Ontario." She patted the side of the jet then descended the steps. "Where have you been? You're dressed for a party." She tilted her head as she inspected Kyra's outfit. "Minus the blood splatter of course."

Kyra glanced at herself. "I... It's a long story."

"Is everything alright? Did you find Alex?" She held a hand to stop Kyra from talking. "Liam and Winston told me you teleported back to Toronto. I don't appreciate the fact you didn't let anyone else know you were going, or that the Void no longer works. I'm just happy you're home safe."

Her voice sounded sincere. There was nothing that indicated a Shadow possessed her. The creature must have lied. Elizabeth seemed completely normal. It made Kyra relax a little. She placed a hand on the plane, still at awe that it actually still existed. It was something she and her Dad were geek over. He would go nuts to see it.

"Dad is in the infirmary…he's in bad shape," she told Elizabeth. Tears stung the corners of her eyes. The anger and fear and disgust at what happened to Alex finally took it's toll on her. "I don't know if he's going to pull through."

Elizabeth's face paled and it took a moment for her to collect herself. "I should go to him."

That made sense, they were childhood friends which continued into adulthood. She went through so much with him and been by his side even after he lost his leg and later Lucas. They were like brother and sister and would protect one another through thick and thin. Normally, Kyra would be happy for Elizabeth to go to him but that fear of a Shadow in their midst made her anxious.

"He's in the Light Room. He'll be there until we're certain no Shadows tagged along. We have a guard locked in a second one. He seems clean but we're waiting another half hour before letting him out. Naomi is watching over him."

"The Light Room," Elizabeth repeated. She sighed, renewing Kyra's suspicions. "I'll visit him later."

Kyra stiffened, her fingers flexing as she reached for the hilt of one of her swords. She paused when Elizabeth turned her focus back to the jet.

"We managed to fuel the jets but it's a time thing. The reserve is pretty much dried up. I give these birds a few hours before they run out but it may just be enough time to fly everyone out," the older woman told her.

"Fly everyone out?" Kyra asked.

"We don't have the Void as an option, but we may be able to get everyone to Iceland on the Hercules then pod hop from country to country until we find a new Sanctuary. Marie is reading the Ley Lines. We should have a location soon…or at least an idea where to go." Elizabeth explained. "I've called for another transport to get us all out. These babies will give us the distraction we need."

It was plausible. They would need at least two transport planes to get everyone out but with the growing number of hostile countries, it was hard to know where it was safe to go. What about Director White and those in her care? Guilt filled Kyra. She had left White and the other EDC agents to fend themselves on their own at the gala. Yes, they were armed but they were up against Shadows and possibly the army. White did have her fellow Celestials to help her, but a part of Kyra wanted the Celestials to fail, wanted the Celestials and Shadows to kill one another and forget about the mountain Sanctuary.

"Do we have enough pilots with combat training?" Kyra asked.

With the Air Force watching their every move they needed a distraction. However, whoever piloted the jets were likely to die. The weapons and speed of modern jet fighters were far superior to the jets of the 1950s…even the Avro Arrow. They could only buy the hybrids a few precious minutes to board the transports and get in the air. After that, it was a matter of how far they could fly and how fast before the Air Force chased them down.

"We do," Elizabeth confirmed.

"Not just that, but these jets are like no other jets out there," Winston gushed.

He waited for Elizabeth to get off the ladder before moving it to the nose of the jet and climbing up himself. He sat on the nose and gestured for Kyra to come up as well. Curious, she did so and gazed into the open hood, unsure what was so fascinating. It took only one look to understand. Inside, hardwired to the engine was an alien artifact. Wires and clamps connected to several crystals as a car engine would to a battery.

"They harnessed a Key to a jet engine?" she asked, utterly perplexed.

"All the jets have been retrofitted with them. The military was trying to fuse Celestial and human tech. I don't know if their meant to go faster or interstellar," Winston explained. "Whatever the case, when we turn on the ignition, they purr like kittens. I bet they can give the Air Force a run for their money. They might even tie into the weapons system…but we need to get them in the air to test anything out."

Kyra didn't know anything about jet engines or weapon systems. To her, it was a mangled mess, like Frankenstein's Monster in jet form. Was this why the Arrow was decommissioned? Did some mad scientist try to mix Celestial technology with human? Did it spook the wrong people enough to try getting rid of it? Was that why the jets were hidden here where no one was likely to find them? A cold chill went down her spine and it was impossible to tell if it was due to the open hanger or the situation. They needed more time to test the jets before going into battle, but time was limited.

"Are there any schematics for the engines?" she asked.

Winston nodded. "We found them sealed in a locker. It took some time to get them out, but everything looks as it should." He leaned back. "Unfortunately, we won't know how well the systems work until we get one in the air."

"Alright," Kyra consented.

She wasn't sure what to think of this new revelation. Finding old fighter jets in a decommissioned military base was one thing. Discovering fighter jets with alien tech was not something she every expected to find. She was a little in shock. Were these even safe to fly? What did having a key give the jet? Would it be faster? Could it go into space? The jets only sat two people, a pilot and gunner. How would this help them? Winston and the others were certainly excited by the find.

"Keep me advised," she told Winston, unsure what else to do.

He smiled brightly at her. "I will."

With a small nod, she climbed back down and went to Elizabeth. Her aunt grinned, obviously happy with mixed technology. She was their only official pilot which meant she would be one of the ones to test the fighter jets. Should the test go wrong...

Kyra banished that thought. She didn't want to even consider losing her aunt. If the jets worked, then perhaps it would give them the upper hand against the Shadows. Nonetheless, a part of her still felt uneasy about what the Shadow told her when she rescued her Dad, but was not yet willing to believe that a Shadow possessed Elizabeth – after all, how would she have gotten past the shield? They were designed to keep Shadows out, even if the were inside a human. It seemed very unlikely. Nonetheless, she needed to speak with Marie and learn more about this idea of evacuating everyone by plane.

Marie was easy to find. She made herself a little command center off to one side with paper maps and scrolls. Liam was with her but looked out of place. He appeared downcast and it wasn't a far reach to imagine he wanted to interact with the jets as well. Without his eyesight, there was very little he could do to help prepare them for flight. There was little he could do to help.

"Hey babe," Kyra said in greeting. She went to Liam first and pulled him in a warm embrace.

He hugged her back with a content sigh. "Hey. I take it Alex is back?"

"He is," she confirmed.

He read her emotions as he often did and hugged her a little tighter. "He'll be okay," he promised.

Kyra gave a nod, unable to say anything more. She was doing everything in her power to keep it together. Now she wanted to break down and cry and let out all the stress she felt in the last few months since losing Lucas. Having almost lost Alex…having seen what these Shadows had done…she felt as if she was going to be sick. Having Liam hold her and rub her back felt strangely soothing and she allowed herself the small comfort.

"How is he doing?" Marie asked. There was genuine concern in her eyes. She stepped around the table and gave Kyra a small hug and motherly kiss to the forehead.

Kyra leaned into her a little. "He's in rough shape. They did a number on him. They…" Her words faltered as Marie hugged her and her son a little tighter.

"I'm so sorry, Kyra. He's a strong man. He'll pull through," she assured. She pulled back and looked Kyra over. "You should freshen up, maybe get some rest. I'll check on your Dad. Is it okay to visit him?"

Relief flooded Kyra. She nodded. Even if Alex and Marie didn't see eye to eye due to Marie being a Celestial, it was nice to see he had her support and she was willing to care for him. She wiped he eyes, brushing away the moisture that gathered there. There was no way she would be able to get any rest but she could at least have a shower and change her clothing. Her feet felt heavy as she made her way back through the village to her little hut. Marie and Liam walked along side her but didn't say anything. She appreciated it but honestly, she was getting tired. Maybe a little sleep would be for the best. A shower, sleep, then clean clothes. Food as well…she needed to eat something. She couldn't remember the last time she ate and her stomach was beginning to growl.

Sadly, that wasn't going to happen.

"Kyra!" a nurse called.

Had it been anyone else, she would have snapped at them but given the situation with Alex she immediately stopped, fear twisting her heart into a tight knot. The look of fear on the nurse's face made Kyra feared the worse.

"Kyra, it's Alex…he's gone into cardiac arrest. We need you," the man told her. "We've pulled in all the medics. I…I'm sorry…I…"

She didn't let him finish. She bolted through the village back toward the infirmary. She pushed past people, mumbling apologies as she shoved her way through. Marie was close behind her. They burst through the double doors. Kyra went straight to the light room where she could see doctors clustered over Alex with a defibrillator. His body jerked with each discharge. The heart monitor beeped once, twice, then gave a horrid whine. They shocked him again only for the same result.

"You can't be in here," Doctor Parish snapped when he spotted Kyra.

The room was crowded. Kyra moved to find a safe place where she would be out of the way but Marie caught her arm and pulled out of the room.

"No, honey," the older woman said sternly. "You can't be in there. Alex needs the doctors, not you…not right now."

Kyra went to pull away but Marie was far stronger than she appeared. She held Kyra fast and made her stay by her side. Liam and Elizabeth arrived a few minutes later. They crowded around Kyra and Marie. Liam went to Kyra, taking her from his mother. They watched as the doctors worked, waiting, and praying that they could restart Alex's heart. Eventually the whining at the heart monitor stopped and a steady beeping replaced it. The doctors waited several more minutes before finally filing out of the light room and removing their protective gear and tinted glasses. Doctors Dobre and Parish went to Kyra, their faces grim.

"Kyra…" Dobre began, her voice holding a small quiver. "I'm sorry…there's more damage than we initially thought."

Parish frowned. He looked angry at the other doctor but directed his focus on Kyra. "He went into shock twice which triggered a heart attack. His body is shutting down. We're keeping him on life support, but… I don't think he'll be able to hold on for long. The internal damage is quite severe. His body going into shook only complicated matters." He placed a hand on her right forearm. "I will call our Healers in. They may be able to fix some of the damage but…all we can do now is wait and hope he pulls through."

Dobre had an empathic smile, but it never met her eyes. They were sad and feared the worse. "He is strong, my Queen, but he suffered through a great deal, both physically and mentally. If he survives the night then he has a chance of recovery."

Kyra's body shook. Her knees felt weak. Marie managed to get her to a chair before her knees gave out completely. She felt sick. She honestly thought she was going to throw up. Marie even got her a trash bin to be safe. Elizabeth cursed under her breath, having arrived shortly after the others. She stood close to the plexi-glass wall to view Alex. Kyra wanted her by her side but could not bring herself to call to her aunt. Instead, she let Marie and Liam fuss over her. There was no way she was leaving her father's side now. She wasn't going to lose him as she did Lucas.

Chapter Thirteen

Everything hurt. His head, his chest, his arms, his stomach, but worst of all...his groin and lower body. He tittered on the edge of consciousness, exhaustion mixed with the ungodly pain making it almost impossible to swim out of the murky depths of his mind. He didn't want to wake up but he knew if he didn't he may never do so and instead fade away into the darkness. There were monsters hidden in there. Beings that hid within him, darker than the Shadows, darker than anything he dealt with before. They clung to him, dragging him deeper into the darkness, away from the light. It felt as if he was swimming through thick muck like molasses. Breaking free was near impossible and took every ounce of strength he had.

His eyes slowly opened. Darkness met him. For a moment fear gripped him. His arms felt weighed down but slowly his left became free and he lifted it up to his face, finding a blindfold over his eyes and removing it. He immediately regretted the move as blinding white light filled his vision. He dropped the blindfold back in place. His arm fell to his side, already too tired to hold it up any longer.

"Fuck..." he groaned. He wanted to sit up but couldn't. He needed more time but was afraid of falling asleep again and being pulled into the darkness of his mind.

He jerked when a hand touched him. He pulled away and tried to shimmy to the other side of the narrow gurney but his body refused to, as if trapped. He fought back a desperate whimper. It stuck in his throat as he steeled himself, mentally preparing himself for the next assault.

"Dad?" Kyra's soft voice came out of the darkness. "It's me, Kyra. Don't move, okay? Just relax and breath. You're alright. I'm here. Can someone turn down the lights?"

"No," he whispered. His hand patted the bed to his left, searching for her. "Keep them on…please."

His hand met hers and relief flooded him. He knew her grasp, felt her warmness, and the bond they shared reconnected as her mind whispered against his, chasing away the darkness. He took a deep cleansing breath and let it out slowly.

"Kyra…" he whispered, his voice hoarse. His throat hurt, the windpipe damaged from being forced to give head to numerous men who were anything but gentle.

His daughter sat on the edge of the bed, careful not to get too close, as if she might spook him. Alex appreciated that. He really didn't want anyone touching him. He had been sexually assaulted before but this…this was something horrific. Raped and tortured to the point he could barely move and his mind was all but numb. His legs felt like dead weights, the right numb yet pulsing.

"You're safe," Kyra assured him. "You're back in the Sanctuary."

"How?"

"Naomi helped me." There was a moment of silence, heavy with sorrow and regret. "I'm so sorry, Dad. I should have been there. I could have stopped them."

"Or had the same happen to you," he pointed out. "They were organized. They knew what they were doing and made sure you weren't able to interfere."

He rubbed his thumb across the back of her hand. The gesture was familiar and comforting. It made everything that had happened seem like a horrible dream. He wanted to believe it was despite his body telling him otherwise. If it wasn't so bright, he would take off the blindfold, but he understand why he was in the light room. If any Shadows were attached to him or made it's way inside, the light room would help dispel them. He was safe here.

"I should have listened to you," Kyra sighed. "You said it was a trap and it was. If I had listened to you, none of this would have happened."

He grunted softly. "Maybe…but they would have found another way to lure us out." He carefully removed the blindfold and squinted at her. She handed him a pair of tinted safety glasses used by the physicians. They were individually wrapped and kept in a protective box on the counter. She must have been anticipating his need for them once he awoke. "Honey, it's not your fault. Besides, we found that journal. Was it any help?"

"I don't know. Marie seems to think it can help us connect with or create a realm within this realm, like how the fae supposedly exists. It makes no sense to me. Now that the Void is verified as destroyed, it doesn't matter." There was an unanswered question in her words, one Alex didn't want to answer but had to.

"When we destroyed it, there was no guarantee that it would shut it right down. I didn't want to take a chance of Celestials or Shadows attacking us again. I was afraid of losing you both. I never knew that one day we would have all these people here. I thought you were the only hybrid and I could keep you safe."

She nodded. "I know." She squeezed his hand and smiled softly at him. "You should rest more."

"How long have I slept?"

"The better part of the last two days."

"Two days?" He tried to sit up but the best he could manage was to roll onto one side. Pain jolted through him, objecting to even the slightest movement. He ignored it as best he could and propped himself up on one arm. "No…no, no, no. We need to get everyone out of here. They have something planned…someone on the inside. They're planning to attack."

"Yeah, I know. We're waiting for another plane to arrive and fly people out," Kyra told him. She sounded sure of herself, as if they had been working on this particular problem while he was unconscious. "Marie is working on where to go while Winston figures out a way to make the planes 'invisible' to radar detection. Elizabeth is coordinating the evacuation. If we can get the second transport then we can get everyone out in one shot. It's going to be tricky but…"

The piercing wail of klaxons interrupted them. Kyra stood, moving toward the door as if to protect Alex. He struggled to sit up. His body objected and a part of him wanted to curl up and hide, fearful of the Shadows that abused him were there to take him once more.

A rumbling sound mixed with the klaxons and a moment later the ground shook violently. Kyra threw herself over Alex, covering his head as rocks fell from the cavern ceiling and hit the roof of the infirmary. While the building was build sturdy, if a large enough section of the ceiling gave way, the entire Sanctuary could be destroyed and everyone killed or buried alive.

The shaking lasted only a few seconds before ending. The klaxons continued to blare but over it the cries of those injured by the shaking. The medical staff rushed outside to help them.

"That wasn't an earth quake, or the volcano awakening," Kyra muttered. She straightened and looked out the window to watch as the injured moved into the infirmary. "The klaxons wouldn't be sounding."

"That was an explosion, not a quake," Alex answered. Horror filled him as did the memory of the last time he felt such a blast that almost buried him and his research team alive. "Someone is trying to destroy the mountain."

She turned toward him, her eyes wide. "They're bombing us?"

He nodded, words failing him.

"Okay…stay here. I need to make sure everyone is alright," she told him.

"Wait, I'll come with you," he insisted.

He forced himself to sit up on the edge of the gurney, ignoring the protests of his bruised and battered body. He dared a look at his lower half and was happy to find he was wearing a hospital gown that covered everything but his legs. His right one was wrapped in linen from his stump to mid thigh but while it seem to pulse with his heartbeat, he had no other feeling in it. He closed his eyes, not wanting to remember the spikes that had been shoved into it.

Kyra's hands gently gripped his shoulders. "No. Lay down and rest. I'll be right back."

He gave her a stern look. "Get my prosthetic. I'm coming with you."

She stared at him for several long moments, her gaze watching his, before letting out a low sigh. "They took it, and other one is at the chalet. There's no way to get it. You need to stay here…where's it's safe."

Another rumble and shake proved otherwise, but the building held up. He would have argued more but she was already heading for the door. She turned back and gave him a worried look.

"I love you," she told him. She opened the plexiglass door.

"I love you, too," he called after her.

He watched as she hurried into the next room, the large plexi-glass wall allowing him to see Marie and Liam meeting her there. They spoke hurriedly, Marie apparently explaining the situation to Kyra. The younger woman nodded, the worry and concern on her face turning to anger. She gave them some instructions then pressed her lips to Liam's in a quick kiss before she ran off. Marie spoke to Liam for a moment of two more before he, too, left. She glanced toward the light room and made eye contact with Alex. For once, he didn't frown at her or give the impression he did not want to speak to her. A lot had happened in the short time he had been missing. He needed to know what Kyra was not telling him. Marie gave a small nod before entering the room.

"How do you feel?" she asked timidly.

"Like hell," he answered honestly. He fell silent for a moment, his hands knotting in the sheets. "What's happening out there?"

Marie was hesitant for a moment then sat down in the chair Kyra had previously occupied. "The cannons engaged. There are multiple fighter jets currently in our air space. They've swept in several times and deployed missiles. From what I can tell, two have been shot down. One crashed a few kilometers from the entrance. It looks like they're trying to take down the shield and cannons. So far, they're holding. A ground team was spotted headed toward the chalet," she explained. "Elizabeth is prepping her team to counter them. It might buy us time but without the Void, we have nowhere to go."

Alex raised a hand, utterly confused. "Elizabeth's team?"

Marie opened her mouth to answer but paused. "You had no idea about the fighter jets stored in the hanger?"

"I did. They're non-functional."

"Winston fixed them."

Alex rubbed the scarred half of his face, pressing his fingers against the remains of his ear. The gesture often hurt but this time it was strangely comforting. "Of course he did. There's barely enough fuel to get them in the air." He inhaled sharply, a thought coming to him. "I need to speak with her...Elizabeth. If she takes them out there...it's a one-way trip. They won't have full functionality. Trying to land back in the hanger will be next to impossible, especially this time of year. Half the water coming from the waterfall are slates of ice. It will crush they're wings. They'll be lucky if they can even make it out." He forced himself to the edge of the bed. "I need to talk to her."

"You should be resting," Marie argued only to be interrupted by the cavern shaking again.

"Get me to her," Alex said sternly, leaving no room for debate.

For the first time ever, Marie looked nervous and not the self assured Celestial hidden within a human form. She glanced outside the room, frowned, then nodded. "Alright. Give me a minute."

Surprised, Alex watched as she hurried out of the room only to come back a moment later with a wheelchair.

"No...no, no, no... I can walk," he argued. He hated wheelchairs with a passion. He never wanted to be confined to one as he was when he first lost his right leg. He went months through physiotherapy before being given his prosthetic.

"Have you seen your leg?" Marie countered. "Even if I had your prosthetic, it would be of no use to you. Now stop being a man-child and let's get your butt in the chair. We don't have a lot of time."

She was right and he hated that. He let her help him into the wheelchair, and – despite his better judgement – let her push him. Just the little movement from the gurney to the wheelchair caused unimaginable pain. It took all his willpower not to cry out. Exhaustion hit him once he was seated. The pain didn't ebb. The new position hurt more than he was willing to express and caused his entire body to tremble. Sweat dotted his forehead but could be felt all over his body.

"Are you sure about this?" Marie asked once he was settled.

He nodded. He had no choice…he needed to stop Elizabeth.

She carefully pushed him out of the infirmary as more hybrids hurried in for cover and safety. Medics rushed about inside and outside the building. Searching for those injured and getting them to safety. The infirmary would not be able to take them all. Others were making their way to the great hall. It was built similar to the infirmary and was also reinforced to protect people in case of earth quake. Nonetheless, there was a very real chance of them being buried alive if the Air Force continued to fire missiles at the mountain.

He caught sight of Kyra from the corner of his eye. She had a group with her, including Naomi, their best fighters, and most gifted hybrids. She ushered them onto the large lift that would take them to the old mine several stories above. She looked toward him as she closed the gate. Alex bite his tongue, stopping himself from telling her not to go. She needed to. She was the only one who stood any chance of stopping the attack. He wished there was a better way than to engage them, that her teleportation power was strong enough to move everyone, but she could not hold it open for as long as it was needed. Had she more time to learn to control her new gift, then perhaps it would have been able to save them. Instead, he gave her an encouraging nod and sad smile, fearful of the outcome of the battle.

"They'll be alright," Marie said.

She placed her hands on his shoulders. He placed one of his over hers. He could feel her fear. That part of him that was still part Celestial connected with her emotionally. He squeezed her fingers. She needed comforting as much as he did. He didn't want to tell her everything was going to be okay because the chances of that being true were slim. They needed to focus on doing what they could to save those trapped in the Sanctuary.

The trek to the hanger was not an easy one. The rocky landscape was not meant for the narrow wheels of a wheelchair. Marie almost dumped him out of the chair twice when the small front wheel caught on a crack in the ground. The cavern shaking and falling rocks did not help matters. They reached the hanger just as the huge door was beginning to close. They managed to make it inside but both instantly regretted it when the ear-splitting whoosh of engines met them.

Alex waved frantically when he saw Elizabeth about to climb a ladder to a white, red, and black plane that resembled the Avro Arrow. She paused when she saw him. An endearing smile lit her face but she didn't stop to greet him. Instead, she began climbing up the latter and into the cockpit. She gave him one last glance before the hatch closed.

"No!" he yelled after her.

It was useless. She couldn't hear him. He couldn't even hear himself over the roar of the engines. He tried to take control of his wheelchair and roll toward the jet fighter but Marie wheeled him off to one side, away from the back of the planes where the heat and exhaust were dangerous. He tried waving at her again. There was someone seated behind her and for one awful moment he thought it was young Winston. The boy was a genius but not trained for arial combat like Elizabeth. He would be useless to her in the air other than to fix a malfunctioning system. Thankfully, the youth was at what appeared to be an old computer, monitoring what was happening. A small bit of relief filled Alex but only for a moment. Anxiety and fear drowned it out as he watched Elizabeth taxi the Arrow along the short runway toward the waterfall.

Marie rolled Alex to Winston. She took the headset the young man was wearing and handed it to Alex. He quickly put it on.

"Elizabeth!" he all but yelled into the device.

"Alex!" she called back with a small laugh. "I'm glad you're awake. How do you feel?"

"I'll feel a lot better once you park that bird and get out," he responded.

His hands shook as he pressed the headphones to his head to block out the sound of the engines. He had no idea how she was able to hear him over the noise.

There was the sound of a small sigh. "I'm sorry."

Another violent shake had larger chunks of rock falling from overhead. One piece landed on the cockpit of another jet, breaking the nose, and killing the pilot and gunner. Chunks along the entrance broke away, enlarging the waterfall and putting debris in the way of the remaining jets.

"We can't stay here," Marie told Alex.

He nodded. They needed to get everyone out of there immediately.

New klaxons began going off. Winston pushed past Alex to get to the computer. "Fuck! The shields are down!" He took his headset back and yelled into it. "The shields are down! Beth, if you're going to go, do it now before they make it to the entrance. If they hit our power supply, we're finished!"

Alex sat in stunned silence as watched Elizabeth fire a missile at the debris. It destroyed enough of it to reopen the hanger. The Arrow sped out at high speed. It's wings cut through to flowing water of the falls, not catching in ice at all. A moment later the second and third planes followed suit. People attended the last one, hoping to save those trapped inside. Alex wasn't given the chance. Winston opened the doors to the Sanctuary and yelled for everyone to get inside as he turned on the overhead flood lights in hopes of stopping Shadows from entering through that entrance. They, like all other lights, were powerful ultra violet, but like much of the Sanctuary, there was still quite a bit of darkness that could not be dispelled.

Marie got him back into the Sanctuary, moving him off to one side so everyone else in the hanger could get pass safely. Alex silently counted each person as they came out, some on gurneys. Once they were out, the door was sealed. Even if Elizabeth and the others survived, they were not coming back through the hanger.

"Now what?" Marie asked. Her shoulders sagged, desperation and fear finally taking a toll on her.

Alex looked up at her in surprise. He didn't know her very well but he knew Celestials were normally above fear and almost god-like. Emotions were rare, despite Marie displaying so many, fear had never been one of them until now. Alex felt the same. He was afraid but determined. If the Shadows managed to get in, they were not taking him again. There had to be a way to stop them or at least get everyone out. Lucas would know what to do.

Lucas...

His eyes brightened. "Marie, do you have Lucas's journal?"

Marie gave him a confused look then a slightly embarrassed one. "Kyra asked me to review it. The fae..."

"It's okay," he said, interrupting her. "Can you do it? The pocket realm?"

"Only with access to the Void."

He nodded. "Celestials created the Void. Can you recreate it?"

She shook her head. "It's not that easy. It took the elders with knowledge of the universe to create it. I don't have a coven of other Celestials, or the knowledge required for it."

"No...but we do have the human-born Queen and King of the Celestials," he pointed out.

Marie was silent for a moment. "It might work," she breathed.

A shadow of doubt fell over her face but she said nothing. Instead, she grabbed the nearest person and told him to find Liam and tell him to meet them at the temple. The engineer nodded and rushed off. Marie watched him go before glancing up at the temple.

"I really wish we installed side doors," she quipped with a small grin.

"It would have helped," Alex agreed.

He bit back a chuckle as Marie grabbed two more people and ordered them to help Alex up the temple steps while she folded and carried the wheelchair. It was not an easy climb with the ground shaking and parts of the ceiling falling. They had to dodge large chunks of rocks but eventually they made it to the top. Alex looked back over the village and the buildings that were damaged or destroyed. There was no telling how many may have been killed inside them. Even the infirmary and mess hall were taking a beating. However, the temple was in much better condition, having survived thousands of years and numerous wars before being hidden underground.

"We need to get everyone inside," he told Marie. "The temple can withstand an outside attack."

"You're right," she said.

A small bit of hope filled her as she looked out over the village as well. She reached out to everyone telepathically, accessing the hive mind they all seemed to share, as well as touching the few human among them, instructing them all to enter the temple. She could have done the same with Liam by himself but choose not to, most likely due to her own fear and not wanting to panic her son more than either of them already were. It was why Alex would not reach out to Kyra right now. She needed to focus on the battle at hand. He only hoped her and Elizabeth remained safe.

Bit by bit, people braved the shaking and failing debris to make their way to the temple. Alex and Marie waited only a few minutes before heading into the inner sanctum of the temple itself and the long journey down into its heart. The thumping of rocks falling on the temple echoed all around them and for a moment an age-old fear of the temple collapsing all around him filled Alex. He had to pause several times, stopping the two hybrids helping him down the long twists and turns and stair case after stair case. He fought back the memories of the attack on his research team so long ago and prayed that the cavern didn't completely collapse. There was no telling how much air they would have or for how long if that happened.

He couldn't afford to keep thinking in such a manner. He needed to focus.

The Vault was wide open and Alex had to bite his lip not to snap. He had told everyone that the Vault was off limits. Of course, given the fact that Kyra knew the Void no longer worked meant someone – most likely Liam and Winston – had been down here while he was missing. As angry as he was, he was also grateful. It saved him from having to unseal the Vault. He wasn't sure if his plan was going to work but if it had a chance of success, they needed as much energy as possible. If Marie could open a pocket realm then this generation of hybrids would never be hunted again. If they were only able to reactivate the Void, it would buy them time and get them somewhere safe…for now. Either way was better than what they were facing right now.

Chapter Fourteen

Utter carnage met Kyra as she stepped out of the mine into the woods. There were helicopters everywhere. Several hovered above while others landed in the distance, close to the chalet and Elizabeth's plane which was nothing more than a burning pile of rubble. It effectively cutting off that route of escape for the hybrids. Soldiers made their way through the woods, weapons drawn in search of the refugees. They were human, otherwise they would not have made it through the shield. The large cannons protecting the property could not keep up with the helicopters and jets invading their space. The jets were obviously meant to be a distraction so the helicopters could land. It worked for the most part but Kyra took some satisfaction in the vehicles that were shot down. She could see several that were shot down and crashed into the mountainside. She did not, however, like the sight of missiles being fired into it.

"Move!" she yelled at the team she had formed to combat the soldiers.

She shoved aside a young woman as a missile sped toward them. It slammed into the rock face only a few feet away from the entrance to the mine. The shock of the impact threw the entire team to the ground. Kyra rolled onto her side, her ears ringing so loudly she could not hear anything else. She rolled onto one side and turned to access the damage. The cave entrance to the mine was collapsed. It would take hours to dig it out to get back inside. On the plus side, it also meant their attackers would not be able to easily get into the Sanctuary, at least not those with human hosts. The Shadows themselves was another story...if they made it past the shield. Given the force of the attack, the shield coming down wasn't a matter of if but rather when.

"The soldiers on the ground are human," she yelled to her team. "Shoot to kill. If they shut down the shield, the Shadows will swarm us. If you're unsure then shoot first and take their head second."

The EDC agents nodded in understanding. The hybrids, still new to their powers looked unsure. They were forces to be recon with nonetheless, and nodded in agreement. This was their first battle, in some cases their first time facing off against Shadows or soldiers. Killing was not something any of them were truly prepared for. They were each armed with guns and machete knives, as well as their own powers. The training they received from the EDC was now going to be put to the test.

"Naomi," Kyra called. "Can you enter all their minds?"

Naomi went to her side. Her voice was louder than it should be, her ears obviously still ringing as well. "I need to be closer...but I may be able to take control of a few."

Kyra nodded. "Stick close to me."

She unsheathed both swords, nodded to her team, then moved forward, using her other senses to track the soldiers. The Guardians that normally patrolled the perimeter were useless in this battle. They had no physical form and could only watch until the Shadows broke through. They were only able to fight beings like themselves. She kept low to the ground. Her hearing was slowly coming back, but she didn't rely on it. Instead, she listened to nature. The snow was deep in areas but Kyra knew the woods like the back of her hands. She knew where it was deep and where it was shallow. She knew the crisp smell, untainted by people, machinery, or weapon fire. Everything that now trespassed on her home changed the scents around her, making them distinct and easy to follow. The others mimicked her but spread out. There were more missiles, more explosions, but they learned to maneuver around most of them, keeping low. Those that could, used their gifts to blend in with their surroundings. Kyra reached out to each of them mentally, silently instructing them and watching over each one. It was easy to dodge the soldiers at first. Despite their weapons, they were in foreign territory and hiking up into the mountain to reach them. The hybrids had the higher ground. However, it was still a battle between novice hybrid warriors and experienced soldiers, and the soldiers were not afraid to kill without question, doing exactly as they were ordered.

Guns shots echoed through the woods, followed by shrieks and cries of those hit. Kyra and Naomi kept low, both having to shield themselves from their fellow hybrids' sudden pain and the echo of death from those that fell. Naomi used her gifts to mask the sound of her and Kyra moving through the snow as they crept toward a lone soldier. They took him by surprise and before he could raise his weapon or call out to the others, Naomi took control of his mind and twisted it until it was under her control.

"Your teammates have betrayed you," Naomi said just above a whisper. "They are the enemy…they are the aliens you seek. You will protect us and help us find them…and kill them."

She glanced at Kyra for approval before letting the man go. The soldier stared at them both for a long moment before bowing his head toward Kyra, acknowledging her as his new commander. Kyra returned the nod with a gesture to move forward. The soldier obeyed, his loyalty now to them. They moved forward, eyeing other prospective soldiers they can turn, but the man Naomi turned took his new duties to heart. He began firing at his former team the moment he saw them, killing many within seconds, effectively saving several hybrids. Kyra and Naomi left him to his mission and darted into thicker coverage as the man moved toward the chalet, taking out the intruders one by one. Eventually the soldiers realized what was going on and began firing back at the man, killing him, but it bought Kyra the time she needed to reach her house. She dashed into the side door, determined to reach her Dad's laptop. It controlled all the defenses for the old base. It's satellite uplink ensured the shield remained up and the cannons' tracking system. Without it, everything would fall apart and not only would soldiers raid their home but the Shadows would be free to roam their land.

"Kyra!" Naomi yelled from the door.

She ignored the other woman as she hurried through the kitchen to the living room. The laptop was there, on the low coffee table where they had left it. She moved toward it when Naomi screamed at her. She looked up just in time to see a missile headed directly at the house. It was moving too quickly. There was no time to grab the computer, let alone escape the house. It slammed into the front of the building, destroying all in its path. Kyra had no time to brace for impact. It was the second time in less than a week that one of her parents' home had been destroyed by a missile. The blast lifted her off her feet and threw her backward toward her fathers' bedroom. Instead of hitting a wall, she slammed into another body whose arms wrapped tightly around her. Naomi's soft voice whispered in her ear, triggering Kyra's powers. A portal opened just before they hit the wall. It dumped them several meters from the house, on the edge of the forest where they watched in horror as the chalet exploded, destroying everything inside.

"No!" Kyra screamed.

Kyra stared at the remains of her home, unable to believe it was gone. It was nothing more than a smoking pile of rubble with only the back deck and hot tub left. It was gone…just as Lucas was gone. Tears stung her eyes. It felt as if her heart had just been ripped out. She sat in the snow unable to move but thankful Alex was in the Sanctuary and was not home when it was demolished.

The sound of cannon fire ceased and a darkness swept over hold of the mountain as the chatter of thousands of voices were heard over the cold winter wind. Even the soldiers paused, uncertain of the sudden change.

"Kyra…" Naomi whispered, fear dripping from that single word.

The already cold air dropped even lower and the natural shadows cast by the trees and tall mountains grew darker.

"They're inside the perimeter," Kyra answered, snapping out of her sorrow. She looked around. They were surrounded but now the enemy was unseen, hiding all around them. "Get into the light! Get out of the woods and into the light!" she screamed both vocally and mentally to the hybrids and soldiers alike.

She didn't realize her mistake until too late. The moment the hybrids came out of hiding they were gunned down by two helicopters hovering just over the lake. Kyra managed to grab Naomi and pull her back into the forest just in time to avoid either of them being shot. She stopped who she could but at least five were killed members of her team. Murdered in cold blood. Those not killed instantly were dragged away by the Shadows. Their screams of agony echoed through the woods before being abruptly silenced.

Kyra quickly placed a hand over Naomi's mouth to stop her from screaming. They were already in a dangerous spot. The last thing they needed was to attract the soldiers or the Shadows. No matter what they did now, they were faced with enemies on either side. Their only escape was to portal back to the Sanctuary, but Kyra was not willing to abandon the others. If they ran away now, it was only a matter of time before the Shadows entered the mine. They could be doing it right now as the opening was already shrouded in darkness and even with the opening collapsed, the Shades could move freely around the rocks and slither into Sanctuary. There was nothing she could do to stop them.

She slumped into the snow, defeat pressing down on her shoulders. Gun fire continued to echo all around her. This was it. There was nothing more she could do.

The whistle of another missile made her roll over and cover Naomi. There was an ear shattering explosion and a moment later the ground shook violently beneath them. When Kyra looked up, she was surprised to discover one of the helicopters that gunned downed the hybrids was shot down and crashed into one already on the ground.

Another fell a few moments later. It triggered a small avalanche. While the trees held back some of the snow, there was enough to make some of the soldiers flee toward the remaining helicopter on the ground. It too was destroyed, exploding into a brilliant ball of fire.

The whoosh of a jet caught Kyra's attention. She looked toward the lake in time to see the Avro Arrow zip just above the frozen water, firing at the helicopters before banking sharply to the right, rolling vertically then shooting skyward. Naomi whooped with glee next to her. It was echoed by the few surviving hybrids. They rushed into the clearing to take on the soldiers, now having the upper hand and able to go where the Shadows could not.

Kyra's fingers flexed around the hilts of her swords. Now was their chance. She stepped around the ruins of the cannons. Fires burned all around her home, making what was once a serene paradise into a burning hellscape. It felt as if everything was in slow motion, as if she could see everything clearly. Every move the enemy made, every flicker of flame, every bullet that passed by her head. She moved with them, avoiding gunfire, and countering it with a swing of her blades, beheading soldiers without emotion, feeling numb. They took her home, just has they had taken her family years earlier, before Alex found her, before Alex and Lucas gave her a home and adopted her, making her part of their home. Lucas was dead now, Alex was trapped underground, recovering from unspeakable abuse. Kyra was done being a victim. She was done seeing the ones she loved most suffer.

She killed without discriminatingly, taking out soldiers swiftly as she shifted into her true form. A small grin lifted her lips at the horror on the soldiers' faces. It was as if they were looking upon the face of death and knew they could no longer win and it gave Kyra a sick sense of satisfaction to behead each one.

It didn't stop the air attack, but it seemed Elizabeth and the EDC had that covered. Once there were no more assailants on the ground, Kyra turned her gaze skywards. She had never witnessed a dogfight before but knew that must be what was happening up above. She hoped

Elizabeth and the EDC could hold their own. As much as Kyra wanted to help them, she needed to stop the Shadows before they entered the Sanctuary…if they weren't already there.

Retracking the swords, she hurried back to the mine. It was unlikely she could stop all the Shadows, but she could stop as many as possible. Her body shifted completely to her Celestial form as she ran, lighting up the forest and consuming every Shadow in her path. Naomi stayed close to her, keeping within her light so that the Shadows would not touch her.

"Kyra, where are you?" Elizabeth asked through the small ear piece in Kyra's ear.

"Heading back to the mine," Kyra answered. She made it to the path and raced up it. "Thanks for the save."

Elizabeth was silent for a moment. "You need to stop."

"What?"

"Kyra, stop!" the older woman said sternly.

Kyra stumbled to a stop in surprise. Elizabeth never spoke to her in such a way. Not since she was a child a least. A cold shiver ran down her spine. "Elizabeth?"

"The satellite is moving into position. They're going to take out the whole mountain," her aunt explained. "You need to get Alex and portal out of there."

"I can't leave my people."

"If you leave the Shadows will stop attacking. You'll be free. So will he."

That made no sense. Why would the satellite be moving over the mountain now to destroy the Sanctuary? The could have wiped them out months ago. Realization hit Kyra like a punch in the gut. Elizabeth had lured her and Alex to Toronto. They were supposed to be gone long enough for the satellite to move into place and destroy the Sanctuary and hybrids hidden within. That didn't make sense though. Why would Elizabeth willingly go to the Sanctuary if it was to be destroyed? Why show them the Arrow and other jets? Why help them repair them?

She closed her eyes and took a deep breath. "They did get you," she whispered.

"What's wrong?" Naomi asked. She stood next to Kyra, worry filling her face.

Kyra raised a hand to silence her.

"I was trying to protect you," Elizabeth continued. "All we needed was Alex."

"What do you want?"

"To end the war. To be free," the Shadow whispered.

Kyra nodded to herself. "Why do you need Alex? How can he possibly open a new Void?"

"He is the Key. He has always been the Key. He cannot be controlled, therefore he must be broken in order to create a new Void."

"I don't understand," Kyra pressed. "Why save us if you planned to kill us all along?"

There was silence, as if she had stumped the Shadow. Perhaps the creature was not as fully in control of Elizabeth as it believed. It must have used Elizabeth's codes in order to pass through the shields. This one was different. It had not done so to let in the others. Nor had it harmed any of the hybrids, and it had led the defense using the hidden jets. There was some humanity left in it. The tidbit of information regarding Alex being able to create a new portal wasn't said in passing, that was Elizabeth telling them how to escape. Kyra glanced at Naomi, a small smile lifting her lips. She mentally reached out to see if there were any survivors from her team and called them to her location. Disappointment filled her. Naomi and she were the last.

"I'm sorry," she told Elizabeth.

She didn't wait for an answer, instead opened a portal to the Sanctuary. She and Naomi hurried inside just as the Avro Arrow flew overhead and opened fire. Bullets whizzed past them but none hit.

They arrived in the Sanctuary. UV floodlights were engaged, making sections of the cavern a blinding white. There were large pockets of darkness where the lights had been smashed from falling chunks of the ceiling. The Shadows were confined to those pockets of darkness, searching for a path to take or a human to attach themselves to. However, there were no humans or hybrids within the cavern. It was empty. Everyone was gone, not a soul in sight. Buildings were crushed under large boulders. The mess hall was collapsed on one side. Even the infirmary was damaged beyond repair. Thankfully, no one was in either building. At least she couldn't sense anyone alive in them. She could still feel Alex and Liam, their thoughts echoing in the back of her mind. The were safe, as was the majority of the hybrids.

The large door to the hanger was shut and likely sealed. The only thing that still stood, damaged but sturdy, was the temple. It was designed to withstand just about anything. That's where everyone would be. Thankfully, it was fully lit with only a few boulders and rumble in the way. The steps were the most damage. Kyra's light still shone brightly as they made the difficult climb, and avoided the debris and Shadows. Both were winded by the time they reached the top. There was no one waiting for them in either the Tlaloc temple or the Huitzilopochtli temple, meaning they had to be deeper inside, likely the Vault. Unwilling to make her way through the entire temple to the Vault, Kyra opened another portal to it. Or more precisely, to her Dad. The moment she stepped out of the portal, she ran into his arms. She was happy to see he was safe, as were Liam and Marie, and the rest of the hybrids. There are several missing, likely killed in the attack, but most were safe.

Her Dad didn't ask if she and Naomi were alright or if any of the others survived. He merely hugged her tightly, expressing his joy that she was alive and with him. It brought a small lump to her throat. She wanted to tell him what had happened, the lose of their home, the numerous deaths but all she could say was: "It was Elizabeth. They took Elizabeth."

His body stiffened, her words catching him by surprise, but he didn't pull back. Instead, he held her tighter. Warm tears dripped onto her shoulder, as he grieved for his childhood best friend. There was nothing either of them could do for her.

Chapter Fifteen

He was numb. Every part of him felt like ice as he sat back in his wheelchair and listened to his daughter explain the battle outside. He had no words to express the turmoil of emotions that filled him. Elizabeth, of all people, being taken over by a Shadow? A part of him felt as if he should have expected as much, after all, what better way to get to him and Kyra than through the ones they loved. Another part of him refused to accept it. Elizabeth was in the Sanctuary for days and had not attacked anyone. She alerted them to the jets, led the arial assault on their attackers. If she was a Shadow then why go out of her way to protect them? Something was off. It didn't feel the same as when others he knew were taken.

"Dad?" Kyra asked, drawing him away from his thoughts.

Stared off into the distance for a moment before returning his attention to her.

"Give me your ear piece," he instructed.

He held out a hand for it then promptly inserted the tiny device into his own ear. He hesitated a moment. His heart was racing, mind refusing to accept that his best friend, his sister in every way but blood, now hosted one of those demons within her. He refused to believe his Elizabeth was gone. He tapped the small button on the earpiece.

"Beth?" he called, keeping his voice calm.

There was a moment of silence before a relieved voice answered him. "Alex."

A tiny smile tugged at his lips. Her voice still had a way of calming him, despite the situation. After everything he had been through, he should be terrified speaking to a Shadow, but this was Elizabeth, his Elizabeth. He couldn't let himself think of her as anything else. Not yet. There was a chance Kyra was wrong.

"Are you okay, hun?" he asked.

"I'm fine…we're fine. Is Kyra with you?"

"Yes. Do you want to talk about what happened out there?" He waited, fearful of what she may say.

"I'm sorry, Alex," she responded after a moment.

He frowned and looked to Kyra. He had to approach this another way. "Hey, Beth, remember when we were kids? We made that promise…that if anything happened we'd…"

"Be there for one another. Alex, it's me. It's still me," she assured. There was a sigh of resignation in her voice. She wasn't trying to hide who or what she had become.

He nodded to himself, remembered she couldn't see it, then said. "I know."

"You planted the journal in the penthouse, didn't you?" he asked.

"Alex…" There was desperation in her voice.

"I need to know. Did you plant it? Did you set all this up?"

"I didn't want to…I…I didn't want to lose you…"

Alex's eyes widened. He was talking to the real Elizabeth. There was some sort of separation between her and the Shadow inhabiting her. That was why she had been able to move freely through the Sanctuary. She was somehow able to contain the creature and keep it from escaping

200

her. She was still protecting them despite everything that happened. He dare not ask why she set him and Kyra up for the attack in Toronto, or if she knew what the Shadows would do to them. Nonetheless, fear was inching it's way back into him.

"Alex, listen to me," Elizabeth said suddenly. "There's not much time. The satellite is almost in place and more fighter jets have been deployed from North Bay and Trenton. They'll be here soon. In the journal you have everything you need to reopen the Void. You're the Key. You've always been the Key. It will take everything you have but you have to do it. It's the only way to save Kyra...to save all of them. We'll hold them off as long as we can."

"How do I know this isn't a trick?" he asked. What she was saying didn't make sense. If she knew about the journal, why not give it to him before now? Why this elaborate scheme? Was Elizabeth fighting the Shadow? There were so many questions and no answers.

"Remember when we were little and your Dad took us to Niagara Falls for the very first time?" she asked.

It was an odd question. He hadn't thought about that trip in a very long time. "Yeah?"

"We watched that video about the history of the falls," she continued, her voice soft despite the sound of engines in the background. She gave a small laugh. "You made me promise to never tell anyone you were scared of going over the falls and refused to go sightseeing anywhere near the top in case you somehow fell in. I told you if that ever happened, I'd jump in after you."

His jaw dropped. She had sworn to save him if anything bad ever happened to him. First the falls and in school as they grew older. She had been there almost his entire life, protected him, searched for him, did everything to care for him. She had literally been taking care of him since he lost his leg. A part of him felt she was always care for him.

"I remember," he answered, concealing a sniffle.

"Tell Kyra something for me," she told him. "There are good and bad Shadows, just like there are good and bad Celestials and Humans. Not everything is black and white."

His head bobbed up and down in agreement. "I know."

""They've aimed the satellite at the mountain," she told him. "I'm going to try to take it out."

"No! Elizabeth, no! We can figure this out."

She gave a small laugh. It was one of her teasing ones that was meant to tell him he was being silly. "I will always be there for you." There was long pause. "I still, and always will, love you, AJ. You've always been my best friend."

She ended the conversion, the earpiece going silent.

The old nickname brought tears to Alex's eyes. It was a nickname his father gave him as a child as they shared the same name. He stopped using it shortly after the elder was killed. Elizabeth was reluctant to the change but eventually began using his given name. He blinked away tears and tapped his earpiece once more.

"Beth? Elizabeth…whatever you're doing…don't. Please…we can find a better way," he begged. He didn't like the finality in her words and feared what she may do. Taking out the satellite, that meant going into space. The Arrow wasn't designed for that. "Winston, can you get a reading of how many jets are approaching?"

Winston looked a little startled. He quickly looked at his tablet, mumbled something to himself, then looked back at Alex. "Maybe a dozen. They're coming in fast from the east."

"How many jets do we still have?"

"All three, sir." He hesitated. "They're moving to intercept."

"Keep tracking them," Alex ordered. He wheeled himself toward the altar. "Marie, I need the journal."

"Dad, what's going on? What did Elizabeth say?" Kyra asked. She followed him, surprised by how quickly he was moving in the wheelchair. Her gaze met Marie's as she and Liam met Alex at the altar. "Dad?"

He held up a finger to silence her as he looked over the altar. He slowly moved around the structure, his fingers tracing over the craved stone and metal. It controlled the entire Vault. If Elizabeth was correct and it could essentially be rebooted, then there had to be some sort of switch or connection. He was tempted to tear the entire thing apart to rewire it…if that was even possible.

"Okay…let me see the journal," he told Marie.

He held out his hand for it. Once he had it, he began flipping through the pages in search of anything regarding him or the altar. He went back and forth a few times before finally finding it. It was an image of his scarred hand, each intricate mark left by the artifact that burned him expertly drawn. Lucas had studied his hand many times and would trace a thumb over his palm for hours on end when they would snuggle late at night together. This image was almost photo quality. His hand was a "key" to the Void and fit against the groves of the altar that would normally fit the true key which was an ancient stone tablet with carvings and gems that fit in the groves. It couldn't be as simple as him placing his hand over the lock. Pursing his lips, he placed his hand on it and waited…and waited…and waited. Nothing happened. The energy that would usually course up his arm didn't happen.

"We've got movement in the Sanctuary!" Winston suddenly yelled.

Alex's head jerked upward, but Kyra was already on it.

"How many?" she demanded. Her long stride took her to the engineer in four quick steps.

"Impossible to tell." He paused as the lights in the Vault flickered. They went off, causing some to cry out in fear until the backup generator kicked on with a loud rumble. "They've killed the power. The solar grid has been destroyed."

"They can't get inside the Vault," Marie assured, but there was uncertainty in her voice. Her words were a lie meant to keep everyone calm.

Alex nodded, not about to contradict her. "If we could tap into the volcano, we could draw enough power to the Vault to raise the shields." Except it was dormant. There was no way to access it's vast power.

"Don't worry about the shield," Liam said, surprising them both. "I've got that covered."

He strolled toward the large door and placed both hands on it. A ripple of power moved through the Vault. It felt as if they were placed in a bubble, sealing out all outside noise despite them already being isolated. The energy he produced ran across the altar, lighting several of it's hieroglyphics. They faded quickly but did not go unnoticed.

Alex stared at those hieroglyphics for a few moments before looking up at Marie. "Can *we* generate enough energy to power it?"

Marie worried her lower lip, her gaze thoughtful as she studied the altar as well. "When the Void was first created our most powerful elders infused their life forces into it."

"It killed them?" he asked, surprised.

She nodded. "They sacrificed themselves to find us a new home, fearful the Vault would not sustain us. They were meant for short range planet hopping. The Void could take us anywhere on the planet and so much further. Suns and volcanoes were the only substances that equaled the power of the elders."

Alex sat back. He grimaced in pain but ignore it and ran a hand through his hair. They didn't have Celestial elders to create a new Void, and while Kyra was powerful, he was not willing to lose her in an attempt to make one. There had to be another way. He slowly reread the section of the journal about the scars on his hand then flipped to the section about faeries and pocket dimensions. He pursed his lips. What was he missing?

The ground shook violently, almost knocking him out of the wheelchair. A familiar groaning sound came from above. Alex's stomach knotted with the memory of nearly being buried alive so long ago. The Shadows were likely dismantling or possibly trying to collapse the temple, knowing they were taking refuge in the Vault. The fact the satellite had yet to fire was surprising. If it malfunctioned then they were safe for now and may be able to survive several days. Eventually they would need food and water, something not readily available. It was likely that if the Shadows could not reach the Void then they would make sure the hybrids starved to death while in hiding. If the temple fell, it would bury the Vault, trapping them.

"Liam?" Marie called. She hurried to her son to help him.

"I'm fine," the young man insisted. He didn't move from his spot and continued to hold the shield he created.

He wasn't fine. Alex could see he was struggling to hold up the shield, especially now that the temple was beginning to collapse. He touched Kyra's arm and nodded toward Liam. He was her mate and needed her more than Alex did. She opened her mouth to object but stops, instead giving a tiny, resigned smile before going to Liam's side. Marie hesitated before returning to Alex. She met Alex's gaze and raised a curious brow.

"Do you have a plan?" she asked.

He nodded. "Maybe…the portal realm…you need the Void for that, yes?"

"Yes."

"What if you didn't?"

She frowned at him in confusion. "What do you mean?"

"It took a group of elders to create the Void, but that was a huge network that covered the entire Earth and who knows how many other planets. We don't need to do that. We need to simply get out of here to somewhere safe...somewhere the Shadows can't follow us."

"Without an active Void...I'm not sure that's possible," she answered honestly.

"Marie, you're the only one powerful enough to do it," he pointed out. "You're the only Celestial, and the only one with the knowledge to create a pocket realm."

She glanced back at their children, pressed her lips together in a thin line. With a sigh, she turned back to Alex. "It's worth a try."

She rubbed her hands together, clearly nervous, then took a step back. What happened next Alex had only witnessed once before when a Celestial left his body. The Celestial within Marie exited her body in a cloud of blinding white light. Marie's body arched, as if the being leaving her had to pull itself free. Given the decades they had been together, this was likely the first time the Celestial had left its host, making their bond so solid that separating the two must have been painful for both. Everyone stared at them in awe. No one had seen anything like it before. The light being floated before its host for several long seconds before taking on a more humanoid shape similar to Kyra's true form. Where Kyra was light within human flesh as strong as diamond, the Celestials didn't have true mass. They moved like the Shadows but were polar opposites. They were the light within the darkness, pure energy more powerful than anything on Earth.

Marie, the real Marie, stumbled back several steps. She blinked rapidly for a moment, as if just waking up. She looked to the Celestial but did not recoil in fear, instead, she looked concerned for the other being.

"Mom?" Liam called. He turned slightly, one hand leaving to door.

Marie held a hand up to stop him. "We're alright," she assured. Her voice sounded different, softer than before. A distinction between herself and the being that inhabited her moments ago. "Focus on the shield, love."

Alex stared at her in surprise. She didn't seem frightened of the Celestial or confused by what was happening. She and the Celestial truly co-habited one body, something he fought against when he was possessed.

"Kyra, call to the Guardians...all the Guardians," Marie instructed. "We need them there. They will fight for you."

In all of the panic, Alex forgot about the Guardians. He had not seen any in the rush to get everyone to the Vault. They were the ghosts connected to the temples either by rebelling against the Celestials, or researchers who discovered the temples and were killed because of it. Some had died defending the temples. Unlike the Shadows, they were not enslaved and were made of light much like the Celestials themselves. They kept the Shadows in check...usually. Kyra inadvertently destroyed several when her powers went out of control months ago. That was why there were so few left in the Sanctuary and likely overtaken by the Shadows.

"Alex," Marie said. She placed a hand over his, her voice low for only him to hear. "Are you sure you want to go through with this?"

"I don't think we have a choice," he reminded her.

Her gaze searched his. "You don't understand. There's a reason why you were marked as a Key. The Guardians must have known this day would come or they never would have marked you." She turned his right hand over to view his palm and the markings. One finger traced over the scarred and puckered skin. "Celestials possess human as a way to survive in our world. This realm is not their own...but the other reason is because of our imagination, our ability to virtually be in more than one place at a time, to live many lifetimes within one. This Key isn't so much to the Void but to realm created of your imagination."

"I don't understand."

"The Fae came into existence through the imagination of one human-hybrid tens of thousands of years ago. You have the ability to do the same and save us all, but it comes at a very high price." Her fingers continued to trace the lines but Alex knew what her words meant.

"I'm not going to survive, am I?"

"Neither of you will." She looked back at the Celestial as it took it's place next to the altar.

There wasn't any other choice. Either they stayed in the Vault and either wait for the laser to cut through the mountain and destroy them, starved to death, or suffocate…or they attempt to open a pocket realm where they could exist outside the normal world. Where neither the Shadows nor humans could reach them. The answer was pretty simple.

"Let's do it," he said.

Marie let out a breath and nodded. Her Celestial half placed its hands on either side of the altar and motioned for Alex to take his position. He flexed his fingers, rubbed his hand against his hospital gown, then, with a deep breath, placed his hand in the grove reserved for the Key. Electricity immediately ran up his arm. He bit back a cry. It wasn't so much painful as it was surprising. He had not felt such energy course through him in many years, and like then, his hand became fused to the altar, unable to pull away.

"Ignore the sensations," the Celestial whispered in his mind. "Open you mind…imagine a place beyond this one. It's safe and has everything your daughter needs to survive. It is peaceful…a paradise. See it as if you were there…as if everyone you ever loved were there."

An image began to form before his mind's eye. A vast landscape with towering trees, fresh flowing water, and fields breaming with vegetation. The sun, a brilliant orb of pure light shone above. He imagined homes, simple and sturdy, enough to house every hybrid with more than enough space for more if needed. The weather was warm, not quite tropical but warm enough year-round to ensure there was always food. Birds chirped happily in the bright blue sky while a mixture of animals roamed freely all around. In the distance was the temple, looking identical to the Templo Major just like all the others. Why he envisioned it in this new realm was beyond him but he imagined this was how things looked tens of thousands of years ago when the Celestials ruled the Earth. That thought left a bitter taste in his mouth. He changed it, ridding this new world of such an awful reminder of oppression. No, this land was new. It was a new beginning for his daughter and those she protected. She may be their queen but she would not rule them as the Celestials had humans long ago. Instead, he designed her a new home, recreating the chalet. It brought a smile to him. Kyra could change the chalet however she wanted, but it would give her a sense of home even if he could not be there with her. He poured his heart and soul into creating every little detail, wanting it perfect for her.

The energy running through him no longer hurt. If anything, it was relaxing.

There was a shift in the air. A warm fresh breeze washed over him. The scent of pine filled the air. He opened his eyes and gazed toward the Void. A bright opening appeared several feet from the altar, not quite part of the Void yet a portal all it's own. Inside, he could see the very world he imagined. It was dazzling.

"Keep the image in your mind," the Celestial told him. "You need to hold it while I stabilize the new realm."

"Kyra," he called to his daughter.

She hurried over, awed by what was happening. He didn't need to explain what he wanted her to do. She used her powers to help the Celestial reinforce the realm and portal needed to pass through to it. He continued to create this new world, adding more details even as Kyra ordered the hybrids to enter this new realm. They hurried inside as the ground shook and thumping increased above. It shook Alex's concentration for a moment and almost caused the portal to close. Kyra held steady, but it caused her to strain herself. Her portals normally lasted a few precious seconds. This was more than she could normally handle.

The Celestial said something in a language neither of them knew before moving forward, fusing itself with the altar. It sent a rush of energy through Alex. His eyes widened as he felt the energy move through him, changing him as well. The world he created finalized, becoming a permanent fixture within it's own realm.

"Dad?" Kyra asked worriedly.

"I'm alright," he assured. He felt different, not himself, as if he was floating. "Winston, where's the Arrow now?"

The young engineer was urging people to enter the portal. He looked away from the group he was helping to assess his tablet. "It's overhead...increasing altitude rapidly. It's alone...they must have shot down her wing mates."

Alex closed his eyes. With his free hand, he tapped his earpiece. "Beth?"

For a moment, there was no answer, then an exasperated: "AJ, what are you doing?"

"I just needed to hear your voice," he said honestly. "Where are you?"

"Finishing the mission."

Alex sighed. She wasn't going to tell him, even though he could see the Arrow's location on Winston's tablet. He tried removing his hand from the altar but it was firmly stuck there. The energy he felt before now seemed to move in reverse, pulling his energy into the altar much as it had absorbed the Celestial. He absently watched as the hybrids entered the new realm. He had to hold on until all of them were inside.

"Tell me about the mission. Where does it end?" he asked.

Kyra looked at him, confused, but didn't interrupt.

"I'm sorry I couldn't help more," Elizabeth told him. "I wanted to stop them before they took down the shield. I never meant for you to get hurt."

"I know, Beth, I know." He glanced at Winston, signalling him to leave the tablet on the altar before the youth entered the portal. He watched as the Arrow flew into space, the virtual map changing with it's flight plan.

"Dad, we've got to go," Kyra urged.

The last of the hybrids passed through into the new realm. The few remaining EDC agents were right behind them, leaving only Kyra, Liam, and Alex behind.

"Go," Alex said. "I'll be right behind you."

She stared at him for a long moment. "Promise?"

He nodded. "I promise."

She hesitated a moment longer before hurrying to Liam. She took his hand and lead him to the portal, pausing long enough to give Alex one last look. He smiled back at her but didn't follow. Instead, he watched as Elizabeth's plane moved across the tablet. He felt exhausted, utterly drained. His hand was still stuck to the altar, as if glued and taking every bit of his life force.

"Beth…talk to me," he said. He closed his eyes, willing the portal shut before Kyra realized he would not be joining her.

"I'm almost there," she answered. "Stay with me?"

"I'm not going anywhere."

Their connection wavered the further she got away from the planet. The Arrow wasn't designed for space. How she planned to destroy the satellite was beyond Alex. He wasn't sure what sort of

211

arsenal the Arrow was packing or how it had enough fuel to make the trip. Static cut in as Elizabeth spoke, making her words incoherent. Nonetheless, he continued to talk to her. He told her Kyra was safe, that everyone was safe now, hoping it might make her turn around and come back. Maybe save her life as well. He heard her apologize for setting them up, that she never meant for him to be hurt, that none of it was supposed to happen like that.

Movement within the Vault caught Alex's attention. The Guardians and Shadows battle moved into the Vault now that Liam's shield no longer protected it. Alex relayed that to Elizabeth but she didn't respond. Their connection broke leaving only silence in it's wake. Alex lifted his hand off the altar as the last of the power within it seeped away, along with it, the rest of his energy. The portal closed with an audible snap before the Shadows could reach it.

"I'm sorry," were Elizabeth's last words before the transmission turned to static.

"Me, too," he whispered to himself, his words meant for both Elizabeth and Kyra.

He turned to face the Shadows, ready to fight, regardless of his condition or being trapped in a wheelchair. He felt different, stronger, no longer afraid. Something in him had changed. He was given no time to ponder this, though. The ground shook violently, knocking him out of the chair and onto the ground. An ear-piercing shriek filled the Vault. He clasped his ears, trying to shut it out. It was the only warning he received before the Vault ceiling ripped to shreds by the blinding white light of the laser. Elizabeth had failed to destroy the satellite in time. Alex closed his eyes against the unbearable heat and curled in on himself, but it was not enough to save himself as the laser consumed him and all in it's wake.

The last thing he saw before fading away was Lucas kneeling before him, his arms open wide to welcome him to the world beyond.

Chapter Sixteen

Death is the only constant in life. No matter the person, rich or poor, young or old, it eventually comes for them all. It was a darkness that exceeded all others. With it came a quietness, a sense of peace and calm. In the end, it was less frightening than all the wars and battles faced worldwide. For some, there was nothingness, a simple void that left one numb until eventually consciousness faded away and there was nothing left of the person, nothing but a vague memory that would fade away with time as well. For others, it was a long tunnel that led to possibilities, reincarnation and new life, a chance to begin again. Yet for a special few there was a light at the end of that tunnel. It was so bright one might fear their soul would be burned, destroyed, and shattered into thousands of tiny pieces. However, sometimes, just sometimes, that was what one needed to pass into the next realm of existence.

"Alex! Alex, wake up!"

"Dad? Dad, come on, open your eyes."

There should have been pain. His entire body was nothing more than a roadmap of agony. Yet, there was none. He felt nothing. It wasn't the usual numbness that came with shock. This was something different, almost like floating. Birds chirped in the distance. The sweet smell of dew on grass filled the air, and the steady lapping of water against the shore flooded him with a sense of peace. If he was dying then this was a good place to do so. In fact, he could sink into the ground beneath him and it wouldn't matter.

Except for the voices nagging him to wake up.

He opened his eyes slowly, expecting to awaken back in the Vault and the intense brightness of the laser that ripped through the mountain to destroy the Sanctuary. Instead, he was met but Kyra's worried face and next to her…

"Lucas?" he breathed.

His husband smiled down at him. He was exactly as Alex remembered him. His dark unruly hair moving in the spring breeze and bright brown eyes staring down at him adoringly. His shoulders were just as broad as before and his chiselled jaw still spotted the goatee Alex came to love even though he liked to tease Lucas of looking like a villain. If this was a dream, he didn't want to wake up. There was only one problem…Lucas had no colour to him and was almost transparent like a ghost but radiating light. Like the dream he had in Toronto.

"Hey, babe," Lucas greeted him.

He held out a hand. Alex hesitated a moment before reaching out to take it, only to notice his hand had the same transparent quality of Lucas. He pulled back and held both hands in front of his face. He stared at the back of his hands, then the palms and was taken back when there were no longer any scars on the right one. The flesh…if you could call it that…was pristine and clear, as if it had never been burned. Confused, his gaze moved up this arm where older burn marks should have been after he had stepped on a landmine resulting in the loss of his leg. The skin there as well was normal, no tight, puckered patches. His heart began to race. Did ghosts have hearts? Was he a ghost? He sat up and looked down the length of the rest of his body. The hospital gown was gone, replaced by a simple pair of jeans and graphic t-shirt. His legs were both fully intact, and with them his feet. He had two feet once more. He wiggled the toes of his right foot, having not had it in decades. A small laugh escaped him at the sensation of feeling his toes. This wasn't possible. It had to be a dream. A wonderful, crazy dream he did not want to wake from.

"Am I dead?" he asked, even though he knew the answer.

Lucas grinned as he helped Alex to his feet. "One does not give his life force to open a portal *and* face a killer laser beam and live to tell the tale…but you can as a Guardian."

Alex stared at him dumbfounded. "I'm a Guardian?"

"You have no idea how hard it was to pull your essence from your body and get it here. It's a good thing Guardians are not bond by space and time," Lucas teased. He pulled Alex into a tight embrace. "I've missed you."

Alex melted into Lucas's arms. They were real and warm. He could even smell Lucas, his natural musk making Alex's stomach tighten with a need that went far beyond sexual. He was home in Lucas's arms. Every emotion he bottled up since Lucas's death now released themselves. He sobbed into the larger man's neck, rejoicing in the feel of prickly flesh. Lucas hugged him a little tighter, the fingers of one strong hand carding through Alex's hair as he whispered words of love and support. He let Alex express himself however he felt he needed to. Alex could not voice how appreciative he was.

He caught Kyra's gaze when he looked up. She was standing several feet back with a look of pure joy on her face. He smiled at her then looked past her to the world around them. It was almost identical to what he imagined. It was much larger though and far more developed. He pulled away from Lucas to look around, unsure what he was looking at. The buildings were larger, more sophisticated. There was still vast fields and rolling hills with several large mountains, but it appeared they were on an island of sorts, not quite tropical but warm and comfortable without the excessive heat. It reminded him of the cottage towns on Manitoulin Island.

"Where are we?" he asked, confused by the changes.

"There's an interesting fact about becoming a Guardian," Lucas explained. He wrapped an arm around Alex's waist and followed Kyra into the town. "You don't quite die and become a Guardian…it takes weeks, even months for your soul to regenerate into a new form. It's a little like being reborn only less messy."

"How long was I gone?"

Lucas shrugged. "A month, maybe two. Enough for us to find and move the rest of the hybrids here. That's why things have changed so much. We needed to accommodate a lot more people that you envisioned."

He wasn't kidding. There were thousands of people moving about the town. Large vegetable gardens were being tended to while others cared for livestock. The hybrids had formed their own community. It was the utopia he hoped for, except one person was missing.

"Elizabeth…" he whispered.

The sadness on Lucas's face told him everything he needed to know. She was gone and not a Guardian like them, despite her desperate attempt to destroy the satellite and stop the laser before it was fired at the Ishpatina Mountain Range. His heart fell in mourning. He loved her like a sister. Losing her was just as hard as losing Lucas, maybe worse. There was an emptiness inside him.

"I don't know," Kyra told him.

She reached out to take his hand but her fingers passed through his. She stared at her hand for a moment before curling her fingers, not happy. She shrugged it off but Alex knew having him as a Guardian, a virtual ghost, was hard for her. They could never embrace or even touch one another as they used to. Alex automatically reached for her before stopping. There was no point in the gesture. He could not comfort her which was likely why Lucas didn't make a move toward her.

Kyra hugged herself. "We have no way of communicating with the outside world...except when I go back to bring more hybrids. I haven't found her."

"She's gone," Lucas interjected. "She sacrificed herself. The Sanctuary may be gone but that weapon will never harm another. We're safe...thanks to you...and Marie." Before Alex could ask if the Celestial survived, Lucas gave him a small squeeze. "She's recovering marvellously considering she hosted a Celestial for decades. Whatever illness she had in her youth the Celestial cured while inhabiting her. She'll have a normal long life."

That was good. In the short time he had known Marie he had only seen her as a Celestial who had possessed a poor woman much like one had possessed him decades ago. He had tried to avoid her because of it, despite how much she tried to bond with him. He felt a little guilty for that now, but grateful Marie – the real Marie – had her life and health back.

As they strolled into the small town, Alex was pleased to see the town was self-contained. Small shops dotted the streets including bakers, a café with bookstore. Little comfort needs and all for trade rather than money. Alex paused at the book café, curious as to how such things made it to this new realm yet happy to see them. He was happier still when he saw Marie and Liam inside, organizing their stock while chatting away with a few customers. They looked perfectly at home in the setting. As did many of the hybrids that traversed it. There was no fear here. People were happy. Children played in the streets which were nothing more than a dirt path. There were no vehicles. Most of the homes and buildings were build by hand, other than the few Alex had created when he envisioned this realm.

Guardians mingled amongst the hybrids, many unseen, like ghosts inhabiting yet another plane of existence within the same realm. Alex had seen them before but usually as faint outlines of their previous selves. Here, they were clear. Still translucent but completely visible. Perhaps it was due to his own status as a new Guardian or maybe this realm reinforced their power. Whatever the case, Alex was able to recognize several, including his father and members of his research team that had been killed years ago, and Owen, Lucas's older brother. In this realm, everything that had been taken from him was now returned. He leaned into Lucas, thankful for this blessing.

They were home.

About the Author

Canadian born and raised, M.J. Spickett has a long history of writing, both as a novelist and freelance journalist. However, her primary focus is to write primarily urban fantasy, erotic paranormal thrillers, young adult fiction. In recent years, she had branched out to write screenplays with the hope of one day turning her novels into film. When not writing, M.J. enjoys traveling and research. Often times, family vacations turn into exciting road trips to find new, exciting locations and experiences to feature in an upcoming novel.

To become an ARC reader and join our newsletter for chances to win swag and/or gift cards visit:

www.mjspickett.ca